Historical Fiction

A Rancher's Woman
Victorian Native American Western
by E. Ayers

Historical Fiction
A Rancher's Woman
Victorian Native American Western
A novel by E. Ayers
Published by Indie Artist Press
Eagle Mountain, Utah
www.indieartistpress.com
Large Print Edition
copyright © 2013-2015
All rights reserved.
ISBN-10: 1-62522-033-2
ISBN-13: 978-1-62522-033-2
April 2015

Cindy, reader

"I can't wait for another E. Ayers book! Her stories pull me in and hold me to the last word!"

Jan, reader

To George, who believed in me.

Acknowledgements

I'd like to thank the people who have made this book possible. Many thank yous to my wonderful editors, to the folks at BNSF, the BIA, and to so many wonderful people in Wyoming, Montana, and San Francisco, California who have taken the time to answer questions and provide me historical information. And a very special thank you to Indie Artist Press.

Author's Note

I'm not a historian, but what I've had to learn in order to accurately write western historical fiction boggles my mind. Hundreds of hours of research have been poured into this book. From social customs, clothing, furniture, appliances, forts, government surplus, shipping boxes, cardboard, and trains, it was all researched. Even the plague that hit Bombay and the trading ships that anchored, but supposedly never picked up supplies had to be researched. So many historians have helped me along the way from the wonderful folks at BNSF Railway to the Bureau of Indian Affairs aka BIA.

I'd start to write a paragraph and then spend

six hours in research. A previous job had me spending hours looking at old photos and deciphering everything from plants to clothing and even possible colors. Those skills were applied to so many old western photos taken in Wyoming and of the Crow tribe for they are often more accurate than the written history of the time. It's been a labor of love.

The atrocities that we, as white men, have imposed on our Native Americans/American Indians are unforgivable. As an author I hope I can help people understand what we did to the American Indians either directly, or indirectly by our presence. The Crows have always respected their environment, the wildlife around them, held their women in high esteem, loved their children, and truly were the stewards of this great land. Mark "Many Feathers" Hunter is fictional, but he's based on their heritage, the white man's pressures, and human nature, which we all share. I hope he is worthy of being an

Apsáalooke (Crow).

A very big thank you to my friends who happen to be everything from harbormasters to ships' captains, train engineers, modern day importers, or married to American Indians for all your help. Their ability to point me in the right direction to find necessary information and explaining things has made a huge difference.

Today, most of us cannot imagine a young woman going to another city to marry a man because her father said to do it. Yet, in that day and age, women did and still do in places around the globe. My own great-grandmother's marriage was arranged. I know from my father, she had no say-so in it. She did as her father instructed.

My heart and soul went into this book and I hope you, the reader, find it a worthy of your time. It's a cold, hard glimpse at life in the West, minus the glamour and romanticized notions that romance readers have come to expect. But through it all is a love between two people that can't be ignored.

Part One

"We're here." Frank Coleman called from his buckboard.

Malene Goddard kept the quilt tucked tight to her body and watched as her sister, Adie Reiner, pulled herself to the edge of the open wagon and looked around.

"What do you see?" Malene asked.

"Nothing. A wooden fence and more nothingness. Frank is opening a gate."

Malene protectively slipped her hands over her lower abdomen where the child within her grew. As Adie snuggled back between the quilts that failed to keep them warm, Malene groaned and her teeth chattered. "I will never travel in the winter again. Never."

The wagon jerked forward a few feet and stopped. She listened to Many Feathers jump from the driver's seat of their wagon. Then she heard the squeal of the gate being closed. She pulled the wool scarf once again from her nose and lower face to speak. "I'm going to die of cold."

Adie giggled. "*Ja*. But we are warmer than they are."

"We can't get any colder," Malene whined. Frank had promised they would have a bed and a warm place to stay tonight, but she was beginning to doubt it. She tried to remember the last time she'd had a real meal or slept in a bed.

It had taken Frank almost three weeks to ride from his house on the Coleman ranch to the Reiner house in Montana. He had come to ask Adie to marry him. But this return trip had already taken thirty-two days. Bad weather had caused them to stop twice. They spent two days under the open wagon while rain mixed with sleet drenched everything. Travel days were slowed by snow or wet ground. Malene had never been so cold or miserable in her life.

When they passed through a small town, Malene begged for them to stop for a few nights at a local boarding house. Frank said no, as any delays would put them in worse weather. They only stopped long enough to buy more firewood. Now that was gone. All they had left were branches and twigs they had picked up yesterday.

The cloud-blanketed sky had darkened hours ago. Her stomach rumbled from hunger. Wind blew and threatened to lift the quilt that covered her and her sister.

She was certain that she was bruised from her feet to the top of her head, because every bone in her body hurt. The bumps in the road had bounced her against the wooden floor of the wagon too many times and the bouncing just got worse. She folded her fur muff in half and tucked it behind her head.

The wagon slowed to a halt and Frank called, "We'll be warm tonight."

Malene sat up, and through the darkness, she spied a small house that looked like a shed. "*Nein, nein, nein!*"

Adie stuck her nose over the edge of the wagon. "It cannot be. It is too small for a whole family to live in there. It must be a mistake."

Frank helped Malene and her younger sister from the wagon. "We'll light a lantern and get a fire going."

He opened the door to the small wooden building and rummaged around in the dark. A few minutes later, the glow from a single candle tossed some light into the shabby room.

Malene could see several primitive bunk beds, a table that looked to be in worse shape, and a small stove. Near the stove was an almost empty shelf.

"Someone has been in here. We have supplies missing," Frank announced.

"Not us," Many Feathers said.

Frank sighed as he lit another candle. "When your people use our property, we know it. This was probably trappers. Where did they put the lantern? You'll need light to use the privy."

Adie found an empty tin and handed the can to Frank. "Can we use this?"

Frank took a knife and punched holes in the rusty thing. "We'll give it a try. Nothing open will stay lit in that wind."

He forced a small nub of a burning candle through the hole he had created. "It's not much and it might get hot."

"I doubt anything can be hot in this frigid wind." Malene knew her patience had been pushed to the limit. She couldn't remember the last time she could actually feel her toes, and her fingers didn't want to work.

"You're doing fine, Malene." Frank chuckled. "It's almost over. I'm as anxious to be home as you are to get out of this cold."

Malene took the candle and scurried to the privy behind the small house. Opening the door, she put one foot inside. She held the candle and checked for spiders in the tiny building. But when her other foot entered, it bumped something. Her mouth opened, and a scream blared until she closed her lips. Then she listened to the cadence of heavy footsteps making their way to her at high speed.

"Malene, what is it?" Frank asked as he yanked on the partially opened door.

Malene looked behind her at both men standing there and pointed towards her feet.

"It's dead. It's not going to hurt you." Frank picked up the frozen snake and tossed it far from the buildings.

"Hurry up, Malene. I need to use it, too," Adie whined from behind the men.

***

Many Feathers laughed and walked to the lean-to where the horses were spending the night. Malene reminded him of a child who had not learned that life would be full of rocks. She was the daughter of the sun. Her hair was the color of light and her eyes were like deep pools on a summer's day. He'd never seen such beauty.

He fed the horses, checked their blankets, then walked into the night, and relieved himself. He tried to understand the white man's ways, but many made no sense. He thought Malene had feelings towards him, but every time he got near her, she would back away. Adie didn't back away from Frank. She let Frank hold her in his arms and kiss her.

Many Feathers pressed his lips together and went back to the small line shack. Frank had a fire going in the tiny stove and the room was warming.

"Shall we try for water?" Frank asked.

He followed Frank to a spot not too far from the buildings, then watched Frank raise and lower the water pump's big handle over and over. When Frank gave out, he took over. No water. "Is it ice?"

"You mean frozen? It might be. But I don't think so."

They both took two more turns and, as they

were about to give up, Frank managed a small trickle of water.

They filled a kettle and the coffee pot while strong winds swirled around them. Frank carried the coffee pot and they each grabbed the handle on the kettle, taking care not to slosh the water.

"You brought enough water for a bath." Adie grinned.

"Tomorrow night, we will all have baths."

Many Feathers listened to their banter and wondered how they would bathe in this cold. He shook his head with bewilderment.

Frank made coffee and looked through the shack. "This is the last of the beans. There might be enough for one more pot of weak coffee. The thieves took whatever food we had here, and all we have left is oats."

Adie sat on a lower bunk and wrinkled her nose. "Feed mine to the horses."

Malene held up both hands. "*Nein*. I'd rather die of starvation than to eat another bite of oats."

Frank looked at Many Feathers. In his own tongue, Many Feathers asked how much further. Frank replied another long hard day.

Many Feathers shook his head and climbed onto a top bunk. He hadn't felt his toes in days, and now his feet felt as if he were being stuck with the needles women used for sewing. He closed his eyes. Sometime later, he opened one eye to see what had awakened him. He became fully awake when he realized he'd heard the screaming roar of the wind. He peered through the darkness. "Frank."

Light snoring and Adie's sleep-laced voice answered, "*Ja*. He sleeps."

Many Feathers jumped down from his high perch and went outside. Almost solid blackness surrounded them, but the roaring winds contained snow. Not big flakes of a light storm, but tiny ones traveling sideways. The ground was already coated in a thin layer of white. These strong winds from the north brought dangerous storms. He had seen men and animals buried and frozen to death in these snows. Unsure how much sleep they had, he sighed. They were all tired, including the animals, but they had no choice. They needed to leave before they were trapped.

He poked his head inside the shack. "Adie, wake everyone. We have to move fast. The storm is bad."

He took what was in the buckboard and loaded it onto the wagon. Then he removed two wheels, making the buckboard unusable, and loaded the wheels on the wagon. He saddled his horse, harnessed the two mules to the wagon, and tethered the other horses to the back of it. Frank could decide who would ride ahead to find help.

With food and a fresh team, they might make it. But worn out animals, no food, two helpless women, and a snowstorm meant trouble.

Adie made a small pot of coffee using the

last bit of beans, while they prepared to leave.

Many Feathers pulled Frank to one side and explained his plan. Frank immediately agreed.

Frank turned to the women. "We don't have too many choices. Many Feathers will drive the wagon. I'm going ahead for help. Bring your cups with you. We can't waste precious time."

Malene groaned as she extinguished the fire in the stove and poured a cup of weak coffee.

Many Feathers helped both women into the wagon and started the long trek south. More snow blanketed the ground. He knew that it would take skill and a large measure of luck for them to outrun the ominous grip of the storm. He kept the mules at a steady pace and watched them for signs of serious fatigue.

Malene left her spot beside her sister in the back of the wagon and sat next to him. "Are we going to a real house?"

"I do not know. I have never been here."

"Then how do you know where to go?"

"If I can see the way, it is good." Using his hand, he pointed towards the east and then the west. "The sun comes up here and sleeps there."

Malene sighed.

"Are you still afraid of me?"

Malene shook her head. "Maybe still...a little... You are a man with different ways."

"So you fear?"

"Maybe I fear all men."

"Why do you say that?"

She turned her head away and looked at the spot where the sun should be rising.

"Your husband was not kind to you, so you fear me because I am a man, or because I am Crow?"

She looked at him. "I heard stories of how the Indians killed our people and stole things from us. But Frank told us other stories of your tribe, and what we have done to all the Indians. He says it is because we do not understand your ways."

"He is right. This is grassland. Home of the big...big animal...I do not have the word in your language."

"Deer?"

He shook his head. "Big."

"Bison?"

"Bison. Yes. That is it. Our water becomes hard with cold. No food, no water. We are trapped on the reservation."

She took her gloved hand out of her fur muff and put it on his.

He looked down at their hands. Hers was covered in gray material with tiny, even stitches that created individual fingers, then the glove was trimmed in beaver fur at her wrist. It looked small resting on his mitten made from pelts. He raised his gaze to her face and smiled, as the thought of her touch sent a warm pulse through him.

She returned his smile. "I am sorry. I would never do such a thing to people. I thought you were...I mean...all I ever heard was that you were like animals."

"We are all animals, but we walk on two feet."

She shook her head. "You do not understand."

"Yes. I understand more than you realize. You are the one who does not understand. The difference between us is that we pay honor to the animals that we kill. White men kill without feeling and often for no reason."

"You have been kind to us…to me."

"You are very beautiful, a daughter of the sun." She looked away from him and he nudged her with his elbow. "You fear me as a man?"

She nodded.

He looked over his shoulder at Adie cocooned in a quilt. "She is asleep. Yes?"

Malene looked back. "Yes. I hope they have a real bed for us, and warm food. I am tired of traveling."

"Yes. Tired. We are all tired and hungry.

You not answer my question. I am only a man. Why does that scare you? Is it because your husband was bad?"

"When I was a little girl, I dreamed that one day I would be married and have babies. I wanted a pretty house and a handsome husband. When I married, I discovered that I didn't want..."

He listened to the muffled clomp of hooves in the snow. "Why you stop talking?"

"I cannot tell you. I cannot tell my sister. It hurts."

He tried to decipher what she wasn't saying, but came up blank. Bitter cold winds whipped around them. It made conversation a wasteful struggle.

A finger's depth of snow lay on the ground and it was getting worse. Horses know their way home, but these mules belonged to the women, they did not know the way. He had no stars to show him direction, no sun rising, only wind pushing more snow to the ground.

The path was becoming more difficult to see. He slowed the pace of the mules. It wouldn't do them any good to veer off course. His worry was given to the wind and to the large bird that watched over him. He and the children of the sun were in the hands of the spirits of the land.

An immense weight settled upon his shoulders. He put his arm around Malene and tucked her closer to him. Frank said to keep the ridge to his left. But with the blinding snow, it was impossible to see that far.

***

Malene sat next to the bold Crow Indian who called himself Many Feathers. Snow covered his leather jacket and wool blanket that draped him. She reached over and brushed the snow from his shoulders. His eyes remained focused on the ground ahead.

She thought about how Frank had grown a

wooly full beard, but not Many Feathers. His face was smooth, but his long eyelashes were now dusted in snowflakes. The blue, painted lines on his face were fading.

Wearing a hat made from the head of a buffalo, he barely looked human when she first saw him on the reservation. He had sent ice water racing through her veins. Then she noticed the painted lines on his cheeks and one that went from his hairline down his forehead to the tip of his nose, he looked even more scary, yet the lines accentuated his chiseled features. But when he removed that horrible horned hat, he had a strange hair adornment made of feathers.

In spite of everything Frank had said about the Indians, she was certain he would cut her into pieces and eat her for breakfast. Fear had consumed her. Instead, he was more attentive and kinder to her than any man had ever been. For that, she was grateful.

She'd spent weeks with him on this trip. His

kindness never wavered. Looping her arm through his, she snuggled tighter, hoping it would keep her warmer. He dropped his hand to her skirt-covered leg and rubbed it. The touch was higher than would be considered decent, but somehow it felt natural. She put her hand on his.

He looked at her and smiled. "I will never hurt you."

For some reason, she believed him. Something inside her quivered from his words. She pulled her scarf over her mouth and nose, and watched the mules. Puffs of steam came from their noses. They wore blankets that had been tied to their bodies with rope, but now those blankets were laden in snow.

The clouds seemed lighter in color, but just as angry. The wind blew hard as if determined to push his body into hers. She did not mind his closeness. Human contact seemed good in this storm.

She had panicked last night, thinking that the little shack was the house where they were going. Adie had read the letters where Frank had described the family home, but it was possible that he did not tell the truth.

That thought led her back to her husband, Albert Goddard. She had fallen easily for him. He dressed in the best of clothes and always bestowed her with expensive gifts. First, it was a necklace of emeralds and opals with matching earrings. Thrilled with the gift, she ordered a green dress to match them. Then shortly after they were married, she couldn't find them. They had vanished from the fancy jewelry box he had given her. He threw a fit, told her she was a stupid fool for losing such a thing, and then accused Cook of stealing them. After he vented his anger on everyone in the house, he left. Cook would never steal, and Malene knew she did not lose them, but the beautiful jewels were missing.

Then he sent her a cameo brooch

surrounded with diamonds. It was the most beautiful thing she'd ever seen. She wore it for him the night he returned. When she took it off, she placed in the jewelry box. Before he left, it too had vanished. She bit her cheek and kept her mouth closed. Somehow she had angered him in some way, so he took it from her. *Just as he had taken the emerald and opal set?* Never would she know for certain.

A sudden bump in the road made her open her eyes. Then there was another bump and another. The world around her was white. She looked over her left shoulder. All white. Certain they could drive past a house that was only twenty feet away and never see it, she shuddered with cold and fear.

***

Many Feathers pulled the wagon to a stop. "We not on the path."

He traded the mules for the horses while

Adie and Malene scurried away from the wagon. He would have laughed, had they not been in grave danger from the storm. White women acted as if he were not supposed to know what they were doing. Everyone did it. It was not a secret.

They returned as he had the last horse in place. He helped them onto the back of the wagon, then he climbed into the driver's seat. He figured out where the path was. They had only missed it by a few feet. He hoped these horses remembered where home was.

The wind abated with only occasional strong gusts, but the snow kept falling. The horses were trying to pick up their pace. They wanted to be home. But the snow was thick and the wheels were having a difficult time getting through it.

He looked back once and saw that Malene had her head in Adie's lap, and Adie seemed to be nodding with sleep. Since cold will create a sleep that cannot be awakened, he called the women to come sit with him.

They both climbed onto the bench with him.

With Malene on his left and Adie on his right, he attempted to smile. "I am sorry you have no food or hot drink. You teach me your song about the bird in the grass."

Adie giggled and lowered her scarf from her face. "*Ja.* You want to learn *Turkey in the Straw*?"

"What is *ja*?"

Adie giggled again, and again pulled her scarf from her face as she spoke, "*Ja,* is yes in German."

"What is German?"

"Our father was from Germany. It is a far-away place and they speak a different language. We speak German and English in the house, but my schooling was in English."

He wondered where such a place existed, for he had never heard of it. "You teach me the words to your song?"

Adie's voice shook with cold, as did

Malene's, but he picked up the words and the tune. At least now, he had them awake.

The pace of the horses had slowed then slowed more as the dray team pulled the wagon through the snow. Wheels cut into the mounding, cold, white cover and each turn packed more snow between the spokes until they would no longer turn. Twice he got down and cleared the wheels of their burden. He needed to lighten the load.

The wheels to the buckboard he tossed to one side of the path. They could be found when the snow melted. Then he helped the women mount the mules and he made them wrap whatever blankets they had around them. He walked beside the horses, fearing they would all be found frozen.

A large bird circled overhead then flew off. He said a prayer to the great bird and continued, trying not to stumble. He no longer could feel his feet or anything below his knees. As time passed, his legs no longer wanted to support him. The world was turning into a white blur.

Several sharp calls rang through the air. They were friendly calls of his people and the great bird that soared in the sky. He heard it again and then again. Each time it came closer. He belonged to the spirit of the great bird and it was calling to him.

Everything was white. Where was his wife and baby daughter? Were they not in the white spirit world? He tried to reach out to find them, but he couldn't move his arms. There! He saw them.

His beautiful wife. His heart reached out to her. She was laughing and playing with their baby daughter. He mustered strength and called to them. A great spider's web separated them. He could hear her. Why didn't she hear him calling?

Dazed, he felt hands upon him. He was being dragged upwards into something. Warmth covered him, surrounded him. Warm liquid touched his lips and he drank. The liquid was sweet. Was this the other side? Was he passing over? Voices were all around him, yet he understood nothing. More warm liquid, smoky and sweet, ran over his tongue and down his throat. His toes throbbed. Heat radiated through his legs and at his sides. It was on his chest and his hands. His entire body tingled with needle pricks. He was warm. For the first time in weeks he was warm as if it were summer. He cried out for his wife. Where had she gone?

***

Malene watched as they unloaded the wagon into two sleighs. She did not know these people, but she was too tired and cold to care. Some of the men looked as though they were Frank's family, and they seemed to know exactly who she and Adie were. The others were Indians.

"Do we have it all?" The older man asked.

Adie spoke up, "I have a gun under my seat."

"What?" The older man brought his horse around and called to the youngest male.

She pointed to the wagon's seat. "Feel."

Malene watched a young boy climb up and find it.

A few minutes later, they were on their way. Except this time, they had cups of warm tea poured from a metal jar and sweet rolls filled with even sweeter honey. Malene looked down at Many Feathers tucked by their feet. He was mumbling words she did not understand. They were each given a warm rock from a knapsack and the rest were used on Many Feathers.

Between those on horseback and the two sleighs, Malene counted nine males. The youngest was probably ten years old, but the oldest, she had heard them call him Pa. She chewed on the honey-filled roll, and when she was done, she poured a little more tea into the metal cup they had given her and added more tea to Adie's. It was wonderful. No longer steaming hot, but it was still delicious. Warmth filled her mouth and she could feel the heat as it went down her throat and into her chest.

Many Feathers lay there cocooned in a heavy fur blanket, still mumbling as if he had a high fever. She poured a little more tea into her cup, lifted his head, and put the cup to his lips. He drank it. She partially refilled her cup, and he drank that, too.

"Not too much," Adie warned.

Malene sat up. She had no idea how much further they had to travel. Snow still swirled around them and it was getting very dark again. She didn't want to complain, didn't want to say a word to Adie, but her lower back and tummy ached. She didn't want to lose the child she was carrying. She'd come this far. It was her baby, and she wanted it.

Adie elbowed her and pointed. "There!"

What appeared to be smoke came out of a far away chimney. *Oh, please let that be the house.* Snowflakes continued to swirl around them partially obscuring their view, yet slowly, in the distance, a house appeared through the gray-white gloom of the snowstorm. Then she realized there were several houses nestled together along with a barn and numerous other buildings. Lights from the windows cast a yellow glow on the white snow. It looked pretty.

She wanted to relax, to feel safe, but she was a long way from home and in a strange place. Would the Colemans accept her? Her insides clenched with apprehension.

A few minutes later, she and her sister were ushered into a warm house.

A golden-blonde woman greeted them. "Which one of you is my Frank's Adie?"

"I am." Adie curtsied. "And this is my sister, Malene."

"I'm Alisa Coleman, Frank's mother. Let me show you to your room and to the bathroom. I'm assuming you will both want to bathe after such a long trip. It will help to warm you."

Malene and her sister followed the woman through the house and up the stairs. They were given a room that contained two beds. The room was large, clean and tidy, but plain.

"We did some last minute switching of rooms when I heard Frank had brought home two women with him. I think you will be comfortable here." Alisa smiled.

"Thank you." Malene curtsied and so did her sister. "You are kind."

"You're welcome. Follow me."

Alisa took them down the hall and opened another door. There was the bathing room with a white porcelain tub and a smaller, old-fashioned metal tub had been brought in and set up. Piles of towels were stacked on a shelf.

"If you don't mind taking care of your own, I will go downstairs and check on the young man who came with you, and prepare food for everyone. I'll see to it that your things are brought up to your room immediately."

As Alisa pulled the door partially closed, Adie turned to her sister and giggled. "Where is the pump?"

Malene looked around. "I do not know."

A little knock on the door turned their attention to a young girl. "I need to use the toilet."

She was probably no more than seven years old and dressed in a light brown skirt and cream-colored flannel shirt. She came in, smiled, and when finished, she pulled the chain.

"Wait!" Adie pointed to the bathtub. "How do we fill it? There is no pump."

The child turned the faucets and suddenly water poured into the tub. "You need to use this to put water in that one. Ma makes us all take our baths at once. She says it's easier. Pa said he should have put two tubs in here." The child's wide smile showed off the odd mix of baby and adult teeth. "My name is Virginia. What's yours?"

"I'm Malene." She pointed to her sister. "This is Adie. Thank you for your help." Malene grabbed the bucket.

The child held up her hand in a wave as she scurried from the bathroom. As she closed the door behind her, Malene could hear the little girl say, "You're welcome."

Soon the two tubs were filled with water. Malene and Adie ran back to their bedroom where their trunks were waiting for them. They found clean clothes and took them to the bathing room. The water was not exactly hot, but it was not cold.

When they were done, they dressed in plain skirts, their fashionable Nell blouses with high collars and comfortable sleeves, and pulled their freshly washed hair into braids. Adie wore a gray wool waistcoat over her black skirt, and Malene pulled on a pretty sweater decorated in embroidered edelweiss that matched her green skirt. Together they made their way downstairs.

When they reached the bottom, Malene looked to her left. There was a large parlor, painted the pale gold color of dried wheat. A braided rag rug covered most of the floor, and scattered over it were quite a few upholstered chairs in golden brown and a few with prints containing gold. Two couches faced each other and contained the same print of the chairs. One wall was covered in shelves that contained a myriad of books. Malene found herself instantly drawn to the books, for she had never seen so many in a house. She quickly scanned the titles, knowing she'd enjoy reading quite a few. There was a kindred spirit in the house, and she suspected it was Frank's mother.

Opposite the parlor, a room had been set up as a schoolroom. There were more books on shelves. Several tables and a few desks occupied the room. Against the wall next to the books was a small cupboard. There was a pile of slate boards and a small stack of lined paper. A large world map hung on a wall.

She and Adie nosed around until they made their way to the dining room where the family had begun to gather.

Frank and Many Feathers were missing. Apprehension swirled around Malene. Were both men all right?

She and her sister were offered seats facing each other at the long table. The Coleman family was large, but there were also several who were Indians, the ones who had been with the Coleman men and saved Adie and Malene from the snow. The food was simple and delicious.

"Frank said you left before Christmas, but you've had bad weather," Alisa Coleman said, as she passed a bowl of mashed potatoes to the youngest boy at the table.

Adie nodded. "*Ja*. It has been over a month

since we have eaten a real meal. The bad weather slowed our progress."

Guilt crawled through Malene. If she had not been with them, they might have arrived sooner. Maybe she should have gone home with her father when he caught up to them at Christmastime on the Crow reservation.

Adie shoveled her fork through her potato. "Frank told my family about the Crow Indians and how they were starving." She glanced at the Indians sitting at the table before turning to Alisa. "That's when Albert said some terrible things about the Indians. Frank left and we came with him."

Malene frowned and lightly kicked her sister's shin, startling her.

Alisa Coleman shook her head. "Adie, who is Albert? I've not heard that name."

Malene glared at her sister. "My husband." *Act natural. Change subjects.* "Frank was upset, and said he would not stay with my family. That's when Adie decided that she was going with Frank, and I came as a chaperone. Frank bought the Indians some supplies."

Alisa passed the soft rolls to her youngest daughter. "So, your husband will be coming for you?"

That did not work. Malene shook her head. "I have run away from him. He was very cruel."

Alisa knitted her eyebrows.

"My father discovered, after we had left, that Frank's words were true, and so were mine." Malene took a sip of her cream-laden milk. "Our father brought several steers to the Indians so they would not starve, and he caught up with us there."

"That was kind of your father." Mr. Joseph Coleman looked like an older version of Frank. He wore a homemade, knitted wool shirt without buttons that crossed at the neck. He was clean-shaven without any trace of sideburns, but his hair was slightly longer as if he needed a trim. "Frank told us of the troubles on the reservation. For several years, they have had problems. He said this is the worst."

"Do not dwell on it," Alisa Coleman said. "They need to change their ways, but they are proud and stubborn people. We help as much as we can, but we have our own family to feed."

"Many Feathers told us that the white men have killed all the buffalo, so there is nothing to hunt," Adie said.

Joseph nodded. "It's been an ongoing situation. There are many people who hate the Indians because they are different. Yet, we moved onto their lands and we took from them. We hunted their game. We put fences where the bison grazed and put our cattle on that land. The Indians were very upset with us, some more than others." He waved his fork in the air as he spoke. "My father and mother made friends with the Indians. We have always allowed them use of our land for hunting or to set up their camps. But once they were put on the reservations, they were trapped in one place."

"I do not understand why we would do something like that to them," Adie said between bites of food.

"Someone thought it was a good way to protect them. It is easy to understand why they were not happy with a small amount of land, when they once had everything." Joseph ate his last forkful of food, then ran a piece of roll over his plate, sopping up every speck of food before devouring the roll. "Someday people will realize the injustice that was done to the Indians, but it will be too late."

***

Many Feathers opened his eyes and looked around the strange place. His last memory was being in the other world and trying to reach his wife. Where was he? It had to be a house. He'd never been in one, but he'd heard about them and seen them on the outside.

He was lying on a soft bed with an even softer pad under his head. If he turned his head, the soft cushion blocked his view. He sat up. On him were layers and layers of material. Someone had removed his clothes. Across the room was a fancy box with a fire in it. He tossed the material off of him and noticed his fingertips were covered in black spots from the cold. His toes looked worse. He stood and stretched. The room was warm.

A man stood looking at him. In one swift move, Many Feathers jumped and sucked air into his lungs. He walked towards the figure, watching the man watching him. He'd seen his reflection in water, but never like this. He touched it. It was hard. He looked behind it. Whatever it was, it was thin. He looked at himself again.

Without removing his gaze from the image, he turned around. On his back was a set of jagged scars. His mother had cried, and he had stayed with the medicine man for many nights. The memory of his left arm being bandaged and splinted for weeks ran through him. He held his arms out and looked at them. They looked the same and both were strong. It had been a nasty fall and he had bumped his head on his way down. Battered, confused, and in pain, he remembered the large bird who watched over him until he was rescued. He laughed to himself. At least, he wasn't called boy who fell from rocks.

The man before him was handsome. Puffing out his chest, he admired the curves of his body. The lines on his face had faded. His hair fell past his waist and one lock of hair, on his right side, had the feathers from the birds he had killed over the years. He stood close to the reflection and stared into his eyes. He liked what he saw.

He looked around the room. There were drawers and trinkets. Books sat in a pile on a table. He picked one up and studied it. His people never wrote their words. He wished that he could read what was there. Did their books tell tales of great men and brave deeds?

There were words on his pass. He'd watched the agent write it. Using a pen, the man made tiny squiggles on the paper, then made more in a book. Before handing him the pass that allowed him off the reservation, the agent blew on the paper to dry the ink. Many Feathers wondered what it would be like to hold such a thing and make words.

A rapping on the door made him turn around.

From the other side of the door, Malene said, "I have breakfast, if you are ready to eat."

His stomach rumbled at the mention of food. "Yes."

She opened the door, her eyes grew wide, and she gasped, turning away.

"Is something wrong?"

"You are..." She put the tray down and vanished.

He sat on the floor of the long room where she had placed the food and devoured the salty strips of meat, several eggs, and sweet white bread. There was coffee in a tiny cup decorated with flowers that matched the plate, which held his food. He tapped the cup with his fingernail and listened to the sound it made. Everything was delicious.

Footsteps came and he saw a woman of the sun approach him. He stood and looked at her. Her hair was a golden yellow and fell in one long braid. He wasn't certain, but she was probably old enough to be his mother, yet her skin was smooth with a youthful appearance.

"Many Feathers, you have much to learn. Men don't walk around naked in front of women. Come."

She pushed against his shoulder and took him to another room. He watched her as she made water flow into a large container. She showed him the toilet and told him what he was to do there in his own language.

He rolled in his lips and pressed his teeth to them. He was not a child and yet she treated him as one. She told him how to take a bath, promised him some clothes, then she slammed the door behind her.

He stuck a finger into the water and discovered it was warm. Everything in the house was warm. After lowering his body into the water, he picked up the bar of soap that smelled like a meadow filled with spring flowers. Maybe Malene would like him more if he smelled of soap.

The woman had showed him a bottle and told him to use it on his hair and then he was to rinse it out of his hair. He picked it up and sniffed it. The sharp odor made him finch. If Malene would like him more, he would use it.

The door opened and the woman returned to the room. "Put the Union suit on first." She held up a red thing. "This goes in the front. Your legs go here and your arms here. Then put on the pants and the shirt. Can you manage socks? Toes here and heel here." She walked over to him, picked up a pitcher, and poured water over his head, not once but twice. "Next time, make sure you get it all out."

He was still sputtering from the unexpected dousing, as she left the room. He rubbed his burning eyes. Memories of his wife playing in the river with their daughter flowed through his mind. She would blow in the baby's face before dunking her. His darling daughter would emerge laughing, as if begging her mother to do it again, then cry when they left the water. He called his daughter Laughing Brook, for she giggled and tumbled like a tiny stream as she ran into his arms.

The memory of carrying them to the funeral platform ripped through him, leaving an ache within his heart like a gaping hole. There was life and death. Too many of his people had found death too soon. Being a great hunter was no longer enough. There was nothing to hunt. His world had changed. He and his people needed to change to live in the white man's world.

He got out of the water, which was now cold, and rubbed his body with the cloth she had left him. Today, he would wear white man's clothes. It was important that he learn from these people. Deep in his heart, he knew he would never turn his back on who he was, but he had to learn new ways.

The red thing she had called a union suit was difficult. Putting his arms in first, meant he couldn't get his feet into it. *This is the front.* He tried putting his feet in first and this time, he got it on. It was soft - warm and soft. The feeling against his skin was wonderful. He managed the other pieces of clothing easily enough.

Downstairs, he found the family. The children were all sitting at tables with books. The woman barely acknowledged him. He frowned and decided he'd look for Malene.

"Many Feathers, come back here." The woman pulled out a chair and turned it around. "Sit."

He did as directed, but didn't like the way she treated him. He was a man and a warrior and not to be ordered around by a woman.

She picked up his feet and removed his socks. A young girl laughed at him, and the woman scolded the child.

"You have frostbite on your toes. That is not good." She examined his other foot. "Do not move."

The young girl was using a pen. He wanted to try it. Did he dare just take it from the child? He'd give it back. The aura of the woman told him he'd better not take it. Maybe he would ask the woman when the time was right.

He had many moons before he would return to his people on the reservation. He needed to learn from the white man to keep cattle and raise crops. Men do not learn from the women, but his gut told him that this one was different. He had much to learn from her.

The woman returned and put something creamy on his feet. It smelled of mint and other herbs. Then she put his socks on. This time the socks fit better.

"Good?" He smiled at her.

"Yes. Good." She smiled back and ran her hand through his hair. "Come, sit where your hair will dry. Virginia, please bring him a comb."

He followed the woman to the room she called a parlor. From where he sat, he could partially see the other room where the children were.

The young girl, who had held the pen, took off and returned a moment later with a comb. This one was fancy. The teeth were carved from bone, but the handle was silver and had flowers sculpted on it. He smiled as he took it, but he had no token to give her in return.

He would find something to give them. He combed his hair and slowly it dried in front of the warm stove. His gaze traveled the room. It was meant for people to gather and sit.

A small stand caught his attention and he went to it. He'd watched his wife bead, but he'd never seen such fancy stitches and in so many colors. He turned and looked back at the seats that contained fat, square pieces of cloth. He picked one up and looked carefully at it. It was a picture done in tiny stitches. The back of the square was covered in a soft, fuzzy, black cloth, and between the two pieces, feathers had been stuffed, making a soft pad. Curiosity sent him back to the children.

The woman was working with one of the older boys who belonged to his people. She was talking in numbers, but he didn't understand. He sat and listened to the conversations. His people called the woman Miz Alisa. The others called her Ma.

He stood and began to look around the house. The house was warm, but it was also filled with so many soft things. Color was everywhere and on everything. He touched the hard wall that was blue like the sky on a cloudless summer day. A house was very different from the tipis of his people.

Another room was set up like the agent's with a desk. He found himself in the room for cooking. Something smelled delicious. Remembering the taste of the sweet bread, he hoped that was what he smelled, and there would be more of it.

In a room near the cooking room, he found his clothes hanging on a rope. They were wet. There were many clothes hanging on the ropes that were strung across the room. He sniffed his clothes and they, too, smelled like a meadow. Another stove made the room too warm so he left.

He went back to the cooking room and discovered Adie standing there. Her hair was the color of the sun on a bright day and it was braided and wrapped around her head. Her cheeks looked extra pink and her lips were almost the color of blood.

She smiled at him. "You feel better?"

"Yes." He breathed in the fragrant air. "You make sweet bread?"

"*Nein*. I must learn. Mrs. Coleman will teach me." She touched his arm. "You look very different."

"Yes. Different…like white man? Is that good?"

She wrinkled her nose and pointed to his face. "Your stripes are gone." She walked around him. "Different, but the same. You look like an Indian, but in our clothes." Her smile broadened. "You are still handsome. I think Malene will like you."

"It is good." A pleasant feeling bubbled inside of him.

He walked down the long, narrow room by the staircase and spotted Malene. Her hair contained more yellow than her sister's and Malene's eyes were bluer. Her milk-white color instantly changed to bright pink, and she turned her head. He caught her by the shoulders. "What is wrong? Why did you run from me?"

She turned her head as far away from him as possible and squinted her eyes.

He cupped her chin and turned it back to him. "Malene, we need to talk. Alone." He pulled her into the small room with the desk. "I will never hurt you. Why did you run away?"

"You were naked."

"Naked? What is that?"

"Without clothes." She turned very pink.

"I am a man." Laughter rumbled from within him. His fist flew to his chest. "I am great hunter and warrior."

She looked up at him for a split second and giggled. "Oh, yes. You are a man."

"Why did you run away? I do not understand."

She scooted past him and out the door.

He had hoped his new scent and white

man's clothes would make him more acceptable, but she still ran from him. He shook his head and wondered what he needed to do to win her affection.

2

Malene found herself without purpose. At home, she would stitch or read, but here she had nothing. For a month, she had done nothing but ride. But for a month, her body had been shook and joggled as if she'd been beaten. From her head to her toes, she hurt. But it was the ache in her lower abdomen that worried her.

She watched Mrs. Coleman and said nothing. She was too uncomfortable to help, but Adie had been quick to offer assistance. Mrs. Coleman had showed Adie how to make bread and add wood to the stove. The woman stayed busy with so many people in the house.

Guilt poured over Malene. She went to her room and stretched across her bed. It was still rumpled from morning. No one made it. Other beds in the house had been made, but not hers or Adie's, and she didn't know why.

She looked around the room. It was plainly

furnished with a wardrobe, an old washstand, and a chest of drawers. None of the furniture matched and all had been well worn with time and use. On one wall, a fancy sampler hung in a pretty frame. On another wall near the door, there was a long, embroidered bell pull without the bell. Someone had very carefully stitched Noah's ark and several sets of animals down the long piece of cloth. Something told her the room had belonged to the two older girls, Issy and Clarissa, even though their personal things were missing.

She ached and she feared for her baby. Tears welled in her eyes but never fell. Exhaustion enveloped her and with it came a feeling of loss.

The thought of going back home held no appeal. She had started this journey as a chaperone for Adie. Rolling onto her back, she stared at the ceiling. That wasn't exactly true. Adie didn't care if it wasn't proper to run off with Frank even though they weren't married.

It didn't take much convincing on Adie's part to come with them. Malene knew she never wanted to see her husband again.

The images of Albert during their courtship ran through her head. He was handsome and impeccably dressed with a handlebar mustache. His curly hair was a reddish brown and his eyes were green like the tender buds of new leaves. He'd take her in town and stroll the streets with her as she held onto his arm. Or on a warm day, he'd have Cook pack a picnic, and they'd sit under a tree and chat. He'd talk about the railroad, and the big cities like Baltimore, Philadelphia, Chicago, and San Francisco. He dazzled her with his tales of money and power. She'd been a fool to believe it. He was but a child spinning yarn that had unraveled after she left him.

Then her wedding drifted through her head. The whole town was invited. Her mother had ordered her dress directly from Paris. It was silk with short sleeves that had been stuffed with feathers to keep them puffy. She had to wear a special corset, for the bodice fit so tight that she felt as if she could barely breathe. The dress tied with a big bow at the back and had a lace train that was extra long.

She was so excited. To wear such a beautiful dress, made her feel like an angel. Her mama had worn a plain frock on her wedding day and insisted that Malene have something very special. After all, she was marrying the wealthy Albert Goddard.

Memories of her father protesting the outrageous cost for a dress that would be worn once rang in her ears. But her father never denied his daughters a thing when it came to clothes. The warm pulse of her father's love flowed through her.

Malene had been excited about going to San Francisco for her honeymoon, for Albert had painted a glorious picture of this new and exciting seaport. But when they got there, he left her alone in the hotel room most of the time. He had too many business meetings to attend to be bothered with her.

With child and no husband... She didn't want to think about her predicament, yet she couldn't stop thinking. She and Adie had decided they would tell everyone that Albert had died in a tragic accident. She didn't have the courage to tell anyone the truth.

Albert had married her when he was already married to other women. He was a liar and he had swindled her father for a large sum of money. Three times she was with child, and twice something had happened to prevent her from carrying that baby to its birth. Coming with Adie meant she could protect this baby from Albert's wrath.

Frank knew of their plan and had laughed, but agreed it would work. Her first letter from home would send the sad news. She would be forced to wear black, but what difference would it make? It was better if she was a widow with child, than divorced or worse, never married and with child. For now, she was merely Adie's chaperone. And what was wrong with a little lie?

***

Many Feathers kept checking his clothes. They were still wet. He ran his hand into his winter moccasins. Lined with thick fur, they came up to his knees, but they had not been warm enough to protect his feet on the long trip. They, too, had been washed and stuffed with thin bows of wood. He assumed it was to protect them from shrinking. He was trapped in the house, and Malene had fled from him.

He wanted to learn to read and write. The white man was always cheating the Indians, and he didn't trust them. Yet, he was here in a house with them. Except, he knew the Colemans were good people, and had heard the tales of their friendship with the tribe. But if he could read and write, he could protect his brothers. He went back to where the children were sitting. "Miz Alisa, you teach me to write? I want pen."

She looked up at him and smiled. "Yes. That is a wonderful thing for you to learn."

She crossed the room and brought him a wooden board. "This is where we start." She turned back to the children. "William, help Andrew with his math while I work with Many Feathers." Then she smiled and took Many Feathers' hand. She curled his hand into a fist, extended his index finger, and dragged the tip over the first letter on the board. "The arrows point the way."

He let her guide his finger over the big letters.

"Every letter must be formed properly. Every letter has a name and a sound. We put them together and make words."

She went over each letter, again and again. By that night, he knew almost all the letters and how to form them.

The next morning, he took Frank hunting. They returned before noon with three turkeys. Many Feathers plucked a feather from each one and wove it into his hair. He thanked each bird for providing for this family and for honoring him.

As he handed over the turkeys to Miz Alisa, she grabbed his wrist and pointed to the soft red fabric of his Union suit under his clothes.

He grinned. "It is warm and soft."

"Yes, flannel is very soft and comfortable." She smiled as she took the turkeys. "We will enjoy these. Thank you."

That night at supper, he noticed that Virginia had turkey feathers stuck in her blonde braids. He grinned at her. He had won over one female in the house, but that was not the one he was trying to impress. The one he wanted kept running away from him.

Over the next few weeks, a pattern developed. He'd work with the men during the day, then at night he'd join everyone in the room with all the soft seats, and he'd work on forming his letters. He learned the letters, the sounds they made, and worked on putting them together to create words.

When he was alone in his room, he'd take out his pass and look at it carefully. He could recognize some words and he sounded many of them out until they made sense. Pride within him blossomed.

Miz Alisa got a book for him to read. It was a child's book with simple words called <u>McGuffey's First Eclectic Reader</u>. Sometimes he'd stare at picture instead of trying to decipher the words on the page. But he worked hard on it until he could read it with ease. Then she found him another book.

***

Adie and Malene worked together in the kitchen. Malene now appreciated what Cook had done to keep their small family household running. Adie could make a pie that looked better than anything Malene could do, but Malene took pride in her loaves of bread and her rolls that were always perfect. She didn't mind washing clothes, and Adie hated it.

Malene never wore her fancy dresses. They were getting tight on her, and she didn't want to wear a corset. She settled for simple Nell blouses with skirts that rode a little higher than they should. Besides it seemed as though she was always rolling up her sleeves to do something.

Her hands became red and chapped. Mrs. Coleman gave her a lotion that had been made with beeswax to use on her hands. It was similar to what she had given Adie to use on her chapped cheeks and lips when they first arrived, except this lotion was thicker and smelled of cinnamon. It helped.

Alisa taught Adie and Malene how to use the sewing machine that Frank had given Adie. Malene tried it but when she pricked her finger on the needle that moved up and down so quickly, she decided she'd rather not use it. She preferred to hand sew while Adie worked the fancy machine with her feet. As soon as they finished their chores, they'd run up to their room and practice sewing. Adie made an apron for herself and then one for Malene from some cloth Alisa Coleman had given them. With the smaller remnants, they made clothes for Malene's baby.

When Frank and his father went to town, Frank brought home letters from the Reiner parents. Malene and her sister took the letters, raced upstairs to their room, and jumped on their beds. Malene's hands were shaking as she opened each one according to their dated postal marks. She didn't want to lie. But when she opened the one envelop, she discovered a Wanted flyer for Albert Goddard along with a letter from her father. Not only had her marriage to Albert been a sham, and he had bilked her father for several thousand dollars, but he had also stolen from the railroad. It was the railroad that had posted the reward.

"Adie." She passed the flyer and the accompanying letter to her sister.

"Oh. This is terrible. It is best that no one knows Albert was your husband." Adie sat beside her big sister and gave her a hug. "I will tell no one. He was cruel to you and even more deceitful to marry you when he was already married many times. Surely, Goddard is a common name."

"If Frank had not come to ask you to marry him, I would still be in Montana waiting for Albert to return."

Adie nodded. "*Ja*. The best thing that happened is Frank confronting Albert over his bigotry and hatred of Indians."

"Papa knew that Frank was right. He spoke the truth and that made Papa stop and think."

"Yes, but the fact that you ran away with me as my chaperone forced Papa to look at all the things that were wrong with your marriage.

He had to face the situation. His inquiry is what set all this into motion."

Malene nodded as her sister spoke, but the hard lump that was forming in Malene's throat was difficult to swallow. "I'm scared. What if Albert finds me?"

Adie shook her head. "He will never find you here. Besides, what reason does he have to be angry with you? Is it not our father who prodded the sleeping bear?"

Malene tried to shake the sensation of dread, but its talons were in her very fiber. "You are right. Let us open the rest of our letters. I know this one is from Mama."

Malene's father had sent both girls money.

Malene looked at her sister. "We need to pay rent. We are living off this family. We need to give something. *Ja?*"

"*Ja.*"

Malene spread the money on the bed. "But how much is rent?"

Adie raised her shoulders and let them drop.

"I do not know."

"Neither do I." Malene realized there was so much that she did not know. She had never handled money, never had to handle it. Now she was far from home and had no idea what anything was worth.

Adie sat on the edge of Malene's bed. "What about Albert?"

"I do not want to lie."

Adie sucked in her lower lip. "It is better not to lie. Albert lied. That is what got you into this mess. Do not make it worse with more lies."

Malene nodded.

Adie smiled. "I know what a steer is worth."

"That doesn't help us."

Adie's expression turned into a frown. "We don't sit on our fingers and expect Mrs. Coleman to wait on us."

"That is true. We have taken many chores from Alisa."

"Mama kept a stash of money. That is what

she gave us. I think we should save some for us. For an emergency." Adie selected a few bills and put them to one side. "I will need money for our wedding." She put several more in a different pile. "I want to contribute to the house Frank will build." Again she made another pile, then wrinkled her nose. "I need a ledger to keep track. Maybe Mrs. Coleman has a book in which I can write, but I hate to ask. Also, I need a book to keep recipes so I can cook for Frank."

"We shall ask to go to town the next time, and you can buy exactly what you want. For now, write on a sheet of paper." Malene smiled at her little sister. "At least you have a future here." She split her money into several piles. "I save some, I spend some, and I have this." She bit her lower lip.

Adie shook her head. "You are alone with a baby on the way." She took the piles and redid them. "There. That is better. You need money for you and this baby."

Malene counted what she had left. "If it were not for me, Many Feathers would not be here. I should have gone home with Papa when he met us on Christmas day."

"Do not say that. I am glad you are here with me. I do not think I would have survived the journey here without you."

Malene shook her head. "I will give Alisa Coleman this for my room."

Adie tossed an equal amount down.

Malene smiled and doubled what her sister had contributed. "This is for Many Feathers."

Adie debated the situation and then agreed with her sister. "We are paying for more than our room, we are paying for all the things she is teaching us. She is like a tutor to us."

"And we are also paying her by helping." Malene put the rest of her money in her trunk and pocketed the amount for their room. "We shall give it to her tonight."

***

Many Feathers listened carefully to Joseph Coleman and made careful mental notes of how much grain each steer would eat, how much land each needed for grazing, and how many acres would be needed to grow grain. His own people grew some crops, but nothing like the white man did. It would take money for him to buy a plow. He wasn't certain he could convince his people to give him the money from selling horses, and a plow wasn't something he could make. But if they wanted to survive another winter...

Joseph showed Many Feathers how to survey and mark land. He would have much to do when he returned to the reservation, but in his mind, he had already chosen the piece of land that he wanted. Drilling a water well would take more money, but he knew he wanted one. He would build Malene a house so she would be happy and would not have to live in a tipi. Besides, he liked being warm in the winter. His dreams were big, but under all of them was the white man's money. Obtaining that money would be the most difficult thing. If he could find a white man's job, it would take years to save up enough money. And he wasn't certain that Malene would wait that long.

He sat at the table with the Coleman family for his meal and picked up the fork. It was awkward in his fingers. The spoon he could use, but the fork seemed odd. He chased peas around on his plate until he gave up and stabbed them. *Why do they not use their fingers?*

Virginia elbowed him and whispered, "Like this."

He smiled at the youngest female child of the sun and copied her. He was learning their ways, and it wasn't always easy. But Virginia was always quick to show him. It didn't surprise him when she begged to go hunting with the men in the morning.

"I was hunting at her age. I do not mind if she comes with us," Many Feathers said on the child's behalf.

Frank frowned. "She does not need to go."

"Our women do not hunt, but it is not unusual for our children to follow us and see what we do."

Mrs. Coleman spoke, "She's a little girl. I'm sure you would not take your daughter hunting."

"My daughter was too young. She was--"

"You have a daughter?" Malene asked. Her eyes were wide and her eyebrows were raised.

"My daughter and my wife have crossed into the spirit world."

"I'm so very sorry. My condolences to you."

He cocked his head and looked at Malene. "I do not understand."

Virginia nudged him. "It means we feel bad that you've had so much sadness."

He nodded. "Virginia is welcome to learn from great hunters."

Frank chuckled. "Ma, how often will she have the chance to be with *great* hunters?

"It's not funny," Alisa answered.

"Ah, let her go," Joseph said. "It's one day of missed lessons and a morning of learning life skills. I'll go with them."

Many Feathers looked at Virginia. She was busy shifting her gaze from her mother to her father.

"Virginia, you may go with the men, but you must mind them. I don't want you hurt."

"Thank you, Ma." Then she looked up at Many Feathers. "I'll be very good. I promise."

"You will earn your own feather tomorrow."

***

Malene watched Many Feathers throughout the meal. He wore the white man's clothes and she wondered whose clothes he actually wore. She'd done enough washing to know the sizes and they were probably Mr. Coleman's clothes, because Frank and John were taller. John was the oldest brother. He and his wife,

Lydia, lived in the house with their two small boys. Virginia was the youngest child of Joseph and Alisa Coleman.

Lydia was probably Malene's age, but she kept to herself and kept her two little boys busy and away from the rest of the family. Sarah was the oldest daughter, and she had married another rancher and moved to a house nearby. She would visit her parents once a week for a few hours and then leave.

At least she visits her parents. A wave of depression washed over Malene and sunk into her bones. Far from home, the only contact she had was through letters.

Malene and Adie cleared the table and washed the dishes. When Malene joined the family, Many Feathers was busy with his book and Alisa was sitting quietly stitching. Malene went to Many Feathers and whispered, "I have something for Mrs. Coleman, and you are part of it. Come stand with Adie and me."

He stood with the two women.

Malene's nervousness took the form of butterflies that flittered through her abdomen. "Mrs. Coleman, we have something for you." She put her hand into Many Feathers' hand and gave it a little squeeze. "We've been here for several weeks, and we've learned much from you." She looked at her younger sister. "I know we are spoilt, and there are many things we have had to learn. All three of us have tried hard to contribute to the household and be useful while we are here." She reached into her pocket. "This is for our rooms and for being our tutor. If it is not enough, please tell us."

She passed the bills to Alisa who counted them out. "This is a generous amount." She smiled. "I ask for no money. I've never asked for compensation. Adie is to be my son's wife, and you and Many Feathers are guests. I appreciate the gesture, and I thank you."

Malene watched as the woman pocketed the money. She seemed genuinely pleased. As Malene attempted to let go of Many Feathers' hand, he held it tight to his.

"If you will excuse us," Many Feathers said, "I wish to speak to Malene." He yanked Malene out of the room to where the coats were kept. "We need to talk."

"Yes, I agree. You never told me you were married."

"Just as you never told me that you are with child." He helped her into her coat before pulling on his. "Frank told me when we first met. But you have never been honest with me. And where did all that money come from?"

Malene walked into the cold night air. "My papa sent the money."

"What else should I know?"

"There is nothing. Albert Goddard was a cruel husband." Tears filled her eyes and ran down her cheeks. She brushed them away. Her entire life was a huge mess, and she had no idea how to fix it.

"I am not Albert Goddard. I loved my wife and my daughter, but I could not save them."

"Why did they die?" She wasn't certain she wanted to know.

"Sickness that comes from lack of food and cold, the same with all my people. Never in my lifetime can I remember eating the way we do here. I must learn from these people so that I can take the lessons back to my own. My people are trapped by the white men." He paused and looked into the far distance as if he could see something in the dark night. "White men like Albert hate us. They kill anything that moves so that we have no food. They do not care. They leave the carcasses in the sun to rot." He took her hand into his. "We must learn your rules and learn to live the way you do. I know what I am saying will not be popular with my people, but I am certain that I am right."

She sat on the steps of the porch. "You make my complaints seem small by comparison."

"What are yours?"

"You have asked many times if I am afraid

of you, and the answer is yes. Not because you are an Indian, but because you are a man, and because you are an Indian." She stared out at the open field before her. "I have no interest in living in a tipi and being your squaw."

"Squaw? What is squaw?"

"Is not that the term for wife?"

"I've never heard it." He took her hand in his. "I do not know how I will do it, but I will build you a house."

His words sliced through her. She was tainted. Being a widow was acceptable, but being a woman who thought she was married...only to find out her husband had other wives... Was her life now reduced to marrying a red man? Tears welled. Except she didn't see Many Feathers that way. She leaned against his shoulder and cried.

He put his arm around her back and tucked her to his side. "I will never hurt you."

The warmth of his tender embrace comforted her. She gazed up at his face and discovered his dark eyes were staring at hers. "It is more than that. I don't know how to tell Adie."

"What are you talking about?"

"To lie with a man."

He laughed. "I do not lie. I tell truth."

"*Nein.*" She rubbed her forehead with her fingertips. How could she tell him? A warm flush ran from her chest to her cheeks. "No. One word, two meanings. To be with a husband..."

"Yes."

She leaned away from him. "I cannot talk about it."

He took her hand, and they walked to a spot behind the barn. She had never felt so alone with a man since her time in San Francisco. She wanted to run to the safety of the house, but part of her didn't want to let go of his hand. Her insides knotted and her mouth went dry.

He leaned her against the barn and put his

hands on her shoulders. "I do not have the words in your language. So I will show you."

Fear pulsed through her body. She was trapped. Too scared to scream, she closed her eyes and waited.

His lips touched hers. With soft kisses, he nibbled on her lips, across her cheek, under her chin, and he continued to kiss her entire face, only to return to her lips and nibble some more.

She wanted to tell him to stop. She was being crushed between the barn and his powerful body. That beautiful body. She should have never looked that morning, but she couldn't help herself. He was very much a man and that had frightened her even more. His lips continued to caress her face, but his hands found her body. Her knees weakened. She didn't want the sensation to stop.

His tongue parted her lips. Her body warmed until she thought it would explode into flames. She kissed him back. His tongue found hers. Whatever he was doing, she didn't want it to end.

His fingers were now on bare skin, and she was powerless to stop him. Fireworks went off inside of her. His lips were on her ear. It was his language that went into her ear and straight to her heart.

She arched her back and let her head rest against the barn. Every part of her tingled from his touch. A whimper made its way up her throat and escaped.

He answered it with a deeper one.

Then she heard him say, "If I go on, you will be my wife. You must decide."

She put her hand to his chest and pushed. "No. I cannot."

"You need paper of divorce?"

She nodded and wiped her mouth. The cold air chilled her giving her a case of goose bumps. That's when she realized her blouse was unbuttoned. She grabbed the cloth and fisted it closed.

He chuckled and moved her hand away. "Do not hide from me. You are beautiful."

His lips caressed her exposed skin as his fingers began to close her buttons. He reached under her skirt and tugged her blouse into place.

She covered her mouth with the back of her hand. He moved it away and dropped another kiss on her lips as his fingers closed her coat.

"I will build you a house and make you my wife."

Her knees were no longer willing to support her, and she clung to him. Emotions rolled over her as if she were being bounced over railroad ties. The security and strength in his arms comforted her, but her previous hopes and dreams had shattered with Albert. Had not her father vowed in his letter that he'd make it up to her and find her another husband?

***

Many Feathers worked hard on the ranch. He went with Frank to the property that Frank had claimed and helped mark off the land for a house. Together they began to drill a well. It was hard physical work. The sun shone brightly, but the air was still cold, yet both men wiped sweat from their foreheads.

Three times they drilled and three times they ran into hard rock before finding water.

Frank's frustration level rose to the point that Many Feathers began to worry about his young friend. He'd seen that frustration in young boys trying to throw a spear and consistently missing their targets. Was this not the same?

"You spend too much energy on anger. You waste your body on it. Let it go on the spirit's wings." He walked away from his friend and studied the ground. On the north side of the property was a ridge. After scrutinizing the ridge, he started to walk back towards the spot that would hold a house while trying to maintain a straight line between the ridge and the pond in the distance. Then he saw what he was looking for, a slight dip in the land and a patch of grass that was greening quickly. He called to his friend, "Bring shovel. This is where we dig."

"What makes you think we're going to find water here?" Frank asked when he made his way to where Many Feathers was standing.

It would take too many words to explain that he knew where the water ran from the ridge. He put his hand out and patted the air over the grass. "I feel it. I am Indian."

Frank furrowed his brow and looked back to the spot where he planned to build the house. "It's awfully far away."

Snatching the shovel from Frank's hand, Many Feathers lifted a clump of grass and soil. "There is water here."

They dragged the equipment to the new spot and began to drill. They had barely started when Frank hit water. It was only a trickle.

"Keep drilling," Many Feathers said.

Soon Frank had a little spurt. Water began to slowly flow.

Many Feathers took the drill from him. "Get your cap. I'll keep turning."

"Don't. We don't want to go too far and lose what we have."

Many Feathers shook his head at the young man. He knew what he was tapping into and it would be good, fresh water. A few more feet and he had a geyser. It took both of them to get it capped. They were soaked, and the sun was setting.

It was dark when they put the horses in the barn. Chilled to the bone, both men raced into the house. Frank grabbed Adie and kissed her. "We have water and plenty of it!"

Alisa stood there with a frown. "Kissing leads to more and you are not married. Take a bath."

Many Feathers looked at Malene and she blushed. He nodded at Alisa and followed Frank up the stairs. They grabbed fresh clothes and headed for the tubs.

Warm and in clean, dry clothes, they came back to the kitchen where Alisa served them a late supper.

"Going home tomorrow?" she asked as she sat with the young men.

"Yes. Mr. Coleman has given me a letter of employment so that I might return."

"You are always welcomed on our ranch."

"Thank you. I hope to one day have a house, too, with water that runs into tubs, and stoves to keep it warm. I have much to show my people." He shoveled the thick gravy and vegetable-laden stewed beef into his mouth. "I promise I will practice my letters and my words. There are still so many words I do not know."

"It takes time. As a child, you learned your language. You know enough of ours to get by, but you have learned more being here with us. My children have to be taught yours. My husband grew up speaking Crow. For him it is natural. As you've learned English, I have learned Crow."

He nodded and put his fork into a chunk of potato. "I will miss your food and your cooking."

"I will fix you plenty of food for your trip. And I have seeds for you to take home with you."

"Thank you. My people will appreciate that." He cleaned his plate and she offered him some pie. He ate it and wondered how he had managed to put so much food inside of him. Stuffed, he rubbed his abdomen as he joined the family in the room with all the soft chairs.

Adie and Malene wanted him to take the wagon and mules back with him, but he declined. It would be easier if he were on horseback. He could make better time. Snow was still a real possibility this time of year and he didn't want to be pulling a wagon. He promised he would write and let them know he was safe.

"Walk with me, Malene?"

"But your coat is wet."

Joseph Coleman looked up. "Take mine."

He put Mr. Coleman's coat on and walked out the back door with Malene. "You know I must go back."

She nodded, but even in the dark, he could tell her eyes were filling with tears. He did not understand her tears. Crow women almost never cried. They accepted life and saved their tears for mourning.

When his wife and daughter died, he told the tribe he was going hunting, but he found a quiet spot far away in the hills to shed his tears. That was when he realized the ways of his people were dying, too. If he wanted to survive, he needed to adapt to the ways of the white man. And with Malene, he had another chance at happiness.

He bundled Malene into his arms and she clung to him. *The white man's ways are different. I must give her time. I must prove myself worthy of her in a white man's world.*

"I will be back." He put his hand on her newly bulging belly. "The child who grows between us knows my voice and my touch. She will grow up with the wind in her hair and the sun always smiling on her."

"What if this child is a boy?"

"Then he will grow up with the sun on his face and be a great hunter, too."

She tilted her head to his, and he kissed her tears away before settling on her sweet lips. They would only be separated a few weeks, and then he would return. He had much to learn, and spring was on its way.

His heart was heavy as he prepared to leave the Coleman ranch. Morning light bathed the world in a golden glow. He had food, seeds, and a wooden box that contained paper, envelopes, stamps, and a pen with a bottle of ink. But he had something even more precious. Malene had given him a dictionary. Joseph Coleman had also paid him for his help. He had money. It was a start, but it was far from being enough for a house for Malene.

***

With tears streaming down her cheeks, Malene said her goodbyes in the upstairs hallway. Many Feathers hugged her so tight that she couldn't breathe, then planted a quick kiss on her lips and vanished down the stairs. By noon, John and Lydia's two little boys occupied his room. Malene wrote two letters, one to her parents, and one to Many Feathers. It wasn't until after dinner that she discovered that Virginia had written to him, too. The child adored him.

Frank took the women into town that week, and they posted their letters, including the one Virginia had written. Frank picked up supplies that had been ordered, and he ordered more things for his house.

Adie elbowed her sister, for there in the post office hung a poster of Albert Goddard.

Malene's insides formed an instant knot and she waved at her face. "I think I need some fresh air. I'll meet you at the general store."

She stepped outside the little town building and onto its wooden porch. The cool air felt good. She inhaled deeply and let it slowly release. There were only a few buildings in the small town where two roads converged. At the far end of town, she saw a man walking. He wore waist overalls and boots. His hair was too dark, almost black, and the handlebar mustache was missing. She stepped back into the shade hoping she wouldn't be noticed."

"Malen--"

"Shh!" She pulled her sister to the shade and whispered, "There. It's him."

"You think?"

She nodded. "I'm positive. I know Albert."

The man went into the saloon.

"There is a reward. You could report him," Adie offered.

She shook her head. "Wife identifies man? Then the whole town would know. I am not going to say a thing."

"*Ja.* You are right. There's no way he knows you are here. He does not know that we left our house, because he left first."

Adie and Malene went to the general store. In the back corner of the store, they found bolts of material. Malene looked at all of them and wrinkled her nose, but settled on a plain yellow fabric, a light brown, and another with a blue and white print.

Adie found a plain, blue linen, and a pretty pattern to go with it. She also found a ledger and a book for writing. She bit her lower lip.

Malene nudged her sister. "Get it. You've wanted a ledger and you need a place to keep your recipes."

Just when they thought they had finished

their shopping, Malene spotted a lamp. It was made of china with hand-painted yellow roses. It came with a glass chimney, and a matching china shade. "Adie, look," she whispered to her sister. "Isn't it beautiful?"

Adie gazed at the lamp and almost swooned. "Wouldn't it be lovely in my parlor?"

Malene looked at the price tag and sucked in a deep breath. It was expensive, but it would make a superb wedding present. They paid for their purchases and walked out of the store. As Malene placed her package under her seat, she looked at Adie, then at Frank, and said, "Forgive me. I forgot something."

She rushed back inside and spoke to the woman who had helped them. "I do not have enough money on me today, but I want that lamp as a gift."

"The lamp is a set. The other is still in the back. If you want me to hold them for you, I will need a deposit and your name."

"Malene God- Malene Reiner. I am staying at the Coleman ranch." She picked out three candy sticks, one for each of them, and then counted out the rest of her coins. She smiled broadly when she returned to the wagon and handed her sister and Frank each a candy stick.

That evening, Adie and Malene laid the fabric on the floor. Alisa Coleman had given them a pattern to use for Malene. Adie marked the fabric carefully, and Malene cut it. Malene's tummy was creating problems with her clothes. These things weren't going to be fashionable, but they would be comfortable, and with summer approaching, she needed them.

Malene found the perfect moment to talk to Alisa without Adie nearby. She told her about the lamps and gave her the additional money for their purchase. Malene's friendship with the woman was based on respect.

Alisa had been spoiled as a child, but when

she married Joseph Coleman, her life changed. She had a large household to run, and a wonderful mother-in-law to teach her.

Frank started working on his house that weekend. All the men pitched in. They had it framed and the metal roof in place. Joseph grumbled about the delays on the ranch, but he, John, and Frank spent another day rolling the seams on the metal roof.

Spring was in the air and the entire Coleman ranch was feeling it. Dirt was placed in wooden boxes and soon tiny sprouts appeared. Rooms were aired on warm days, and curtains were washed and ironed.

Then one evening, Adie and Frank set a date for their wedding. Adie immediately wrote home and told her parents. Alisa extended the invitation for the Reiners to stay at the house with the family. Malene wondered where everyone would sleep.

The following morning, Adie and Malene rode over to Adie's new house. Sun shown on the bright silver roof. The sides were done in cedar shakes that Frank had made from several trees on the property. The view from the front porch looked out over a gentle slope that ended in a pond.

Malene tucked her woolen shawl around her. "It's beautiful."

"*Ja*. It is. Let's look inside."

Adie opened the door and her smile fell from her face. Inside, there was almost nothing. They could walk across the floor, look down between the boards, and see the earth. There was a ladder where the stairs should have been. The house was only a shell.

Malene put her hand on her sister's shoulder. "Frank has worked hard to make the outside nice. I'm sure the inside will be just as beautiful when he is done."

"In six weeks? He will never finish. I do not know." She shook her head. "I wanted us to spend our first night as husband and wife in our own house."

"Four weeks ago, you did not have a house or a well." Malene hoped she was providing comfort, but she knew her younger sister was extremely disappointed.

There were two barely knee-high columns made from rocks. One was in the center of the house and another was against the backside of the house. Malene looked at one and then at the other. "What are these?"

Adie shrugged. "I was to have a fireplace in the parlor. It does not look like I will get one. Nothing looks like the pictures."

Malene waited for her sister's tears to subside, but it didn't happen. They rode back to the Coleman house in silence, and Adie ran to her room. The house was strangely quiet. Then Malene remembered that Alisa and Joseph were going into town with the children.

Malene rolled up her sleeves, washed her hands, and poured the morning milk into the butter churn. It wasn't a difficult job, but without anyone to talk to, it was boring. She plunged and turned the paddle.

Her mind drifted to Adie's house. Frank's enthusiasm while eating late suppers had given Adie much hope. He'd been working hard to make the house ready, and she was planning on filling it with furniture and children.

Malene stopped for a moment and put her hands on her back as she stood up straight. She had no home, no husband, but she'd have a child. Staying in this big, happy household forever, wasn't an option. She'd have to return home before the winter came. *At least Adie has hopes of a house.*

It seemed as if the baby were pushing his or her feet into her ribcage. She winced and arched her back a little further. She hurt.

There were few jobs for women. She did not have enough education to teach, and the odds of finding a job as a governess were slim. Her only hope was that her father would find her a suitable husband. The one thing in her favor was that women were scarce this side of the Mississippi River. She didn't have to love him. All she needed was someone who would be a kind provider to her and her child.

She resumed churning, but her thoughts turned dark. What if he intended to touch her? She never wanted that pain again, never wanted to endure another man inside of her. The scent of whiskey made her stomach revolt, and Albert always smelled of it. Then he'd push her down and take her. *No. Never again. But how do I warn Adie of the pain?*

3

Many Feathers stopped at the agent's office. He posted his very first letter to Malene. He had worked so hard on it. Each night in the fading light, he wrote a sentence or two, as he made his way back to the reservation. His words were few, as it was still difficult for him to make the letters and spell the words in his head. Ink dribbled and smeared, but he'd tried very hard.

The agent tried to tell him he was late, but he pointed to the date on the pass and told the agent he had arrived in plenty of time. "I have arrived three days ahead of schedule. I am not late. You signed this on Christmas day. I have until March twenty-fifth to return. Today is the twenty-second. And Joseph Coleman has signed that I have been employed at the Coleman ranch in Creed's Crossing, Wyoming, as promised. And this pass is renewable. It says so on the bottom, as long as I adhere to the dates. I am in compliance, sir."

The man raised his eyebrows. "And I guess you want firewood."

Many Feathers smiled. "I do not need it today, for I have no way to transport it. But I am entitled to some, and I'm sure there will be plenty of cold nights ahead. I will return on the twenty-fifth for my allotment."

The agent narrowed his eyes. "What did you do while you were gone?"

Many Feathers refused to allow the man to goad him. "I learned how to mark land, and drill a well. I learned how a windmill worked. I learned much about cattle and planting of fields." He smiled, knowing he had one more ace up his sleeve. "I stayed with a Christian family. I learned about their God who is ruler of all, and to say grace at every meal."

The agent nodded. "Come back on the twenty-fifth and your allotments will be ready for you."

"Thank you, sir." He smiled. He had learned

much from the Colemans and the family that called themselves Coyotes. He knew the white man's ways. He turned and started to leave, but turned back. "If I mark off land, do I bring that land claim to you?"

"Land claims must go to Billings, but you need the tribe's permission." He opened a drawer, took out several printed papers, and handed them to Many Feathers.

"Thank you, sir." He left the agent's office and went straight to the main encampment to what he thought was his wife's mother's tent, but she had died while he was gone. It now belonged to his wife's sister, Hopping Bird, and her family. He offered them the food he still carried, found a spot on the bare earth, and slept.

Morning light awakened him. Hopping Bird fixed him coffee and he drank from the gourd cup. Before the white man, very few of his people ever became ill. Now it was common. He thought about the soaps that the white man used on their bodies, clothes, bedding, and on their dishes. The cup in his hand was stained brown. He never wanted to drink from a gourd cup again.

He had changed. He was still an Indian and very proud of what he was. But there were better things and better ways. The Colemans had called him a progressive thinker. He remembered Alisa saying he should teach by example. He would do that.

In the morning, he went to the chief. "While I was gone, I learned much. I would like to stake claim to some land and have it registered with the land office."

The chief listened to him and nodded. Now he would have to wait for the tribe's decision. The chief called the meeting with the tribe elders and Many Feathers was allowed to attend. No one had ever claimed individual land before. He was given an opportunity to explain what he wanted to do and why.

Eagle Feathers was one of the oldest

members, along with Angry Bear. This was not a case of majority rules, they all had to agree. Eagle Feathers asked questions, lots of questions. Many Feathers talked about farming and building a house. He tried to explain that he was not turning his back on his proud heritage, but he wanted to try new things with the hopes of protecting his people. Had they not suffered great losses? Then he told them of the sign he had received on his way to Creed's Crossing, the great bird that watched over him.

He showed off his new feathers from the turkeys to the pheasants that had provided for him. "Each time I went hunting in harvested fields their numbers were many. The Coleman bellies were full." He spread his hands out. "Our bellies need to be filled."

Angry Bear was in favor of such an experiment, but Eagle Feathers believed that marking land would hurt the whole tribe. Were they not already under marked land?

Hadn't that been the reason why they were having so many problems? The chief remained silent, only nodding occasionally.

Many Feathers listened to the discussion. His heart grew heavy in his chest. His mind wandered back in time.

As a young boy, he went on his first hunt alone. He had heard all the stories from those who were older about how difficult it was to hunt, each boy telling great tales of bravery. From the time he was little, his idea of play consisted of tossing things and making them land where he wanted. This time it was no longer a child's game.

He steeled his nerves and made his way into the grassland area. Instead of entering it, he climbed a small ridge and scanned the area below him. Large birds that were good for eating, ate seeds on the ground. Those were the birds he wanted.

He spotted exactly what he needed. A patch of grass that had been trampled and the seed heads were close to the ground. That was where he would hunt.

He sat between the stalks of tall grasses surrounding the flattened area and silently waited with his spear balanced on his shoulder. Bored with waiting, he had made a game of listening to sounds and identifying them. A dragonfly sat on his spear. If he could hear a fly buzz, why would he not hear a dragonfly?

A quail flew to the ripening seed heads. He slowly put his fingers on his spear and tossed it. A perfect shot. He'd speared the quail through the throat. So much for spending the night in the grass, he had a quick, clean kill. Pride filled him.

The smaller birds were prized not just for their meat, but also because of the skill that it took to hunt them. They were faster and more agile. Holding the bird towards the sky, he thanked its spirit, plucked one small feather, and stuck it in his hair. Then he went home.

He brought the bird to the chief, and the man asked him why he did not take the bird to his family. *For I will kill another for my family.* The chief sent him to bring another bird. He went back to the same spot and killed a pheasant for his family before the evening drew long.

When the chief saw him walk into the encampment with another bird, he was surprised. That was when he was given the name Many Feathers. When asked how he managed to kill two birds, he answered, find the right spot, and sit very still.

Today he had to sit very still, for he had found his spot. He needed spirits to guide these men to him, just as the spirits had guided the birds.

Time stretched with no conclusion. The sun had set, and the tipi glowed with light from the center where a meal was being prepared. He continued to sit and listen to the sounds of their voices. Eagle Feathers was against it, and at one point, he almost convinced Angry Bear. But the chief seemed to be on Many Feathers' side, for he spoke to Angry Bear and Eagle Feathers, asking them to give Many Feathers a chance. The chief agreed that doing nothing was worse than allowing Many Feathers to try. The Colemans were known to be good to the Indians and their land productive. Many Feathers had not told tall tales, he had only spoken the truth about the prosperous ranch.

The debate continued late into the night until Eagle Feathers unwillingly agreed to Many Feathers marking land and using it as his very own, but he had to pay for the land and not with the white man's money.

Many Feathers watched the elder as he stood and stepped to him. The man removed a knife from his belt. Many Feathers stood. He steadied his wits and body as he awaited the sharp blade of the man's punishment. Instead, Angry Feathers grabbed the feather-covered lock of hair that held so many years of pride and cut it off.

A different kind of pain ripped though Many Feathers as he stood before the tribal council. He was being shamed for believing he had a better way. One short lock of hair would serve as a reminder for the rest of his life that his beliefs had cost him his pride. He thanked the council and left. From now forward, he'd be between two worlds.

He gathered his things and rode to the spot that he wanted. With a lake and a river on the portion of land he had chosen, he would never lack for water. He had beautiful mountains on one side to guide him, and plenty of open grassland. He climbed up on a ridge and looked all around. Almost as far as he could see would be his. He held his arms out from his sides and let the night breeze whip his hair as he embraced the spirits of the land.

With nothing more than the glow of the moon, he took out the papers the agent had given him. They told what he would need to stake his claim. He wrote to the land office to obtain the forms he would need. Homesteaders were restricted to only marking a square, but he had no such restriction on a reservation. There were five thousand two hundred eighty feet in a mile and he had to mark at least every twenty feet. It would take him a day to mark each mile. The U.S. government had marked the reservation on the lower side with a fence. The river would mark the other side. That left him two sides and not much time.

He wrote a letter to Malene. The loneliness that had once cloaked him vanished when he was with Malene. Without her, it returned. He saw a future for the two of them, and an end to the starvation of his people. Nothing great came easily, and he was starting with nothing, other than determination.

He caught a fish for his meal. It was something that his people almost never did, yet the Colemans often ate fish. Satisfied, he attempted to sleep, but the burden to succeed was great. It weighed upon him, cheating him of much needed sleep.

If Rabbit Hunter would help... He knew he could not run a ranch of this size alone. He had to have help.

The next day, he rode back to the encampment and left a message with Rabbit Hunter's wife. She was about the same height as Many Feather's wife had been, but she was heavier boned with a beautiful smile that matched her sweet personality. He borrowed their sled, posted his letters with the agent, and picked up his allotments. Then he rode back to where he wanted his property and began to collect stones.

It didn't take him as long as he thought it would with Rabbit Hunter's help. The young man and his wife moved to the property and brought their tipi with them. The two men worked hard and when they were finished, Many Feathers had convinced Rabbit Hunter that they were doing the right thing.

There was no wood to build a fence, and if Many Feathers built a wooden fence, he was certain that it would become firewood for his people. Considering he was not under the same rules that the homesteaders had to abide, he merely needed to mark his land. The stones had done that. With careful notation of each stone on paper, he had what he needed to file his legal claim.

It had been weeks since he left the Coleman ranch. As soon as he registered his claim, he intended to return to the ranch. He picked up his mail. But when he opened the forms, he looked at them and groaned. Too many words and he only understood a few of them. The agent gave him a week's pass to Billings.

***

Malene opened her letters from Many Feathers. Her heart soared with each one. Each page was either smudged or full of ink drippings, his words were limited, and written with the scrawl of a child's penmanship. But each one was filled with hope. He wrote that he was going to Billings to file his land claim and that he had planted seeds in a small garden plot. Rabbit Hunter's wife would care for the plants while he was gone.

"Adie, listen." She read the letters to her sister.

Adie nodded. "I am pleased that Rabbit Hunter is working with Many Feathers. Together they will do well. But he has said nothing about horses and our father."

"I noticed that, too."

"I will remind Papa to buy horses from the Crows."

Malene opened a letter from her father and read it. "Oh, hear what Papa has written."

Adie put down the letter she was reading. "*Ja.*"

"*I have found a man by the name of Marshall*

Hamilton. His wife died about a year ago and he has three children, seven, five, and three. He's in business with his father, Hamilton Wholesalers & Importers Trading Company. They are a well-respected firm that supplies dry goods all over the country. The father lives in New York and Marshall lives in San Francisco. He's extremely conservative, wealthy, and looking for a suitable wife. I met Marshall recently, and he knows the details of your marriage. Albert swindled his company, too."

"That sounds very promising. Did Papa say anything else?"

Malene skimmed the next few paragraphs. "Yes, here. He says Marshall is older and portly, but that I should write to this man. for he is a good and honest man. He's given me an address for him."

"Then you must write. But what about Many Feathers?"

She raised her shoulders and let them drop. "Many Feathers is very kind to me." She chewed on her lower lip. "But I cannot marry an Indian. Living here has been hard enough. Can you imagine me living in a tipi?"

"He said he would build you a house."

"Adie, please. To you, this is all a big adventure. I should have stayed home where I could lounge my days away, maybe my back would not hurt so much."

Adie giggled at her older sister. "You hurt because you are growing a big tummy. Mrs. Coleman says you are fine. Working is good for you."

Malene pulled at her blue and white print. "And wearing dresses with no shape makes me look very portly."

Adie giggled. "You will not mind once your baby comes. You will forget all about it."

"You are right. I came here to protect this baby. And if my papa has found a good man for me, then I need to be a good daughter."

"*Ja*. But Many Feathers is in love with you. Do you not love him?"

***

Many Feathers took his paper along with the forms to the office in Billings. Larger than any town he'd ever been in, he reined in his horse and took a few moments to look around. Most of the buildings contained signs and he was glad he'd learned to read. Slowly, he made his way up the street. He almost missed the land office, as it was tucked between two larger buildings.

He tethered his horse to the long wooden rail out front and stood at the door trying to decide if he should knock or walk in. He rapped once and opened the door. It took a moment for his eyes to adjust to the dim lighting in the small brick building.

There was a man sitting at a desk who looked terrified as he asked, "What do you want?"

"I have come to register my claim to property."

The man's grin looked more like a sneer. "Put your X on the paper and we'll call you."

"My X? Do you not want my name?" His gut tightened as he picked up the pen and dipped it in the inkwell. Very carefully he wrote Many Feathers.

"Have a seat." The man pointed to two wooden chairs.

The office looked very official with maps on the walls and several tall cases with locked drawers. He had to sit in a chair and wait his turn. Doing nothing in a white man's building was very strange to him. The air was damp and musty. He rubbed his nose with his forefinger.

Even though the door to the next room was closed, he could clearly hear every spoken word. With nothing else to do, Many Feathers listened to the conversation in the next room. The man in there took a long time, as he had many things to register, including a mining claim.

A man and woman walked into the tiny building. Their clothes were rumpled and dusty. They looked as though they'd traveled a long way to come to the office. The man signed the paper at the desk and then turned to Many Feathers. "Get up. Don't you know your place?"

"My place?"

"When there are only two chairs and you are taking one of them..." The man glared at Many Feathers.

"I was told to sit. You want me to stand so you can sit?"

"Yes. Stupid savage," the man grumbled.

He rolled his hands over facing his palms up and stood so that they could sit. Standing felt better anyway, as the wooden chair was not comfortable.

When the miner left, he spit on Many Feathers. Many Feathers inhaled and fisted his hands behind is back. He was more than aware that the white man held little respect for

Indians, but he could not understand why. He had never done anything to deserve such treatment. Then the man behind the desk called the couple to register their claim.

"Am I not next?"

"No. They go first. You go when there is time to deal with you."

Many Feathers turned his back to the skinny man behind the desk and found himself staring at a map of his land. It was as if it were drawn from the perspective of a great bird high in the sky. The reservation land was washed in red ink, but it was easy to see the two rivers, the mountains, and the lakes. Pride filled him, as he knew he was claiming a large chunk. He stood a little straighter and puffed out his chest.

He would wait if it took all day, for he was going to own his land. He was entitled to it. The agent had given him a copy of the law. The tribal council had agreed and placed their marks on the paper. The agent had signed that paper, too.

Four more people came into the office and each one went ahead of him. Finally, as the day was ending, his name was called. He took his papers into an even smaller room with a desk.

A man with gray hair and glasses said, "Have a seat. What are you doing here?"

Many Feathers sat in one of two wooden seats on his side of the desk and gazed at all the papers stacked in front of the spectacled man. "I have marked my land, and I wish to file my claim, but my form is not filled out completely as I do not understand some of what you want."

The man held out his hand and Many Feathers handed him the papers.

"This is a very large portion of land. Are you certain it is properly marked?"

"Yes, sir. I was taught how to mark land. Each length of chain is clearly marked."

"But according to this, you've not fenced it."

"No, sir. It is reservation land. I am not a homesteader. I only had to mark and have approval of the tribe."

The man sighed. "Who filled out this form?"

Many Feathers flexed his fingers. "I did. Did I do something wrong?"

"You know how to write?"

"Yes, sir. Mrs. Coleman taught me to read and write. But I often must look up the words in a dictionary. This was too many words."

The man chuckled. "Well, I never had a red man come to my office with a claim, nor have I ever known a red man who could read and write. Let's finish this form. For starters, you need to enter your full name. I need that. What's your full name?"

"Many Feathers."

The man shook his head. "Do you not have an English name?"

"English? It is Many Feathers."

The man took a paper from within a drawer in his desk. "What was your father's name?"

Many Feathers swallowed as he translated the name of his father and settled on Hunter. "Hunter. His last name was Hunter."

The man wrote Hunter. "Now you need a first name. Many Feathers will not work. It needs to be an English name. You have marked much land. What do you intend to do with it?"

"I will build a house, grow vegetables and grain, and will raise cattle. I will be the first rancher on our reservation."

The man nodded and transferred the information to a larger map. "As many marks as you have made. I will give you the name of Mark. From now on you will be Mark Hunter. You will no longer sign things as Many Feathers. Your agent should have given you an English name. I will fill those forms out for you. From which tribe are you?"

"Apsáalooke."

"You are a Crow."

"Yes, sir." Many Feathers watched what the

man was doing. Several times forms were passed, and with effort, Many Feathers signed Mark Hunter. In asking for this claim, it had cost him his name, but he had a new one to go with his new life as a rancher. Eagle Feathers attempt to shame had created a new path to autonomy.

Many Feathers left the office with his deed and his new name. He counted several coins and decided he'd buy some food. The bakery was closing as he approached, but he asked anyway.

An older woman, with her hair tied into a knot, slipped several cookies and loaf of bread into a bag. "Here. Now go away!"

"What do I owe you?"

"Nothing. Go!" She pointed to the door.

Money still confused him so he put some change on the counter and left. These people treated him as if he were a wolf that was about to devour them. He had planned to stay in town, but decided it was best if he didn't. He rode until he spotted a stockyard and then what he thought might be the Reiner house by Malene's description. If he could sleep in their barn, he'd be grateful. The sun was setting as he knocked on the door.

A woman with hair the color of fire opened the door.

"Hello, I am Many Feathers. Is this the home of Adelwulf Reiner?"

"One minute, please."

The woman closed the door, and a moment later, Mr. Reiner opened it.

"Yes. You want me?"

"We met on the reservation. I went with Frank, Adie, and Malene to the Coleman ranch."

Adelwulf Reiner cocked his head and intently stared for a moment. "Ah, yes. I remember your name."

"Thank you. I had business in Billings and I am on my way back to the reservation. I stopped with the hope...you allow me to sleep in your barn?"

The man looked up and down at him, and then asked him inside.

Many Feathers stepped into the impressive house.

Mr. Reiner called, "Cook, have your husband take care of this man's horse and prepare a room for him to sleep."

"Come with me," Mr. Reiner offered.

Many Feathers looked around the spacious rooms that were filled with fancy furniture and things on every wall and surface. It was too much and he wondered why people had so many things with no use.

Mr. Reiner motioned for Many Feathers to sit in the chair by his desk.

The red leather chair was soft yet firm. He liked it.

Mr. Reiner put his fingers together when he took his seat behind the big desk. "The man I met had feathers in his hair."

"Yes." He lifted his shortened lock of hair. "I

traded my feathers for the chance to have my own land and create my own ranch."

"How can you do that when your people must stay on the reservation?"

"The land is on the reservation." He reached into his pouch and withdrew his papers. He chose the deed and passed it to Mr. Reiner.

"This says Mark Hunter owns the land."

"Yes. That is my English name. I had to have such a name for the deed. It's official." He passed the piece of paper that recorded his new name.

Mr. Reiner looked at that paper before he handed both papers back.

"My daughters speak highly of you."

"That is good."

"But Malene has said nothing about you losing your feathers."

"I wrote her about it, but she has not seen me. I'm sure it will be a surprise."

Mr. Reiner stood and went to a fancy bottle on a table. "Would you like a drink?"

"I do not drink spirit water, if that is what you are offering, but I would like plain water."

"Would you prefer coffee?"

"No, sir. Thank you. Water is good. It is night and time for sleep."

"Would you like some food?" Mr. Reiner picked up a bell and rang it.

"No, sir. I have eaten. Thank you for the offer."

The woman with hair like fire came, left, and returned with a pitcher of water and a glass.

He gulped the cool water until he thought his insides would explode and his thirst was quenched. "Thank you."

"When will you be leaving?" Mr. Reiner asked.

"Tomorrow morning. I have much to do on the reservation before I leave for the Coleman ranch in a few days."

"Very well. In the morning, I shall give you a packet to give to my daughters."

"I will safeguard it and give it to them."

The man nodded and pointed at the woman with hair the color of flames who had returned to the room.

She also acted as if she were about to be eaten. He did not understand these people. But he allowed the woman to show him to a room, as she pointed to another room down the hall.

"Yes. Thank you." He knew about such a room, except this one didn't have a tub. He washed his hands and face and went back to the room. He took off his clothes and climbed into bed. It was almost too soft, but he loved it. Somehow, he would make such a bed for Malene.

He closed his eyes and opened them when sunshine filtered into the room. The firebox in his room was different and filled with black chunks. He picked one up and examined it. It left black dust on his hands. He put it back and washed his hands before going downstairs.

There he found Mr. Reiner and a big breakfast of eggs and salty strips of meat. It tasted delicious. He drank his coffee and asked about the black chunks.

"Coal. It is what is used on the trains. It's better than wood."

So, that is coal. "And how do you buy it?"

"It comes by train. But you will need a wagon to bring it home."

Many Feathers nodded. It would be good for his house, being there was little wood on the reservation. "Does it work in stoves, too?"

"Yes. Very well."

"There is a coal mine on the reservation, but I have never actually been to the mine. I have only passed it on occasion."

Mr. Reiner handed him a packet tied with string that was sitting on the table. "You will see that my daughters get this?"

"Yes, sir." Many Feathers thanked the man and left. With luck, he'd be on the reservation by sundown.

He spent the night in a tipi with the scouts and then went straight to the agent's office, handed over the paperwork for his name, and obtained a pass to go to the Coleman ranch for sixty days. He gave Rabbit Hunter several instructions and left the following morning. He hoped the Coleman ranch would again pay him for working.

He made good time, as the weather was nice the whole way. Flowers grew amongst the young grass and gave the air a sweet scent. The sun warmed him during the day, and the nights were cool but not freezing. In the clear blue sky above him, he watched a large bird circle several times. His confidence built as he neared the Coleman ranch.

Adie was hanging clothes on a line strung between two trees when he rode up on his horse. She squealed with delight and ran to see him. "Your feathers! What happened?"

"I gave them up for my own ranch. Where is Malene?"

"Inside. Come."

"Wait. I have something from your father."

She waited for him as he went to his horse and brought her a packet. She took the packet, grabbed his hand, and pulled him to the house where Malene was busy sewing.

The minute Malene saw him, her face lit up, and she beamed a big smile at him. "Many Feathers! Where are your feathers?"

He laughed and showed them his shortened lock of hair. "I traded them for my own land. It is now deeded to me. I also have a new name. I am Mark Hunter. And you are heavy with child!"

***

Malene nodded. The other men in the house seemed to ignore her condition as if they dare not speak about it, but Many Feathers came to her and placed his hands on her belly.

"Where are the feet?"

"I think in my back. This is not easy for me."

"Your cheeks glow, but you look sad. I do not understand." He held her in his arms and kissed her.

"Ah, hem!" Mrs. Coleman said, as she entered the room. "No kissing."

Many Feathers grinned at the woman with the single long braid that fell over her shoulder. Then he kissed Mrs. Coleman on the cheek. "Kissing is good. It shows honor."

"Not in this house!" She frowned at him, but the sparkle in her eyes said that she was pleased to see him.

"That is sad. So how do you know that I am happy to be here?"

"A smile is sufficient." She turned and as she left the room, she said, "No kissing."

Malene and Adie giggled.

"Frank and I are always in trouble for kissing. I like being kissed. But I don't think Frank would like you kissing me. He would get jealous and think that I like you better than him."

Many Feathers' smile broadened. "I will let only Frank kiss you, then there are no problems. You do not want a jealous husband."

"Tell us about your ranch," Adie begged.

"I will, but I must tend to my horse and see Mr. Joseph Coleman first."

Malene watched as he left. His hands on her belly felt wonderful. His lips on hers felt wonderful. Everything about him was wonderful. She didn't want him to leave the room. She could barely pack up her sewing as her hands shook with pure joy.

"Malene, Papa gave him a package to bring to us."

They untied the string and removed the plain paper. Inside were several pages from magazines showing fancy furniture for the parlor and dining room. Their papa enclosed a note requesting that they post a letter to him immediately telling him exactly what they received. The packet also contained twenty one-dollar bills, and wrapped in a small piece of cloth, was a simple but favorite pair of earrings that Malene had left behind.

Malene went to the writing desk and wrote back to her papa, thanking him for the earrings, and the twenty dollars, along with the thoughtful inclusion of furniture pages.

Adie hung over her big sister's shoulder. "I do not understand why he wants to know so much about the package. We always thank him for the money he sends."

Malene shook her head. "Adie, it is a test. He wants to know if he can trust Many Feathers."

Adie turned and plopped into a nearby chair. "Oh. Do you think he would steal?"

"I do not think he would do such a thing, but Papa has no other way of knowing. Better to do a small test."

"Twenty dollars is not a small test."

"And horses are worth more than twenty dollars. I think Albert has made Papa more cautious."

"*Ja*. I think you are right." Adie put her elbow on the chair's arm and rested her chin in the palm of her hand.

"It is sad that we will never know what Papa put in the package. He did not tell us."

Adie blew out a long breath. "Because if he did, we might try to hide what Many Feathers has done?"

"*Ja*. He knows we like him and his people." Malene sealed the paper in an envelope. "There's one more thing. Many Feathers can read. He would know if it were a test."

"I do not like this. And I don't like waiting. Do you think Papa would tell us if something were missing?"

Malene shrugged. "Or would Papa say that something was missing to make us distrust Many Feathers?"

***

"Hey, look who is here!" John Coleman grinned as he greeted Many Feathers.

"I have fifty-four days before I return." Many Feathers smiled back and spotted Joseph, Bear, and Frank walking in his direction.

"What happened to your feathers?" Joseph asked.

"It was my payment for my own land. I now have my own ranch."

"Great!" Joseph slapped Many Feathers on the back.

"Not quite. My land is empty. I need to learn more and buy steers." He told them how much he marked off and they all looked at him wide-eyed. A tiny wedge of insecurity stabbed at his chest. "Is that wrong?"

Joseph chuckled. "It's yours. Nothing wrong with that. We can't grab that much land."

"Plus there is more grazing room."

Frank whistled. "All that for feathers? You are one lucky man."

"Not really." He fingered his shortened

strands of hair. "My pride they took from me. I am no longer Many Feathers. They did not give me another name, but when I recorded the deed, I got a new name. I am now Mark Hunter."

Bear looked at him askance. "How did you get that name?"

"All Indians are supposed to have English names. Our agent did not do it. Now we all need them and the name must be registered. You will need one, too." He went on to tell them how the white man at the office in Billings gave him the new name.

"Tonight, we celebrate," Joseph said. "Our new rancher to the north, Mark Hunter! Welcome to the Coleman ranch." He shook hands with Mark.

"I am still Apsáalooke."

"Yes, you will always be a Crow. It is in your blood and it colors your skin. It is your heritage and your past, but Mark Hunter has a future. With luck, he will show his people another way and give them hope."

Joseph's words sounded grand, but the weight of the burden fell squarely on Many Feathers' shoulders. It was one thing to be given a new name, but suddenly he was aware that he had to become Mark Hunter.

That evening after dinner, the adult family members gathered in the kitchen, including John and Lydia, Bear and his wife Abigail, and Bear's brother Falcon. The women sat at the small table while the men stood. They laughed, joked, and told stories, but they all listened as Mark told them of his trip to Billings and the way he was treated.

"You will face that many times in your life. I am sorry, but people do not understand. They have been taught that your people are savages and worthless creatures. We are all God's children. You are always welcome here as a man and as a fellow rancher," Alisa Coleman said.

Mark nodded. "I have much to learn."

"Yes, you do. But you learn quickly, and we appreciate your help," Joseph said as he leaned over his wife and picked up a cookie from the plate in front of her.

Mark looked at Frank. "I am hoping you will help me. I wish to use your well drilling equipment and buy a windmill."

Frank nodded. "I'd still be out there sinking holes where there is no water if it were not for you."

Mark laughed. "You would have found it eventually. You are like a wolf who sinks his teeth into prey."

Joseph looked around the room. "We're plowing fields tomorrow. It's time we all find sleep."

Mark found himself sharing a room with Lydia's little boys. He quietly entered the room and tumbled into the soft bed. The two boys slept together in the bed across the room. The white man kept everyone separate, but not his people. Grandparents, parents and children all shared the same tipi.

Morning broke almost too soon. Mark had lain awake thinking about his new life. Now, it was in front of him.

As he plowed the field, he realized he couldn't have cattle wandering into it. He'd have to prevent that, and he wasn't certain how much a plow cost, but he knew it wasn't cheap. As the sun moved directly overhead, Malene brought him a sandwich and some milk.

He stopped for the midday meal, but his shoulders hurt and so did his hips. Walking behind a horse and a plow took strength, but he didn't want to admit to aching muscles. He skipped his supper and tumbled into bed before the sun set. Had he figured that ranching would be easy?

***

Malene opened the letter from her parents

and squealed with delight. "They are coming!"

"*Ja!* Mine says the same thing." Adie grinned. "They will be here for my wedding."

"I must finish the embroidery on your dress."

"It is so beautiful. You have taken my plain dress and made it very special. Mrs. Coleman has taught us so much."

"She has. I almost dread the day I will leave this wonderful noisy household."

Adie giggled. "Mama will be so surprised. She is used to peace and quiet."

"That is true."

Malene opened all her letters except for the one from Marshall Hamilton. She'd read that when she was completely alone. She gathered her things and put them in her trunk. She had to finish the needlework on Adie's dress since she was going to wear it for her wedding.

The house was strangely quiet when she took a seat by the window, then she realized why. Issy, Clarissa, and Virginia were out in the garden with Adie and Alisa. Beyond them, the men worked in the fields. Lydia's little boys were playing keep-away with a ball while Lydia sat under a tree and read. It was a serene picture of country life, but she did not belong to it.

Her needle pierced the blue linen fabric, again and again. Her white thread created an intricate pattern of flowers within scalloped borders that she had carefully marked on the skirt. The entire dress looked as beautiful as anything that could have been ordered from New York. Adie's seamstress skills were excellent and Malene loved to do the embroidery work.

She found herself staring out the window. In the far distance, two workhorses pulled a plow while Many Feathers steered it. He was easy to spot, for his dark skin glistened in the sun and his long hair fell around his shirtless body. Falcon, Bear, and their father wore their hair short like the Colemans. She smiled. The thought of that hard body and gentle hands sent a warm shiver through her.

Malene didn't want to open that letter from Marshall. She didn't want to know what he had written. A strange man in a far away place, she felt as though she was being auctioned off to the highest bidder. She didn't want to take her gaze from the man behind the plow.

Then the baby kicked her and she inhaled with the pain. Other women didn't seem to complain of pain when they were with child, but this child never gave her any relief. She was tired, and tired of carrying a baby that never seemed to sleep.

4

At the end of the day in the fields, Mark Hunter peeled off the white man's pants he wore and dove into the pond near the house. The other men followed him, hooting and hollering as they splashed and played. The water flowing over him washed the dirt and sweat from his body. Lydia's two little boys stripped and ran to the pond while their mother screamed no.

Joseph called, "Let them come and have fun."

The youngest, Michael, tripped and fell face first into the water. Falcon grabbed him and tossed him to his grandfather who tossed him to his dad. But when Mark caught the child, he realized the little guy still had not found his breath. "You do not swim?"

The child clung to him for dear life as if he were about to be thrown again.

He took Michael away from the splashing to

a quieter spot, and lowered the boy gently into the water. "Kick with your feet. Kick hard and make big splashes."

Mark went from holding the child at the waist to holding his hands. He curled the child's hands into little cups and taught him to use his hands like an animal's webbed paws in the water. Soon Mark was able to let go of the child for a few seconds. He praised the boy, then praised him some more. Children of the tribe usually learned to swim their first summer of life. This child was on his fourth summer. Mark knew the boy would be a strong swimmer by the end of the season.

Lydia was now on the bank calling for her son.

"Your ma wants you. We'll swim tomorrow." He helped Michael swim until the boy could touch the bottom with his feet. Mark watched as Michael scurried to his mom with a proud smile. Mark got off his knees and stood.

Lydia screamed.

"What's wrong?" He looked behind him as if he'd find a snake, then looked at Lydia's bright red face. He got out of the water, grabbed his pants, and pulled them on. "Are you all right?"

The woman heaved a sigh and yanked on her son's hands as they walked quickly to the house. He slipped his feet into his moccasins and buttoned his pants.

When he reached the back door of the house, Alisa stood waiting for him. In one hand, she had a wooden spoon, and she was tapping her foot. He'd seen that look on her face when she was angry with the children, but he had no idea why she was angry with him, until she opened her mouth.

"You have been told that you do not walk naked around here. That is not polite."

"I was swimming."

"You were naked in front of Lydia."

He rolled his palms over and cocked his head. "You want me to swim with clothes on?"

"No. Men do not show themselves to other

people."

"I am a man. I am made like a man. What is the problem?"

She groaned and turned from him. "Do not do it again. Do you understand? We are civilized. Lydia is crying."

He shook his head and went to his room to find clean pants for supper. Malene was waiting for him when he came out of the room. She looked pretty and very feminine in her brown dress with her protruding belly.

Malene frowned at him. "You must be careful. We are supposed to not know what a man looks like."

"You are...I forget the word...jeking?"

She sighed. "Joking? I am not joking." She put her hand on his shoulder. "You are very much a man and a fine one, but I should have never seen you, and Lydia should have never seen you."

"Why?"

"Because it gives us bad thoughts."

He watched Malene blush. Looking in each direction of the narrow room, he turned back to Malene and stole a kiss. "Like kissing?"

Her tongue darted over her lips. "Oh yes. Like kissing."

He could feel the grin pushing his cheeks upward. "Then I will find ways to kiss you more often. We will take a walk after supper."

"You need to apologize to Lydia and to John."

He pressed his lips together as he tried to understand. "We need to eat."

He held Malene's chair and then Virginia's before taking the one next to the young girl. After, he held up his hand and looked at John and Lydia, but Lydia stared at her plate. "I apologize for this afternoon. I did not know that you think seeing a man is evil." Mrs. Coleman attempted to cut him off, but he held up his hand in her direction. "Let me finish. I meant no harm. My people think nothing of being…without clothes. From an early age we are taught not to look, but we know. We do not hide our bodies. I did not know that you think it is wrong to see another person. I don't understand, but I will be more careful."

Virginia giggled.

He turned to her. "Little boys grow up to be men. Nothing changes."

She giggled some more and put mashed potatoes on her plate before passing him the bowl.

John spoke very quietly. "I accept your apology, and so does Lydia."

Mark looked at Malene and her cheeks were very pink. He also figured that this family would not appreciate him showing any signs of eagerness towards a woman. He stuck his fork into his food and ate. Plowing gave him a hearty appetite and there was plenty of delicious food on the table.

Malene and Adie washed the dishes and when they were done, Malene walked onto the back porch where he stood waiting for her. He took her hand and strode off in the direction of some trees that grew along the creek that fed the pond.

"Where are you taking me?"

"Where I can kiss you and not get in trouble for it. I want to kiss you and hold your child. I like kissing."

"Should we not bring a lantern?"

He pointed to the cloudless navy blue sky filled with a multitude of stars that twinkled. "There is enough light for us to walk."

He pulled her into the trees and wrapped her into his arms. His lips crashed onto hers. He parted them with his tongue. She tasted of coffee and cookies. One hand cupped her soft derrière while the other held the nape of her neck. She was sweet - soft and sweet. His tongue danced with hers as heat pooled in his loins. Hitching up her skirt, his hands found soft flesh.

She protested into his mouth, but he did not care. He wanted her as a man wants what he'd not had since before his wife had died. Her protests stopped, and she melted into his arms. He whispered his love in her ear in his own language, and she sighed as if she knew what he said. His lips traveled down her neck to her pink tipped breasts. "Too many clothes."

She undid her buttons, giving him access to her. Her breathing was heavy as he licked and kissed her. She moaned and arched her back. Her milky white skin seemed to glow in the moonlight. His hands cupped the child between them. Tight white skin covered a hard, firm belly. He drew back and moved clothes out of his way as he felt the child growing within her.

He took her hand and placed it on her full belly. "This is the head and this is the child's back. I should be feeling the baby's bottom, not a head. This child needs to turn around and put its head down."

"What does that mean?"

"This child is in danger. You are not a horse.

No one can reach inside of you and turn this baby at the last minute. Pray to your god for this child to turn or you will have a very difficult birthing."

Tears filled her eyes and he kissed them away. His lips followed her jaw to her ear, then down her neck.

She inhaled a deep breath.

He cupped her breasts and groaned as his mouth covered a pink nipple. The beauty of his woman filled with child pulsed in his loins. His need was great, but she was too heavy and would not understand. He whispered in her ear, "Kissing leads to good things."

He turned and walked away from her to spill his seed. He heard her footsteps behind him, but when she slipped her arms around his waist, his body convulsed with pleasure. When he could compose himself, he turned to her.

She smiled and slipped her hands under his shirt. Another round of fire ran through him.

Before he helped her button her clothes, his lips traveled one more time over her sweetly scented skin. His fingers caressed her soft smooth body. "You are special, Malene, and you will be my wife. I will build you a grand house and treat you like a chief's wife. I will bring you the best of everything."

She gripped his shoulders. "I cannot marry you. You are an Indian."

"Your heart and body say you will be my wife. You will be Mrs. Mark Hunter, wife of rancher Many Feathers who no longer has feathers."

***

Malene hoped no one would notice her blush-stained skin and bruised lips, as she stepped into the kitchen. Mark ran up the stairs as she stepped into the parlor. Adie was crocheting a pink shawl, and Mrs. Coleman was mending socks. Malene picked up her sister's blue dress from the large basket next to the sofa and went back to embroidering it. Six inches deep of elaborate needlework wrapped the hem and was to be finished in a flourish that went up the skirt slightly off centered. The sleeves were embroidered, as was the collar. She probably only had another eighteen inches of stitching left to do.

A half hour later, Adie packed up what she was doing and put it in a basket. Malene wiped her needle before dropping it in the tiny glass jar with a cork stopper. "Yes. It is late and we need to go to sleep."

Mrs. Coleman looked up. "Kissing leads to more, and you are not supposed to be sneaking off with him. I know what you are doing, and it is a dangerous game. You are not a child, and you know where it leads."

Malene took a deep breath. "You are right. I am not a child. There is no reason why I cannot walk with him. We talk. I like his company." She looked back over her shoulder.

"And I like his kisses. He is very sweet to me."

"You are also a married woman."

Not for long.

It was after Adie was asleep that Malene got out of bed and opened her trunk. Inside was the letter that Marshall had written. She could not sleep for the baby kicking her, and for her thoughts of Mark. Now was as good a time as any to read what Marshall had written. With a heavy heart, she slipped the sharp edge of the letter opener under the flap and quietly slit it. She withdrew the pale blue paper with the crest of Hamilton Wholesalers & Importers Trading Company at the top and, while standing by the window in the light of the moon, she read.

My delicate position? No one around here considers this delicate. September? I guess that will be fine. At least, it won't be too hot or too cold. The trees should be pretty. She let out an audible groan. *Thirty-nine? That's almost old enough to be my father. A suite of rooms that includes a nursery and will become mine after we are married? That's good. That means he won't be sleeping with me every night.*

She put the letter away. She had no idea what to say to him, or if she wanted to say anything. *I promised Papa.*

The night was filled with noisy insects as she slipped between the sheets. A minute later, she kicked the top sheet off. Perspiration covered her and ran in little rivulets that almost tickled as the beads of sweat headed for the bottom sheet. She plucked at the lightweight fabric that clung to her wet skin. The baby kicked. She whispered, "Settle down, sweet baby, and go to sleep."

But she couldn't find sleep. She ran her hands over her belly and felt the hard bulge beneath her skin. *How does Many Feath-Mark know that the head should go down?*

She and Mark took many evening walks, but they were more careful, as they both knew that kissing led to much more. Yet his touch excited her and she hungered for it.

His skin had darkened in the sun. His forearms were smooth as was his chest. And when the men came in for dinner, if they had not jumped into the pond, the stench of sweat almost gagged her, but Mark had no such odor. He could be dripping wet and not smell like a wet dog.

Having lay awake most of the night it seemed morning came too early. The men jabbered about roping as if it were a great sport. Malene looked across the table at her sister and her sister shrugged. Malene grinned. It was time to discover what exactly the men were doing. After breakfast with the morning chores completed, she and Adie took the buggy to watch the men.

With fields plowed and seeded, the men had begun to brand the young calves. She didn't like to watch what they were doing to the baby bovines, but she enjoyed watching Mark rope them. The other men would toss the rope and usually miss, but not Mark. Joseph had been roping cattle most of his life, but it was new to Mark. It didn't take much to realize that the men were envious of Mark's ability and grateful that he was making their job easier.

Malene's mind wandered as she watched the men and soon settled on Adie's upcoming wedding. Wedding invitations had gone out through the county. But when Adie realized that if she married inside the church, then the Coyote family would not be allowed to attend nor would Mark, she asked for the wedding to take place outside. The preacher said that was fine with him, and Frank seemed pleased.

A smile tugged at Malene's cheeks. Her sister would do well. Adie's genuine kindness extended to everyone on the ranch.

When she and Adie had decided they had watched long enough, Adie turned the buggy around. But it didn't take much for Malene to recognize that Adie was daydreaming.

"Hello?" Malene waved her hand in front of Adie's face, as they made their way from the grass pasture to the house. "You are far away."

"Thinking about my house."

"Are you still worried that your house won't be ready?"

Adie nodded.

"Maybe we should ask Frank to show it to us tonight."

"I am afraid it still looks like an empty shell." Adie pulled on the reins and steered the horses between two plowed fields as they headed to the Coleman house.

"Frank has worked late almost every night. I doubt that the house is still empty inside." Beyond the house and barn, way in the distance, stood a ridgeline and someplace next to that Adie's new house was tucked. Malene squinted her eyes from the sun and still couldn't see an outline of Adie's house.

The Coleman men would be taking a few days after Adie's wedding to move cattle northward for the summer. Frank said they would be spending the night in that shed where they had stayed before arriving at the Coleman house. That was one of the reasons Frank and Mark had worked so late on Adie's house. According to Mark, Frank was concerned about having everything ready for Adie.

Adie wiped the perspiration from her forehead. "One of us needs to churn butter, and I thought I'd make some muffins. By the time they are in the oven, I'll take the churning job from you."

"That sounds more than fair."

That evening at supper there was a big discussion about who would move where to make room for Mr. and Mrs. Reiner.

"I do not need a bed or a bedroom," Mark offered.

Lydia said the boys could move back in with her and her husband. But one of the older boys offered to move to the barn with Mark. That would allow Lydia's boys to take his bed.

Adie asked about seeing the house, but Frank refused her. "I want to surprise you. No peeking. You will like it. I promise."

***

Mark moved his things to the barn. As he lay there, he realized the barn was cooler than the house. Like a tipi, the barn had holes in the roof that allowed heat to escape. He looked at the open areas and the cupolas with their turbines that moved the hot air. In the winter, he needed the hot air to stay inside, but in the summer, such a thing would be good. He had to figure out a way to reverse it for winter. If he made a firebox…

The barn was also darker than the house and he awakened later than he should. He shook his blanket that he'd laid on the straw and folded it neatly. The men were already heading out. He saddled his horse and caught

up to them. But about the time they got ready
to start working, dark clouds began to roll in
and the men headed back to the barn, except
for Frank and Mark. They went to Frank's
house.

Frank had hired a man to do the walls and
they were smooth as skin. The staircase and
newel post was in place, and he was working
on the spindles. He was also working on
something else.

Mark picked up the big chunk of wood that
had been turned on the strange piece of
equipment. "What is it?"

"A poster for our bed, but I am not done."

Mark cocked his head. "Poster?"

Frank showed him the other three he had
done. "One for each corner of the bed."

"Mmm."

"If you will help, I might be able to finish the
spindles today."

Mark pitched in. He ran the machine while
Frank used a chisel to turn the small pieces of

wood into fancy, smooth, rounded spindles. But after watching Frank make several, Mark wanted to try making one. The first time, the chisel flipped out of his hand. Then he figured it out.

Rain hammered the metal roof while they worked. But together they managed to do every spindle for the staircase. Using the hand drill, they installed each one and put on the handrail.

"Want to try to finish the bed before we quit for supper?"

Mark nodded and his stomach growled in protest. Skipping two meals was nothing. Only when he was here, did he eat regularly and have so much food. "I need to sink a well and put in a windmill before winter. Do you think you can help me?"

"Not a problem. You let me know when and I will be there. You've been a huge help to me. If you want, I'll bring help with me. John and Edward will help you. It'll be fun. I'll bring

Adie."

"I doubt Lydia will come." Mark laughed. "She still cannot look at me."

Frank chuckled. "I heard Malene has seen you, too."

Mark shrugged. "I do not understand your ways. Why is it bad to see a man?"

"I don't know. But that is what we've been taught. The most I have ever done is sneak a few kisses with Adie. We will wait until our wedding night. And I pray I do not hurt her."

"Her path will be blocked. There is often blood, but not much. It might hurt her for a second and then it is over. Push her...door open and then be still until she catches her breath. It is often the next day when she will feel the difference. Be gentle with her."

Frank sat on a step. "How do you know so much?"

"We do not hide such things. And I had a wife. Women want to be...apprised."

"Huh?"

"Wrong word?"

"Probably."

"They want to feel special. Take time and let them find joy first. Treat them as if they are the most important human to ever walk the earth."

"Ah!" Frank stretched his legs out in front of him. "Adie knows I love her."

"That is good. Make sure you show her how much you love her every day. Always be tender. I touch Malene and she melts in my arms."

"Did she tell you that she is to marry another man? Her father has found her a rich man in San Francisco."

Mark's heart sank to someplace in his guts. "No! She cannot marry another. She loves *me*!"

Frank stood, grabbed the broom, then swept up the wood chips, and placed them in a box. "I should have not told you."

***

"Someone is coming!" one of the children shouted.

Adie scampered down the staircase and out the door and Malene was right behind her. In the far distance, they saw a coach, and it was traveling at a fair speed, judging by the size of the dust clouds. Malene took Adie's hand as they waited.

"Do you think it is Mama and Papa?" Adie asked as she squeezed her sister's hand a little tighter.

"Adie, my fingers will turn blue."

"Sorry. I'm so excited."

As the carriage drew closer, they both wondered if they remembered how to breathe. Malene let go of her sister's hand and waved. "It's Cook and Dan."

"You're certain?"

"Yes." Malene wanted to run to them, but she could no longer do such a thing with her belly. She turned to Virginia who stood beside them. "Tell your ma that my parents have not traveled alone. They have brought Cook and Dan with them."

A moment later, Mrs. Coleman joined Malene and giggled. "Where shall I put everyone?"

When the carriage came to a stop, Dan jumped from his high perch and opened the door for the Reiners. Adelwulf stepped out first and then he helped his wife, Fredericka, from the carriage. There was a flurry of hugs, kisses, handshakes, and introductions.

Mrs. Coleman said, "Children, go play and leave the adults. When it is suppertime, I will call you." She turned to one of the boys. "Sky, take the carriage and the horses to the barn."

Bear's youngest brother climbed up on the carriage.

"And when you're done, ride out and tell the men. I will not wait supper tonight." She turned to her guests. "Come inside where you are out of the sun."

Dan began to protest the young boy

handling the carriage.

"It is fine for Sky to care for the animals," Malene said. "He loves them."

"But he is a boy."

"Who has been raised around them and is used to doing chores."

Malene walked her mother inside. "There is a toilet upstairs. Wash up while I help Mrs. Coleman with the tea. When you are done, come to the parlor."

Malene went to the kitchen to help with the activities there. Virginia stood off to one side looking a wee bit anxious. Malene smiled at her. "Virginia, will you peel the potatoes?"

The child nodded.

"Clarissa, will you check the garden for any extra vegetables?"

The young teen nodded. "Issy is upstairs taking things from our room." She looked at her ma. "I think we're sleeping in the attic."

"I think you are right." Alisa giggled. "You are good girls and I am proud of your thoughtfulness." Then she turned to Malene. "Go visit with your mother and her friend."

"I think Cook would be happier in the kitchen than sitting in your parlor."

"Nonsense. She is a guest."

Laughter bubbled up her throat. "You do not know Cook."

A few minutes later, everyone was settled in the parlor and Mrs. Coleman served tea with slices of bread and jam.

Malene looked around the room and smiled. It was a picture perfect moment and one she thought she'd always treasure. Her mother smiled and chatted with Mrs. Coleman as if they'd been friends forever. Dan sat with his hat on his knee and chatted with her father, and Adie was chatting with Cook about all the things she had learned to do in the kitchen.

But a few seconds later, it all dissolved as mud-caked men thundered in on horseback and jumped into the pond. Her heart pounded in her chest as she watched the spectacle. The horses were just as coated in mud. She couldn't imagine what they had been doing. She had never seen such a mess.

She excused herself from the room and quickly went outside. "Men, please! My parents have arrived."

They didn't seem to hear her so she stood on the edge of the bank and tried one more time. "Please. I need you on your best behavior. My parents are - ah-h-h-h!"

Her boots slipped on the muddied grass and she lost her balance. The world went in slow motion. Her arms windmilled at her sides and she avoided falling on her back, but her feet kept sliding until they suddenly quit sliding which jolted her forward, and she landed in Joseph's arms with a huge splash.

Mark took her into his arms and kissed her. "You're not supposed to be swimming with us."

Tears began to flow. "My parents are here. I wanted everyone to know. Instead, you are all acting like wild animals."

"I'll carry you out of the water. But I won't put you down until I'm standing by my pants and you'd better not leave me or I'll be in so much trouble with Mrs. Coleman."

"Are you naked?"

He grinned.

"You are bad."

"I am not bad. I am a man and proud of it."

She tried to make a mean face, but giggles burst from within her. "Now I know why you men swim. The water feels wonderful."

"We've been branding in a muddy field. It was not muddy when we started, but it became muddy." He changed his hold on her. "Your skirt needs to cover me."

She allowed him to carry her from the water, and the way he put her on her feet gave her a full view of him as he pulled on his pants. The lump in her throat was large and she swallowed it. She had never really seen her husband, but seeing Mark sent fire through her body.

He smiled at her. "Never fear me."

She nodded then realized that the entire male household had just watched her watching Mark. Heat flowed up her neck and over her cheeks. Yet, somehow she felt no shame. The man she first knew as Many Feathers was indeed a man.

She turned and looked at the men still in the water. "I was trying to tell you to be on your best behavior because my parents have arrived."

She squared her shoulders and walked to the house.

***

The next time Mark saw her, she had changed into her pale yellow dress and her hair was tied in a knot at the nape of her neck. Another table had been pulled up to the dining room table and four more chairs were brought from various rooms. Malene practically ignored him, but he held her chair for her to sit. Then he held Virginia's, and waited for Alisa to sit. Then he sat. He had learned the white man's way and their polite words.

He trusted the Colemans, but he wasn't certain he could trust Mr. Reiner. Mark knew about the parcel because Adie had told him, but had never heard another word about his little test. It had raised his hackles, but he had not touched that packet. So if anything were deemed missing, it would be an untruth.

He placed his napkin on his lap, took a spoonful of peas, a spoonful of potatoes, and a slice of ham. He stared at the pickled apples for a moment while he decided if he wanted to try one. A single ring made its way to his plate. He took three of the baby cabbages, and realized Virginia didn't have one. He found the smallest one and put it on her plate before he passed the plate.

He leaned over and whispered, "Try it. I promise they taste terrible."

She giggled and passed him the butter.

He put a small amount of butter on the small plate next to his roll. He had to prove he was worthy of Malene. She didn't need a wealthy white man. She needed someone who loved her for herself.

Virginia popped the whole little cabbage in her mouth, chewed, shuddered, and swallowed.

It took everything he had to swallow what was in his mouth and not choke on it from the laughter he kept to himself. He leaned over to her and, in a low voice, said, "I never lie."

Malene looked at him, and he could tell by the smirk on her face that she, too, wanted to laugh.

Adie chatted almost non-stop to her parents about the wedding plans. But when Adie mentioned her wedding dress, her mother's eyes grew wide.

"You cannot wear a dress that you made. Why did you not buy one?"

"Because my dress is beautiful. Malene has embroidered it for me."

Mrs. Reiner looked as if a ghost had walked down the table. But Mark also had a feeling that there was going to be a great battle between the mother and the daughter. And Mrs. Coleman was being very quiet.

He finished his meal and said, "Excuse me, please. It's been a long day. It's been wonderful to see you both again. Thank you, Mrs. Coleman, for the lovely meal and those tasty little cabbages." He picked up his plates and looked at Malene. "I hope to see you later. I'll be out back."

Mrs. Coleman looked at him as if she wanted to throw a spear at him. He smiled and took his plates to the kitchen. He knew Adie would not be helping her sister, and Mrs. Coleman should visit with her guests. He lifted the hot water from the stove and poured some into the washbasin, added some slivers of soap as he'd seen the women do many times, and began to wash.

Clarissa and Issy joined him and it didn't take them long to wash, rinse, and put the dishes in the hutch.

Mrs. Coleman walked into her kitchen and inhaled. "Mark, you did not need to do dishes. Did you leave me hot water for coffee?"

He dried his hands. "There's enough for coffee, but not for all the pans. You fix the coffee."

She measured the water she needed, then he refilled the large pan and put it back on the stove.

He grinned as he watched her pour hot water over the ground beans. When she was done, he walked over to her and whispered, "I hope that your garden no longer contains those little green cabbages, and that we never have to eat them again. Virginia feels the same way."

Then he planted a kiss on her cheek. He turned to leave, but found his hair in Alisa's clutches. He grinned, but Clarissa and Issy were laughing. "Yes. You have something more to say to me before I leave?"

Her eyes were narrowed and her lips were pressed tightly together. She still had a tight grip on his hair. He looked at the teen girls and winked. "I know. No kissing. But it's hard to resist a beautiful woman who makes the most wonderful meals."

"Issy, Clarissa, go upstairs. I want to talk to *Mr. Hunter.*"

He couldn't hold the amused feeling inside of him any longer. He tossed his head back and laughed until she yanked his hair so hard that it hurt. "Why did you do that?"

"You set the worst example to the women in this family!"

"I did dishes. Is it wrong for a man to wash dishes?"

"That's not what I am talking about. I'm

talking about this afternoon at the pond. And thank you for your help tonight."

"You are welcome." He took the hand holding his hair in his and smiled. "You are a lovely woman and Joseph knows it." He touched her cheek. "When is your baby due?"

Tears filled her eyes. "Christmas. Kissing always leads to more."

"With a man like Joseph, it is good. You are healthy and strong. You will do fine."

"I have told no one, not even Joseph. How did you know?" She swiped at the moisture that threatened to spill down her cheeks.

"Your..." He curved his hands in front of him. "Your shape has changed. I will keep your secret." He planted a quick kiss on her cheek. "You are like my mother, always watching out for her children and everyone else's children. But do not worry about Malene when we are together, I am very respectful. She has been through more than she is telling."

"What are you saying?"

"Talk to her. Have you not seen the burn mark on her arm?"

"Yes. She burnt herself in the kitchen."

"No. Get her to tell you the truth. All of it."

Malene stepped into the kitchen. He took Malene's hand and walked out the door.

5

Malene tugged on Mark's hand. "Please. I prefer to sit on the swing tonight. I am tired."

"If that is what you want."

"For tonight, it will be enough. You've already set my heart fluttering."

"Good." He pulled her close and lightly kissed her. "Because I love to set my wife's heart fluttering."

"We are not married."

"I will marry you, and we will raise this child of the sun that you are carrying. I will give this child a name." He pressed his hands over her belly. Then he leaned down. "Turn, my dear child, turn."

"I'm scared."

"You will do fine. You are strong. Women are made for babies and for a man's pleasure."

"No. That is not true. Every time...it was terrible. I hate it. I cannot be your wife. That is not what you want."

"With the wrong man, you will never enjoy being with a man. When I kiss you, you will let me do anything to you, but I have not."

She closed her eyes as if she could stop the truth of his words.

"When you love a man, it is wonderful. When you don't, it is…death is preferable."

She opened her eyes and stared into his. "You are right. I did not know."

"Now you do. We will sit on the swing. I will like that. I will build one for you at our house."

She sat next to him and took his hand. Inside she felt as if she were crumbling into a million pieces. "But I cannot marry you. You are an Indian."

"That does not matter. It is what is in our hearts, not the color of our skin."

"I promised my father I would go to San Francisco. He has arranged a marriage for me. He swears this will be a good one."

"Then you must obey your father and go to

San Francisco. But you will never marry that man because you will never love him." He rubbed his thumb over the back of her hand. "Make your father happy, but leave your heart with me, for I shall hold it close and protect it. And when you are ready, I will be waiting for you with a beautiful house."

Tears streamed down her face and she pushed them away. "But it is illegal for me to marry you."

He waved his hand through the air. "By Crow laws, we will be husband and wife. Your government cannot touch our laws."

"Bear and Abigail are not married in the church."

"Then they are married under our laws."

She leaned her head against his shoulder and looked at his hand entwined with hers. Even his color excited her. His hand was calloused and hard, yet his touch was tender and sweet. Her mind drifted. He was good to the children, treating each one as if they were his favorite. He was teaching Lydia's boys to swim.

He had blended into the white man's world as much as possible, learned to use a knife and fork and to read and write. She was amazed at his ways and what he had done. He was different, yet the same. And he loved her.

She heard the door open and she straightened up.

"Here is my daughter," Mr. Reiner said. "I wondered what happened to you tonight."

Mark quickly stood, offered the swing to her father before bringing another chair over and tucking it in the corner of the porch facing Malene. "It is a lovely night, sir. Did you have good journey?"

"Yes. I stopped at the reservation and spoke with a man by the name of Angry Bear. He confirmed your ranching plans and thought it was best if I deal directly with you. I have a buyer who wants six matched horses."

"Six? What does he want with them?"

"He wants horses."

Mark smiled. "For riding, pulling, farming, or racing?"

"Hmm. I must ask, for I do not know."

"That would help me select the best for his purpose."

"I did not come out on the porch to talk about horses. I came to talk to my daughter, who did not join us in the parlor. Is there a problem? Are you and Adie getting along?"

"Oh, yes, Papa. She is so excited about the wedding. Frank has built her a house, but he won't let her see inside of it. He wants to surprise her. But the last time she saw it, it was merely a shell."

Mark chuckled. "Tell her she has a house. I know."

Mr. Reiner looked at Mark. "You have been in it?"

He nodded. "I've helped Frank with many things. The whole family has helped."

"Is it furnished?" Malene asked.

"Fern...ish...?"

Malene smiled. "Furniture."

"Not exactly. I'm not to tell. He wants her to choose, but he has a few things."

Malene rolled her eyes at him. "She has bought some things for the house. And I have a beautiful gift for her wedding."

Mr. Reiner smiled. "Your mama also has gifts for her."

"That is good. I think she needs everything, but I think it is nice that Frank wants her to choose." She watched her papa - watched him look at Mark. She felt the need to fill in the empty silence.

Mr. Reiner spoke first. "I am pleased that my parcel arrived intact."

Mark said nothing so she answered. "Why would it not? Mark is a very honest man. Adie and I have both told you that he is an honorable man. I appreciate his company. He has been wonderful in helping me pick up the pieces of my life."

Mark stood. "I need to beg my leave and get some sleep. There is much to do on a ranch of this size. Write and tell me what your buyer means by matched set."

"You read?"

"Of course. Alisa Coleman taught me the first time I was here. Learning the letters and the sounds took me a whole night. After that, it was just a matter of putting the sounds together. My spelling isn't always perfect. You have too many words that are spelled differently but sound the same."

Malene giggled. "I can always read your letters. I do not have a problem with your spelling."

Mr. Reiner raised his eyebrows. "So you learned to read in one night?"

"Maybe three. It was not easy. She gave me one book to read and then she gave me another. This time she gave me Herman Melville's <u>Moby Dick; or, The Whale.</u>" He frowned. "It is a wild tale of men who do not respect the creatures around them. I do not like it, but I am reading it."

Malene couldn't hold back her giggle as she watched her papa's mouth open and then close.

Mark extended his hand towards her papa and he took it. Then Mark turned his attention back to her. He held out his hand palm up and she put hers in his. He lifted her hand to his lips and pressed a soft kiss to her fingers.

Heat instantly raced through her. It was brazen, but done as if he were some knight in King Arthur's Court. Heat flowed to her cheeks.

"Good night, Malene. May you and your sister sleep like birds in a nest."

"Thank you. And thank you for giving up your bed for my parents. I hope you are comfortable."

He nodded. "I will see you both at breakfast."

Her heart fluttered. She wanted to race after

Mark. The image of him naked was embedded in her mind. Kissing might lead to bad thoughts, but his body was enough to make any woman swoon.

"I'm sorry, Papa. What did you say?"

"He is full of surprises. I cannot believe he learned to read that quickly."

She shrugged. "Mrs. Coleman is a good teacher."

"So, if he opened the parcel, he knew what I wrote."

"He did not open the parcel. He is a man of his word."

Her papa shook his head. "Has Marshall Hamilton written you?"

***

The morning of Adie's wedding dawned brightly with a clear blue sky. Fredericka pulled her daughter's hair into the latest style that was pushed into big puffs on each side of her head, then pinned into a bun at the back. Adie started to cry.

"It does not look like me. Frank will not like it. I want my braids."

Mama sat on Malene's bed and fanned herself. "You'll look like a peasant girl from the old country."

"I do not care."

"Mama, go have coffee with Mrs. Coleman. I will help Adie." Everyone turned and stared at the door when they heard a knock. "Who is it?"

"Virginia. I have something for Adie."

"Come in," Adie called.

Virginia brought a big bouquet of blue flax. "I thought they would match your dress."

"*Ja.* They do. They are perfect." She held out her arms and the child ran into them.

"You look so pretty."

"Thank you. And so do you." Adie fingered the pretty floral print dress Virginia was wearing, which had been specifically made for the occasion.

Malene looked at the flowers. "If I braid your hair, I can tuck flowers through the braids."

Adie nodded. "Let's try."

Another knock had them turning to the door. Virginia's mother brought in a glass of water. "They will all be wilted if they do not get water."

"I was going to put some in Adie's hair." She pinned one braid into place.

"Wet her hair. That should help." Mrs. Coleman took the flowers and put them in the glass.

"What a great idea. Virginia, will you bring more water for us?"

The child nodded and started to leave the room but stopped. "Did you know that Mark bought a new suit for the wedding?"

***

Everyone gathered in the yard of the little church in Creed's Crossing. Mark hung back with Bear's and Falcon's families and listened to the wedding service. Wiping the sweat from his brow, he thought he would die of heat under all the clothes he wore. But if he was going to live with white man's standards, then he had to look more like them. He just couldn't bring himself to cut his hair like his Crow brothers on the Coleman ranch. He was still Apsáalooke.

He watched Adie. Her smile was as bright as the sun on blue water. A white man's marriage was different. No one gave Adie of a robe decorated with beads. Instead, Frank gave her a tiny band of gold for her finger and many others brought gifts to her and Frank. He decided it did not matter how they were married, for all women liked being married.

He remembered his wife on their wedding day. He had seen her from afar many times. Whenever their gazes met she'd smile coyly at him and then look away. Her bones were delicate and she barely came to his chest. She had a long face with big eyes, and the prettiest smile. She was proud to marry him and scared, for they did not know each other, but their love grew strong.

This time, he could protect Malene using the white man's ways. He knew Malene, her weaknesses, her joys, and her dreams. The love was there between them. No man had ever loved her. She might have been with child, but that child was a product of repetitive rape. Hatred flowed through his blood and burned in the pit of his guts. How could any man be that cruel to a wife?

His thoughts turned to the fact that she would leave for San Francisco. He couldn't keep her from going to the man her father had chosen, but her heart belonged to him. She would be his wife, even if he had to wait forever.

After the wedding ceremony, there was

fried chicken, and cold slices of flavored potatoes, pickles of all sorts and cheese filled another table. It dawned on him that many people brought food to the wedding. Off to one side, in the shade of the building, was a big block of ice and people were chipping pieces off it and adding it to their tea.

He watched what they were doing and tried it. A big chunk fell away and he picked it up and put it in his mouth. He could not imagine doing such a thing in the winter, but it was delightful in the summer.

On a table sat a special cake, half hidden under a tipi of gauze fabric that was held by tiny strips of wood. There were several such little tipis that covered the food and protected it from insects. He'd seen the cake in the kitchen of the Coleman house. Lydia had baked it and covered it in something she called icing. She had let him taste the butter and sugar mixture from the sides of an empty bowl. It was very sweet and delicious.

Next to the cake were presents. Many gifts were wrapped in colorful paper. Several men began to play music on instruments made with strings. And people danced.

Adie wore new shoes made with white canvas and tiny buttons. Malene had a pair in yellow. He knew she had planned to wear a different dress, but switched to her yellow one. The material was gathered over her belly. If it was meant to hide her shape, it only enhanced it. He liked her in yellow.

She was a beautiful woman with a bountiful body. He barely took his eyes off of her. The dress accentuated the sway of her hips. He inhaled and held that breath. He wanted to undo the row of buttons that held the material closed over her breasts and belly. He wanted to touch her curves.

An eagle called as it soared overhead and dropped a feather at Mark's feet. He picked it up and stuck it in Malene's braid. "A gift from an eagle. My promise to you, my wife."

She touched her fingers to his lips and he kissed them. She closed her eyes. He was certain that his kiss had gone straight to her heart.

As the sun began to disappear behind the mountains, people slowly left. Every speck of food had been eaten, and the deliciously sweet cake was reduced to crumbs. He helped the Coleman women load the wagon and offered to drive it.

"That is kind of you, Mark, but I can drive. Although I will never turn you down if you wish to accompany us on your horse," Alisa said as they loaded the last of their things into the buckboard.

He smiled and helped her onto the seat. Malene had left a few minutes before with her parents, and the Coleman men had gone back earlier to handle evening chores. Issy, Clarissa, and Virginia were sound asleep within minutes of leaving the churchyard.

"It was a nice wedding, my first one. Very

different from ours, yet maybe in many ways the same."

"How can you say that?"

"Our village comes together to celebrate and the husband's family welcomes the wife. We feast, drum, and hope that blessings are bestowed on the happy couple." The fleeting images from his wedding passed through him. "The groom gives presents to all who attend."

"Do you miss your wife?"

"I will always remember her. But when I am with Malene, I am happy."

"She is happy with you. But you need to watch your behavior."

"I love her and she loves me, but she has promised her father to take another man."

"What?"

He listened to the sounds of the wagon wheels on the road and the thump of horse hooves. "Yes. It is true. Her father has found her another man. She is to meet him after the baby is born."

"I am so sorry, Mark."

"I do not worry about another man. Her heart belongs to me. It is the baby that she carries that concerns me."

"Why do you say that?"

"The baby's head is not in the right place. It is here." He held his hand near his ribcage.

"Mark! You are not supposed to touch her."

"It is not terrible for me to have my hands on the baby."

"Oh, how will I ever make you understand?"

***

Mark had left for the reservation to renew his pass. This time he was going to plead to stay for the remainder of the summer. Frank and Adie moved to their new house but often ate with the rest of the Colemans, as Adie had not enough supplies in her kitchen or pantry.

Malene and Adie made soap with Alisa's help. Malene stood at the stove with one hand on her back as she boiled water and roses.

Joseph had gone to town and had brought home mail. She pocketed the letter from Marshall and read the ones from her mother and father. Somehow that life seemed so distant to her. She was more alone here than she had ever been in her life, yet she was happier. Many Feathers - she corrected herself - Mark was her friend. Adie was glowing with happiness and in her own little marital bliss world. Alisa seemed to be withdrawn lately and Malene didn't know why.

Right now, she wanted Mark's arms around her. She needed that strong male confidence, that man who protected her and made her feel as though she was the most important person in the whole world. He made her feel as if nothing else mattered other than them being together with the sky above and the earth below.

Adie babbled about her new furniture. Papa had given Adie and Frank a substantial monetary wedding gift and Adie used it for furniture and things she needed for her house. If Papa had given such money to Albert, Malene knew nothing about it.

Every month her papa had sent money. She didn't need much to live. She paid the Colemans for her room and board, and in return, they had provided for her.

Alisa brought a cradle from the attic and placed it in Malene's room. The cradle was a lovely little bed on rockers. Joseph had made it and carved it with butterflies and flowers for Alisa when she was pregnant with Sarah.

Malene and Adie had made a whole wardrobe of clothes for the baby, and there were plenty of other clothes packed into a trunk in the attic. Alisa brought those items down and washed them. Drawers that were once shared with Adie were now overflowing with baby items. Malene's baby would lack for nothing.

Malene wasn't fond of cooking meals every

day, but she did it. She preferred to bake. Even making soap was a chore.

When she had time, she enjoyed reading. Alisa had many books and often bought more. Adie was better with math, but hated reading. Malene seemed to spend every spare hour reading. For the last week, Malene didn't want to do anything but lie in her bed and read. Pain radiated down her legs and her back hurt constantly. The baby's constant kicking kept her awake and made her extra tired.

"I don't think I can stand here another moment," Malene whined. "Take over, Adie."

With one hand supporting her belly and another on the banister, Malene made her way to her room. The letter in her pocket bothered her. She lay across her bed on her side with a pillow between her knees as she read Marshall's letter. He had made all the arrangements for her to meet him. She would go by private railcar. It gave the impression of being exciting, but somehow it also seemed as if she were being employed.

The house sounded beautiful, a Georgian with big columns, porticos, and balconies. There were gas lamps in the house and furniture from far away places. He hinted that she might have problems running a house filled with servants. She almost laughed. He had three young children. The house she had been living in for months was loaded with children and there were no servants.

She wasn't sure that she liked the part where he wrote about sailing to China and India on a regular basis. It might have been his job, but that also meant she'd be alone in a strange place. She tucked the letter under her pillow and grabbed the latest book.

She had begged to read the book before Alisa had a chance to even look at it. The woman smiled and handed it over. Malene found it scandalous, and she was certain that the prim Mrs. Alisa Coleman would never allow it to be read if she had read it first.

Malene wanted to ask Mark about such things, for she had never heard of a man liking another man in such a way.

She finished the book and put it on the chest of drawers to take downstairs. Her back ached all the way to her knees. To say she felt miserable was an understatement. She hurt and it waved over her. If she didn't have pain, she had the baby kicking her.

The following afternoon, Adie knocked on Malene's bedroom door. "Are you hiding in here?"

Malene nodded. "My back hurts like always, only worse."

Adie rolled her eyes and sat on the edge of Malene's bed. "Lydia is churning butter. I think she liked it better when we worked. Then she didn't have to do anything."

Malene grinned at her sister. "I've gotten that impression, too."

Adie's smile diminished. "I saw Albert when we went to town this morning. You are right.

He's darkened his hair and cut off his mustache. He was in the general store."

"Oh, no. Did he recognize you?"

"I don't think he saw me. I turned my back to him."

"I hope not. Although, I doubt he'd do anything. He doesn't want to be known. But why would he choose Creed's Crossing to hide?"

Adie reached in her pocket and withdrew several letters.

Malene put the one from Marshall to one side and opened her letter from home. "Finally, my marriage is annulled. It is over. Papa has returned my name to Reiner." She held up the papers. "Now, what good news do you have?"

Adie started reading her letter, then squealed with joy. "Mama ordered the dining room set that I loved. It will come by railroad, and then Papa is sending it down by coach delivery."

"Oh, Adie. That is wonderful. Does she say when it will arrive?"

"Only that I will have it by August." She smiled at her sister. "My china arrived today. Frank took it home and I will unpack it tonight. Please come tomorrow and see it. I will make tea for us. Our first tea party in my new house with my new china. Won't it be grand?"

"If I'm up to the ride to your house. I'm so tired and tired of the pain."

"You need to stop whining."

"I can't help it."

Early the next morning Malene could hear Adie's footfalls as she ran up the stairs. *Adie does everything with enthusiasm.*

"I knew I would find you still in bed. Did you sleep last night?"

Malene shook her head, then stood, and put hands on her back. "I must have gone to the toilet a half dozen times. I need to go again."

She made her way to the bathing room, then

back to her bedroom. She took a few steps and felt the warm flow of water running down her legs. "Adie!"

Adie ran downstairs leaving Malene standing in a puddle and afraid to move. The pain that wracked her body kept her frozen in place. She wanted to hug her belly, but didn't want to let go of her back.

Alisa appeared. She started barking orders at Adie and calling to Lydia. A moment later, Malene was wearing a clean but old nightgown, and she was in her bed with her knees drawn up.

"Have you had any pain yet?" Alisa asked.

"Pain? When have I not had pain? It got worse the day we were making soap. It kept coming and going."

"What do you mean coming and going? How often?"

Malene sucked in her lower lip for a moment as she thought about Alisa's question. "Seems as though it strikes every few minutes and becomes very intense.

Alisa held her hands up. "Why didn't you say something sooner? You're about to have this baby. I'll be right back."

Alone in her room, Malene fought tears. Fear crawled over her skin, but part of her was thrilled to know the child she'd hidden from Albert would finally be here. She wanted a little girl so they could have tea parties and dress up in fancy hats. She wanted to name her Sophia. She'd heard another woman called that and thought it sounded so pretty and worldly. But if she had a boy, she wanted him to grow up to be like Mark, strong and confident. Edward sounded like a good name for a boy, but so did James. She still hadn't made up her mind.

Being on her back, wasn't very comfortable. She held her hard belly and waited for this round of pain to end. Adie and Alisa sat with her. Alisa kept checking to see if she could see the baby's head, but each time, there was nothing. Malene wanted to push, but Alisa said if she did it too soon, it would be very painful. If only this would come to an end. Minutes dragged into hours. Virginia begged to see Malene, but Alisa told her to go back downstairs.

Malene heard the clock in the living room chime two. Alisa called Issy. "Tell Sky to go to town for the doctor and come right back. This baby is coming too slowly. Something is wrong."

6

The agent had extended Mark's pass until October. The man seemed pleased to hear that Mark was living with a Christian family and learning to become self-sufficient. Mark rode his horse hard on the way to the Coleman house. It was a feeling he had and when he saw the great bird circling overhead then flying off in the direction of the Coleman house, he pushed his horse to go faster.

Sky appeared to have just finished grooming another horse and willingly took Mark's sweaty one. Mark opened the back door and Clarissa was the only one in the kitchen.

He smiled at the teen. "Where's everyone?"

"Upstairs." She concentrated on cutting up several root vegetables and adding them to a pot on the stove.

Then Issy passed him on the stairs. He intended to change into clean clothes for supper, but the house had an eerie quiet to it.

Virginia met him at the top of the staircase.

He smiled at her and she didn't smile back.

"What is wrong today? Where is your smile? Did you hide it in a pocket and forget where you put it?"

"No. It is Malene. Ma has sent for the doctor, and she won't let me in the room to see Malene."

Every fiber of his being tightened like a rope "What is wrong with Malene?"

"The baby is not coming."

He practically flew into his room, changed his clothes, and then ran to wash his hands. He knew it was important to keep everything around a birthing mother clean. Babies belonged to the spirits of the sky and wind, and not of the earth.

But when he heard Malene scream, he tossed the towel, ran down the long room to hers, and pushed the door open.

"Get out!" Alisa ordered. "She's trying to have a baby."

Alisa blocked him, and he pushed her away, then yanked Malene up. "Keep your feet flat." He pushed Alisa out of the way again, and then positioned Malene's feet on the bed. "Hold onto my shoulders." He forced Malene into a squatting position. His hands felt for the baby on her bulging belly. "This baby did not listen. The head is up and that is what should come first."

Malene screamed again.

"No screaming. It does not make the baby come out."

Alisa shoved against his shoulder.

"Unless you want to find yourself on the floor, do not attempt to keep me from helping Malene. How long has she been like this?"

"All day."

He shook his head and reached under her nightgown. Her body had opened to this birth, but there was not even a foot to be found. He swallowed his own fears for her well being and concentrated on helping Malene. She was taking shortened breaths, working up to another scream. "When you can't stand it, push down with everything you have. You must work extra hard to get this baby out." He held his hand against her most private of parts. "Push as if you are pushing my hand away."

He watched the expression on her face. He forced her face to his shoulder. "Bite my shoulder and push hard."

She sunk her teeth into him until he wanted to scream, but she pushed and this time he felt the downward movement of the baby. "Adie get behind her. When I tell you to grab this baby, grab it, and don't let it slide back inside. This baby is folded up."

Alisa was the one who got behind Malene. "Never in my life. She's not an animal!"

"She needs this baby out and it's not going to happen lying on her back. I've never seen such a crazy thing." Teeth pierced his skin. "With the next round of pain, push my hand out of the way. Harder! You must do it. I want this baby! Push this baby into our hands." He could feel the blood trickling from his shoulder. "PUSH!"

He moved his hand as he felt the child's movement against his palm, then heard the familiar sound as though something was being forced between wet rocks. "One more time. Push hard. It's almost over. Give it everything you've got."

There was a popping sound.

"I got her!" Alisa held the baby. "It's a girl!"

He wrapped his one arm around Malene's waist. "The worst is over. You may take your teeth out of my shoulder."

Malene tried to lean back.

"Oh, no you don't. There is a second birthing. When that is out, you may relax. You still need to push."

"I want to see my baby." Tears streamed down her cheeks.

He watched Alisa clear the baby's mouth,

then he reached behind Malene and plucked the baby's feet with his finger. She cried, a healthy, hearty cry. "Push hard and get the second birth out. Then you may hold your baby."

He caught the second birth and Adie gave him a basin to put it in. He milked the cord and Alisa tied it off with silk thread before severing it. Malene collapsed onto the bed. There was much blood and that worried him, but he didn't dare say anything in front of Malene.

"Will you leave now?" Alisa asked. "I'd like to clean her up."

Laughter pushed its way from his chest to his mouth. "Put that baby to her breast. It will help stop the bleeding."

He walked out of the room, only to be confronted by Virginia with a wide-eyed stare. His hands and arms were bloody, as was his shoulder. "It's a little girl. Give them a few minutes and they will let you in."

He took off his shirt, washed his hands and arms, and then his shoulder. He chuckled to himself. *Good teeth all neatly lined up, Malene.* Until the day he died, he would bare the marks of this child's birth.

Supper that night was soup and bread. But he didn't care. It was enough for him, and as hot as it was, no one was very interested in eating much food. Clarissa had tried. He told her everything was good, and he meant it. She smiled and thanked him.

"I'll take food to Malene, if you fix it for me."

She nodded and jumped from her chair. "Ma needs some, too."

"And Adie. They have not come down."

"How is Malene?" Clarissa lifted the tray from where it was stored.

"She should be good. The baby was turned the wrong way. She came folded." He held his hands with his palms together in a V.

She started to put three bowls on a tray.

"I have an idea. I will send your ma and

Adie down to eat. I will stay with Malene. Fix their plates at the table, and then make some tea. Malene needs to drink more than she needs to eat. Send Virginia with the tea. She will not spill it." He grinned. "She wants to see the baby and they will not let her in the room."

"I think I need to help Virginia. I want to see the baby, too."

"Ah. A woman with a plan. That is good."

As soon as Clarissa filled the tray, he took it upstairs and opened the door. "I have food for Malene." He looked at Adie and Alisa. "Clarissa has your meals waiting for you. Go eat. I will stay with Malene."

"You can't--"

"Yes, I can stay, and you will go eat your food." He put the tray beside Malene. She looked very pale. "You need to eat. Clarissa will bring you some tea in a few minutes."

Adie closed the door behind her, and he opened it. With the door open, there was a slight breeze in the room. Without it, the room was stifling hot. He opened the window wider and moved the curtains out of the way.

There was a pitcher and basin in the room and he rinsed his hands off before coming back to Malene's bed. The baby slept beside her. He picked the red-faced bundle up and cuddled her in his arms. He touched her cheek and watched as she turned her head. "She's a bright red baby. I thought she would have pale skin like yours."

"According to Alisa, she will in a few days." Malene spooned some soup to her mouth. "Who did the cooking?"

"Clarissa. Lydia was trying to keep her boys quiet. Do you not celebrate a birthing?"

"I've never heard of such a thing."

"Have you chosen a name?" He watched the infant scrunch up her face and move a fist near her mouth.

Malene swallowed. "Sophia."

"What does that mean?"

"It is just a name, but I think it is lovely."

"Like her mother." He touched Malene's cheek. "Sophia. It sounds like the wind coming through the pines."

He took the child near the window and began speaking in his language. He held her away from his body and sang. He asked for blessings on the child and her mother that they live full and happy lives. He kissed Sophia's head, then found her toes hidden in the cloth, and kissed them. Each time, he asked for a blessing. When he was done, he discovered he had an audience.

Clarissa came to him and smiled. "She's so pretty."

Virginia jumped to get a better view.

"Virginia, go wash your hands if you want to hold this baby." He passed the infant to Clarissa and helped Malene with her tea. She looked gray-white yet mottled with pink from the heat. He worried that she had lost too much blood and still might be losing too much.

He chased Virginia to the big chair and told Clarissa to give the baby to her little sister. When he was certain that Sophia was about to protest, he took the child from Virginia and sent the girls from the room. Then he sat next to Malene and undid the tie at the neck of her nightgown. He lowered the infant to her mother's breast and smiled. Warmth flowed through him, for he could not think of a more beautiful sight. He touched the baby's cheek, the mother's breast, and then kissed Malene on the lips. "You have given me a beautiful child. I love her as I love you."

Malene smiled. "Yes. She is beautiful, and you told me it would be hard to give birth to her. I don't think I would have lasted another hour if you had not come."

They both heard the little squirting sound, and Malene groaned. He took the baby to the basin and poured water on a cloth. He cleaned the child and wrapped her in another clean cloth before laying the baby in her mother's arms. This time Sophia greedily suckled and he laughed at the tiny thing. He poured a glass of water for Malene.

"Always drink while the baby is at your breast."

Alisa walked into the room. "Malene, you know better than to allow him to stay here."

Malene grinned. "Having him here makes me smile."

"You need to go."

"Why? What is wrong with my being here?"

"You are the most impossible man I've ever met! And I thought Joseph was bad at times."

The baby's feet kicked and he laughed. "She's been practicing that kick for awhile."

Malene giggled. "She's very good at kicking."

He touched her nightgown where a wet spot had appeared against her other breast. "Move to this side now." He heard Alisa groan as Malene switched the baby to her other breast. He lightly kissed Malene's lips then turned to where Alisa was standing and realized that Adie had entered the room. "I need to speak to Mrs. Coleman. Visit with your sister. I will return later."

He took Alisa's hand and tugged her out of the room.

"How dare you!"

He clasped her face with both his hands and kissed her on the forehead. "How dare I what? Hold our child?"

Her mouth opened well before any sound emerged. "You're the father?"

He laughed. "I did not make that child. But Malene knows that I love that child as much as I love her. It does not matter who put the child in her."

Alisa wiped her brow with her forearm. "Mark Many Feathers Hunter, you will be the death of me."

He gripped her shoulders. "I want the truth. She is too pale. Is she bleeding too much?"

"I will check her again. She...she tore when

she had the baby."

"Because the baby came the wrong way. Keep her clean. Our women wash with herbal water."

Commotion downstairs caused them both to look in the direction of the staircase. It seemed the doctor had arrived, but by the time he had reached the top of the steps, Mark could smell the spirit water on the man's breath. The man's suit jacket was crumpled and stained brown. His shirt was wrinkled and dirty, and his pants were damp.

"You got a baby that won't come out?" The man looked at Mark and spit on his chest. "Filthy savage."

The tangle of emotions that had run though Mark all day came together in a burst of anger. His hand fisted, then his fingers straightened. The scent of the man's breath barely masked the man's unwashed urine-laced odor. The palm of Mark's hand landed against the old doctor's chest with such force that the man stumbled backwards. Losing his footing, the man cursed and fell down the stairs as Alisa screamed. Joseph and Frank rounded the corner, and Alisa ran down the stairs to the crumpled heap at the bottom.

"What happened?" Joseph asked while feeling for a pulse. He shook his head.

Alisa calmly answered. "He was too drunk to stay on his feet. He stumbled and fell." She looked at Frank. "You'd better get the sheriff." She looked up the stairs at Mark. "I'm glad we didn't need him."

Mark went to his room, grabbed another shirt and pair of pants, before taking a quick bath. He had no intention of leaving Malene's side, at least not for the next couple of nights. She needed her sleep, and the baby needed her.

It was late when the sheriff arrived, but the stench of alcohol on the old doctor was obvious. Mark stayed out of sight, but listened to every word that was spoken. According to

Alisa, the man was simply too drunk to stand. But Mark knew he'd lost control for those few seconds. He had not killed for food. He had killed out of anger and disgust, and it didn't sit well with him.

He and Alisa helped Malene to the bathing room, and he waited outside the door until Alisa called him to help Malene get back to her bed. Alisa assured him that Malene was fine. More tea came to Malene's room. She drank it and drifted off to sleep.

He held Sophia and admired the dusting of orange fuzz on her little baldhead. He sat in the rocking chair watching Malene sleep. She was his woman, and he was holding his child. He didn't care about the white man's laws. The only things that mattered to him were Malene's heart and the child in his arms.

He woke with a start when Alisa's hand touched him. The baby was in the cradle, and he was sleeping next to Malene.

"Go down and eat your breakfast. I'll stay

with her."

As he slipped from the bed, Malene stirred but went right back to sleep.

He ate his breakfast and drank his coffee, then poured a second cup.

"Good morning." Adie smiled. "How is my sister?"

"I think she has slept well. Miz Alisa is with her."

Adie put her hand on his arm. "My sister loves you very much."

"I know. And I love her."

"Let her go to San Francisco. She promised our papa." Adie beamed a little brighter. "She will not marry a man that she does not love."

"But if your papa has arranged it..."

Adie shrugged. "She loves you. She will never marry a man she does not love. She has learned a hard lesson."

He barely left Malene's side for the next few days, but he made her get up and sit in the chair. Then he made her get dressed and come downstairs for dinner. As Malene's cheeks returned to their pink color, Sophia's red skin lightened to the palest shade of pink, but her downy hair was dusted in the orange of a setting sun. Eyelashes, sprinkled with gold, matched the color of her hair. They rested on fat cheeks. He held the infant, letting Malene eat her dinner with the family, and when the baby fussed, he stood and paced the room with her.

"You are spoiling her," Alisa said with authority in her voice.

But when Sophia wailed, he laughed. "You are coming with me. You must learn to let your mother eat."

He took the baby out to the porch swing and rocked while he sang to her the tales of his people. She stopped wailing and tried to focus on him. Malene joined him on the swing and leaned her head against his arm. Alisa brought tea for Malene and coffee for Mark.

"She's a beautiful child," Alisa said before

she took a sip of her coffee. "But, Mark, you are not supposed to be staying in the room with Malene."

"In a few more days, she will be stronger."

"I will give you tonight. After that, Issy and Clarissa may take turns watching over them."

He nodded. "I need to get back into the fields. I have a house to build this winter."

"You're leaving?" Malene asked.

"Are you not going to San Francisco? I need to build a house for you and my daughter."

***

When they returned to Malene's bedroom, Malene passed Sophia to Mark and he changed the baby for her. Alisa seemed almost amazed to see a man care for a young infant. Malene giggled. "He's very good with her."

"Yes. He is."

Malene nursed and Mark fell sound asleep at her side. She burped the baby, put her in the cradle, and with one hand resting on the cradle, Malene closed her eyes. Twice that night, she opened them to find Mark holding Sophia. She wondered how much sleep he was getting, but when morning came, it was Alisa who passed the child to her.

"Where is Mark?"

"Out with the men, mending fences."

"Oh."

"I found this envelope on the floor under your bed. You had not opened it." Alisa passed the pale blue envelope to Malene.

Malene groaned and opened it. The man was trying hard to court her through his letters. "I know that Adie and Frank wrote for years. Sometimes Adie would read me Frank's letters and sometimes she would blush and skip parts."

Alisa raised her eyebrows.

"They wrote of the things they did and what they liked." Malene shifted the pillow behind her back. "Marshall tells me what he has done or what he is doing. Sometimes he tells me about the house or garden, but he never says anything important. He never says what he feels. It's very dry with no emotion. I know he has children, but he never writes of them. Instead, he talks about what must be done." She looked at the letter and read aloud. "You will need a coat. Bright colors are the rage. And a shawl would be nice, something black with red."

"It sounds to me as if he's trying to prepare you so you do not feel out of place. Some men are not good at speaking what is in their hearts. Frank did not prepare Adie for living on a ranch." She grinned. "He never told her that we don't wear corsets, but then he would not think of such things. Yes, there are women who wear them, but I like to breathe and move. I do not sit and sew all day. I have dishes and messes to clean up. I have chickens to pluck and meat to butcher."

"True. But we also weren't planning on

coming when we did."

"What happened to make you both decide to come so quickly?"

Malene closed her eyes and remembered Frank knocking on the door. She recounted the tale of Frank sitting at the table, and the horrible things that Albert had said about the Indians. "He wanted them all dead and made a comment that shooting them would be a great sport."

Alisa shook her head. "He is not alone in his thoughts. It is often just a few who have created problems for their tribes. Even a few Crows have raided the wagon trains. They did not understand why we were here or why we killed the wildlife that they considered to be theirs." Alisa Coleman grimaced. "But often it was the trappers that killed only for the fur, not the ranchers. Today, white men kill anything that moves as an attempt to starve the Indians."

She touched Malene's arm. "If you become

Mark's wife, you will discover how hated the Indians are. They will hate you for being with him. Even my daughter must be careful if they go to town together. She treats Bear, as if he were her employee, otherwise she would be shunned. Abigail's children will never grow up to call her Ma, especially in public."

"How awful."

"It is illegal to marry a man of color. You could both go to jail."

Tears rolled down Malene's cheeks and she pushed them away. "But I love Mark."

"Yes, my dear, I know. He is a good man and he loves you very much. Give Marshall a chance. Life with Mark will never be easy. Think of Sophia and give her the best possible life. Choose wisely. Never marry just for the money. You must find love in your heart, or you will be miserable."

***

Every night, after the baby's bath, Mark sat on the porch swing with her and Malene. He'd sing and play with Sophia. Sometimes they would just swing and say nothing. Other times, they chatted about the day's events. Occasionally someone would join them, but usually they had the place to themselves.

But one night, John walked out and scuffed his feet as he looked at the darkening purple sky. "Had an interesting day when I went to town. Did you know there's a Wanted poster for an Albert Goddard? Seems he's embezzled money from the railroad. Any relation of yours?"

Malene inhaled. "Albert was my husband's name, but I can't imagine him doing anything such as that. He was wealthy. And Goddard is a common name back east."

"What did he look like?"

"Not as tall as Frank." She chewed on her bottom lip. "Dark hair, clean shaven, very handsome, and always impeccably dressed.

Green eyes. Slender. And he had a terrible temper."

John leaned over the rail and looked up at the sky that seemed to be missing stars. "Interesting. You just described the man Lydia and I wound up talking to in town. Said he was a trader. Wouldn't say he was dressed very well. Apparently he buys and sells things."

Malene squeezed Mark's hand.

Lightning danced across the sky and Mark said, "It is time to go in and put Sophia into her cradle. You both need your sleep."

When they got to her room, Malene blurted out, "It is Albert. We've seen him in Creed's Crossing, but we do not think he saw us."

"He is there and you are here. Go to sleep, and do not think of him. Issy will be here in a few minutes."

He lay next to her and when he was certain that she was sleeping, he went to his room. Anger boiled in his stomach. Albert was a wicked man. Mark knew he would do everything in his power to protect Malene and Sophia. No one would ever hurt her again.

***

Mark still had plenty of time left on his pass, but he offered to take Malene to the train. He stopped at the agent's office, and the agent extended the pass so that Mark could take her and Sophia to Billings.

Malene was excited and nervous at the same time. Alisa, Issy, and Clarissa accompanied Malene. They spent one night with her parents.

Malene was wearing fancy clothes and he knew she was wearing a corset under the new clothes she had bought from New York. She had traveled in plain clothing, but had switched to her fancy dress before leaving her parents' home and traveling onwards to Billings, Montana.

The train would be there early in the morning. The women decided to go to Billings and spend the night there rather than traveling at the break of dawn. besides they wanted time to look around the town to do a little shopping.

When they reached Billings, the women procured a hotel room. He would sleep in the buggy. Adie bought a few small things for her new house and Alisa made several purchases. Malene bought a box of ribbon candy to take as a gift and another for all of them to share.

That evening they found a small restaurant off the main street with a sign that said all were welcome. Alisa went inside to inquire if that meant their Indian could join them. Assured that he could, they ate there rather than in the hotel. Having never been in such a place, Mark looked around. Everything was clean and neat but nothing was fancy. Two tiers of white curtains hung at the big windows and white cloth covered the table. In the far corner was a pie safe and the aroma of apples filled the air.

A woman with very dark skin and curly hair greeted them. Her dress was a plain green. She wore a white apron over the dress and a matching white cap on her head. He knew about the people called Negroes, but had never seen one. There had been a great war that had been fought over them. No matter how hard he tried he could not imagine a man owning another man. It took him a few minutes to remember the word. *Bigots. Too many white men are bigots.*

Alisa paid for their meals and soon generously filled plates of food appeared. The fare was simple, but tasty. He devoured his beef, mashed potatoes, roll with sweet butter, and squash, then ate a piece of the apple pie.

After the meal, he carried Sophia in her basket while Malene walked though the streets of Billings. He stayed a few steps behind the women as he was taught to do. *Yes, bigots!* Forever he would have to walk behind his woman when they were off the reservation. He would never be allowed to proudly walk with his beautiful woman at his side.

He listened to chatter between the women, but kept a close eye on Sophia who was wide-awake. She kicked her little feet and made cooing noises. He tried to push away the loss that rippled through him. He wanted to watch his daughter grow up, to see her first steps, and teach her to ride. Sophia's excitement soon turned to a wail as they approached the hotel.

Malene took the child. "Thank you for carrying her."

"I am honored to carry my…to carry Sophia. Will you return? Shall I wait?"

She shook her head and vanished inside the hotel with the baby.

He bid the others a goodnight and headed for the livery. Had he not been taught to withstand pain? Maybe sleep would come quickly. The extra hours would normally refresh his body, but tonight he wasn't the least bit tired.

"Good evening. Do you have a sink and toilet where I might wash up before retiring?"

The little man with a generous mustache who stayed at the livery jerked his thumb over his shoulder. "Use the horse trough and don't waste the water. There's plenty in the trough."

Don't waste the water. His insides boiled as he walked through the building and out the back door. The corral contained nothing but a wooden box of dirty water. He relieved himself in plain sight, then went to the trough.

Using the pump that was meant to fill the horse trough, he pumped fresh water into his hands and washed his face, arms, and chest. Then he slurped some water and rinsed his mouth. *A horse trough. I am but an animal to these people, unworthy of a bed in the hotel or a real bath.*

He yanked open the door to the carriage and

climbed inside. The air was heavy with the stench of horse manure mixed with hay, straw, and sweaty animals. It permeated the inside of the carriage and made him nauseous.

As he lay there, his heart ached, for he hated that she would be leaving him. He consoled himself with the fact that she loved him. Deep inside he knew this time apart was only temporary. He tucked one arm under his head. Sleep eluded him. Thoughts of another man in Malene's life pricked him like thorns on berry bushes.

He was a rancher with more prime land than most and she was his woman. Alisa's words filtered through his head. *Count your blessings.* He stretched his legs and propped his feet on the opposite bench. *A beautiful daughter with hair the color of fire. A woman of the sun who loves me.*

In the morning, Alisa handed him breakfast from the hotel. He gobbled it down and then took them the few short blocks to the train station in the carriage. First, he helped the other women out of the buggy, then he climbed inside to say his goodbyes to Malene.

She had tears streaming down her cheeks.

He kept his own tears from spilling as he kissed hers away. She clung to him as if they would never see each other again. In the distance, the train blew its whistle. He cupped her breast and ran his hand up the inside of her leg. She was his woman, and he wanted to make certain that she remembered him. He kissed her lips, her neck, and then drifted lower. She gasped with delight.

"You are my woman. Never forget it."

The whistle sounded again. He picked Sophia up and held her to his chest. He kissed her downy soft hair, he whispered, "You are my child, Sophia."

He helped Malene out of the buggy and handed her the baby. She clung to Alisa and the teenaged girls.

He inquired for her. "The Hamilton car?"

The man looked at him.

"It is for Miz Malene Reiner."

The man pointed to a navy and powder blue car. Mark put her trunks inside. Malene never looked at him again until the train pulled from the station. His very fiber was being pulled apart and she was leaving a deep hole within him. He had three women to take back to the Coleman ranch, but he held Malene's heart within his.

Part Two

7

Malene placed her hand against the glass window as tears streamed down her face. Alisa Coleman had become her best friend aside from her younger sister, and Mark Hunter had stolen her heart. She was leaving them. The railroad car began to shake as it moved down the tracks.

Sophia slept in the pretty handled basket that Malene had bought for this trip. She looked around the private car. Curiosity had her. To keep from being tossed about like a pebble in a tin can, she had to hold onto something as she left the seat by the window.

Opening a compartment door, she discovered there was a bed. And when she opened another, there was a toilet and sink. After checking all the compartment doors, she moved the window curtains away from the end door. There she saw a passenger car in front of her, but the only thing behind her car was a boxcar.

This would be home for the next few days and it was quite nice. On one side of the car, there were two upholstered bench seats and a table. On the other side, were more seats grouped together without the table, but no food anywhere, yet Marshall told her she would be fed on the train.

If she were going to starve to death, she might as well enjoy the scenery. She found a comfy seat facing forward by a large window. She tucked Sophia next to her and gazed at the passing fields and the distant mountains.

Alone in the hotel, she had lain awake, fearful that she might never see her friends and family again. Then Mark's goodbye kiss had pierced her heart. She didn't want to think about any of it. But tears continued to spill down her cheeks, blurring her vision of the scenery.

The rocking that lulled Sophia to sleep was doing the same to her. A sharp whistle blew and she opened her eyes. The train was slowing.

A few minutes later, it came to a stop. A woman appeared dressed in a navy blue dress trimmed in powered blue. Her white cap and apron signaled that she was a servant.

"Good morning, Miz Reiner. I am Juanita. Would you like some coffee, tea, or lemonade?"

"Lemonade sounds delicious. I've not had any in ages."

"Mr. Hamilton wants you to enjoy your trip. I'll be right back." The woman had a slight accent when she spoke, and her dark hair had been styled in such a way that the ends vanished under her white cap.

As swiftly as the woman came, she left through the door that lead to the other passenger car. Sophia woke up. Malene changed the baby's diaper and put Sophia to a breast. But her thoughts stayed focused on the servant. Surely if the woman stood still, she'd blend into the car's décor. Malene bit the inside of her cheeks.

The railcar was done in the exact shades of the stationary with only a few touches of burgundy to relieve the sea of the two blues. While holding Sophia in one arm, her other hand fingered the soft cotton velvet of the chair. Everything was beautiful and also very masculine. These were heavy chairs meant to hold men. She moved Sophia to the other breast. Images of men smoking cigars and making financial deals as they traveled danced through her mind. Is that what Albert did?

A few minutes later, Juanita returned. She brought a pitcher of lemonade with thin slices of lemon floating in it, several sweet rolls with fresh butter, a small bowl containing a handful of grapes, and little sandwiches that had been decorated with bits of cheese and olives. Malene giggled when she realized she was not going to starve on this trip.

She stared at the small town while she ate

her meal. There were flurries of activity that waxed and waned outside of her window. Men shouted as carts pulled up and left.

The whistle blew several times before the train began to move and Juanita vanished out the door. Sophia stayed awake and Malene played with her until the child began to yawn. Now Malene was glad she'd spent the money for the travel basket. It was the perfect bed for Sophia as it sat on the thick-carpeted floor of the private car.

She watched the child's eyes close. Strawberry blonde eyelashes curled over chubby pink cheeks. Sophia smiled in her sleep. *Talking to the angels?*

A moment later, they were plunged into darkness and she understood why Juanita had turned on the small lamps throughout the car before collecting the dirtied plates. She shuddered. Being deep under a mountain was exciting, yet scary.

Even the sounds changed into a loud drone

and she wished she had closed the windows. Covering her nose with one hand, she tugged the lightweight blanket over Sophia's. The acrid scent of smoke and rock filled the car. A moment later, they were back in bright sunlight.

Malene was surprised. Her whole trip was luxurious. Trout, salmon, the finest cuts of beef, along with a variety of foods that she'd never seen, were served daily.

Sophia slept soundly and so did Malene. Juanita was wonderful. Slightly older than Alisa Coleman, the woman looked after every comfort.

Malene tried writing, but the jiggle of the tracks made it too difficult. She would write Adie and her mother when she reached San Francisco. The railcar was warm, but the constant breeze coming through the windows made it bearable.

Aspens cloaked in green and tipped in yellow stood near rivers, and mountains capped in white stretched to the sky. There was always something to see out the windows except when they went through the tunnels. Being plunged into darkness sent a tremor through her. Each time they exited, she breathed a sigh of relief. Doing nothing other than sightseeing was refreshing.

Juanita took care of everything. At every stop she'd appear, prepared to handle any need. Even Sophia's diapers were washed and returned. The days passed quickly and she had enjoyed them.

When Malene arrived in San Francisco, she was rested, elated, and ready for a new adventure. The train yard was packed with people, crates, and coaches. It was noisy and stank of humans and animals.

Relief washed over her when she spotted the small coach waiting for her. The Negro driver held a placard with her name on it. He gathered her trunks and helped her into the coach.

Excitement built inside of her as she rode through the busy city and then up steep hills to an area of finer homes. By the time she reached her destination, the butterflies in her stomach were flittering. Before her was the beautiful Georgian mansion Marshall had described with two wings on each side and porches off the wings.

Marshall Hamilton greeted her. "Welcome! I hope you enjoyed your trip."

She nodded. The slight nasal quality to his voice struck her as odd, but he was quite cordial and not at all what she had pictured. She wouldn't have called him handsome, for he was rather ordinary. She stepped into the palatial home and swallowed, hoping to keep her anxiety from showing. But Sophia chose that moment to squeal as if someone had lit a fire under her basket.

"I'm certain you'd like to freshen up." Marshall raised his voice over the wailing. "Let Ellie show you to your room, and when you are ready, we'll have supper and chat."

She nodded and followed a young woman with golden-brown hair. They ascended a wide staircase to the second floor and then down a long hall to a set of rooms.

"Mr. Hamilton hopes that you will find everything to your satisfaction," Ellie said, as she opened the double doors to the rooms.

Malene inhaled as she glimpsed the sitting room. "It's lovely."

"Mr. Titus will bring your trunks in just a moment. Please relax. I'll be back with your afternoon tea."

Malene nodded and lifted Sophia from her carrier. The sitting room was furnished in creamy-white upholstered chairs with a matching sofa. The walls were covered in shades of white satin that created stripes. Even the fireplace was in the same white. Heavy gold-leaf frames surrounded paintings of far-away places. Pillows were abundant with fancy tassels and trim, but they were all the same white color with touches of gold. The monochromatic color scheme gave the place an air of sophistication, yet it felt soothing.

She peeked into the bedroom that had been done in beiges and accented in pale pink. Paintings of white peacocks and peahens along with another white bird that she did not recognize decorated the walls. She looked out the large window and down at a rose garden that was filled with blooms.

Each room was perfectly coordinated and beautifully furnished. The suite was like a private house without a kitchen. It was as luxurious as anything she'd seen in a magazine, and she couldn't wait to describe it to Adie and their mama.

Ellie returned with tea and offered to draw a bath.

Malene sank into a warm tub with Sophia. The baby calmed and so did Malene. The room was large and the tub stood in the middle of it. Palms were everywhere, and an orchid bloomed.

Ellie took Sophia from Malene and seemed thrilled to care for a baby, which gave Malene more time to relax in the tub.

Ellie returned and offered, "May I help you dress?"

Malene nodded and chose a simple brown skirt with a matching waistcoat, and blue blouse. After months of wearing clothes to accommodate her growing tummy, the new tailored fashions suited her. Ellie helped Malene pull her hair into a simple braid and wrap it into a knot at the nape of her neck. She had never been so pampered in her life, and she was enjoying every minute of it. It was shortly after six o'clock when she joined Marshall for a quiet meal.

The dining room contained a long table and several sideboards. The walls were decorated in dark blue fabric. The ceiling was pale blue and in the center hung an elaborate chandelier made of fancy drops of crystal in varying sizes. The table had been set for two. The blue Hamilton crest decorated each plate and the silver gleamed in the light.

She dined on caviar and shrimp, and ate something called sour dough bread. Dessert was a sponge cake topped with sections of sweet tiny oranges. The entire meal was delicious, maybe because she did not have to make it or clean it up. She had eaten too much and her insides pressed against her corset.

Marshall was older, but far from old. His medium brown hair and long sideburns contained threads of gray, and his brown eyes were warm and friendly. He was rotund, and quite jovial. Plus he didn't seem to be the least bit concerned over Sophia's presence. He ignored the child.

In fact, as the evening progressed and they drank their coffee, Malene felt as though she had nothing to say to this man. She no longer felt anxious, but the need for sleep rolled over her like a heavy blanket for she had stayed awake fretting over this meeting, instead of sleeping through the night. The warm bath had helped her to relax and the heavy meal lulled her into a sleepy stupor. She stifled a yawn and then another.

"Let us go to the porch. It's a beautiful evening," Marshall suggested, completely oblivious to her exhaustion.

The room seemed to be closing in on her, and she figured the cool night air would keep her awake. "A lovely idea."

He held her chair as she stood, then she followed him through the French doors onto a porch that was decorated in wrought iron. She could see the harbor below and the lights from the city shimmered in the water. A light breeze sent a loose wisp of hair across her cheek and she tucked it behind her ear. "This is nice, and the view is spectacular."

It almost made her dizzy to look down after living on flat land for so long. Her mind drifted back to sitting on the Coleman porch with Mark. They didn't have to talk. There was no need to fill the silence, but standing with Marshall was awkward.

He took a cigar out of his pocket and lit it. She backed away so she wasn't downwind of his smoke. The scent reminded her of being in the tipi and watching the older men smoking a pipe.

"Would you care for a cigar, too?" he asked, almost as an afterthought.

"No thank you." She took a seat on the far side of the porch with the hope that his cigar smoke went anyplace but in her direction. "The smell is a bit much. I know my papa would enjoy one on occasion, and I've been around a pipe."

"I enjoy a good cigar after my meal."

He wasn't even looking at her. And she wondered what he must be thinking. Her corset impeded her ability to catch a deep breath and she wanted to rid herself of it. She yawned. Exhaustion waved over her. "It's been a very long day. Please forgive me. I'd like to retire to my room."

He bid her a good evening and she took Sophia to the suite of rooms. Ellie was waiting for her. Malene peeled off her clothes and her horrible restraining undergarment. Released from the imprisoning binding, she took several deep breaths. She had forgotten what it was like to wear one. The talc under her arms had caked and she washed it away while Ellie changed Sophia and prepared the baby for bed. Dressed in a thin white nightgown, Malene sat in a lovely rocker while she nursed Sophia.

This room was smaller and filled with white-framed watercolors of baby animals. White wicker was everywhere, so different from the handmade wooden furniture that had held Sophia on the Coleman ranch.

Once Sophia was asleep, she placed the child in an elaborate crib that was covered with netting. The child had begun to sleep well at night, usually only waking up once. But after the train ride, Malene wasn't certain what Sophia would do. The clacking of the wheels on the rails and the constant jostling agreed with Sophia. Tonight, it would be quiet and the bed firm beneath the child.

The sounds wafting through the windows were so different. In the distance, she heard voices, and sounds of horse hooves and carriage wheels on the roads. A bird tweeted. She rolled over, but in spite of her tiredness, actual sleep eluded her. She got up and lit an oil lamp. She would write to Adie and let her know she had arrived safely.

From in the house, came the sounds of children and someone hushing them. She wondered where they had been and why she had not met them. Maybe Marshall wanted her to settle in before he had her meet the children.

***

Mark took Alisa, Issy, and Clarissa through the reservation and showed them the land that he had claimed. Rabbit Hunter and his wife had tended the garden and followed his instructions to the letter. An old bull grazed lazily and the cows had several babies.

"That's not enough for this winter," Alisa said.

"It's a start. The bull is old, but he was cheap. This year, we will eat chicken." He pointed to a small lean-to made with sod and skins.

Rabbit Hunter's wife came out of the tipi and smiled. Mark exchanged a few words with her and she came to the wagon.

"She understands English better than she speaks it."

Alisa nodded and greeted the young wife in the Crow language. The look on the woman's face was of relief.

Mark bid a goodbye and began to move onward. Pride in his land made him sit a little straighter. "I will build a barn first and add a home for them. Then I will build a house for Malene."

Alisa put her hand on his. "She is to marry Marshall Hamilton."

"No. She will come home to me. She loves me."

***

The next morning, Malene met the Hamilton children. Spoilt and noisy, they were a handful. According to Ellie, he'd employ a governess for them and she would quit usually within a few weeks. Then Ellie would take over until he could find another. The oldest boy, Marcus, was the worst. He had a terrible temper and constantly swiped at his younger brother, Dill, and little sister, Clara.

It only took a few days for Malene to discover that the children ate their meals in the kitchen and most ended in food fights. She decided she needed to speak to Marshall about the children. Since Ellie would take Sophia during supper, play with her, then give her a bath so she was ready for bed when Malene retired, it was probably the perfect time to talk to Marshall. She waited until after supper when she and Marshall went to the porch.

She watched him light his cigar. Then she leaned over the wrought iron railing and stared at the blossoms that surrounded the porch. Even in the late evening light, the place was lovely. She found her courage and turned to him, except now his back was to her. "I'm a bit concerned about your children. They seem to be having problems adjusting without a mother."

Marshall faced her. "Yes. I do believe you are right. But they chase everyone away because they refuse to behave."

"I have an idea. I'd like to invite your oldest son to have supper with us tomorrow. He's no longer a little boy, and he needs to have the opportunity to step into his new older role."

Marshall furrowed his brow. "A child at the table? Are you certain you want such a thing?"

She shrugged. "When I stayed with the Colemans, everyone came to the same table for all meals. Sometimes it was noisy or there was an occasional spill, but the family was together. I think Marcus would benefit from your presence."

Marshall took a puff of his cigar and blew the smoke above his head. "I like to relax in the evening. My work keeps me busy."

"Yes. I believe all men feel that way. We don't need to do it every night, but I think it will be good for your son. Boys learn from their papas and..." Her mind raced as it tried to find the best words. A smile tugged at her face. "What better way is there for him to learn the importance of your job? He will grow up knowing what you do and how you do it from conversations. If you say yes, I will speak to him tonight before he sleeps."

"If you insist."

With the antagonist missing from the kitchen table, Mrs. Ellsworth, the cook, might be able to control the younger ones, and with a whole lot of luck, Marcus might learn to behave. She tucked her shawl tighter to her arms hoping to stave off the chill of the autumn evening and decided she'd go to the nursery to talk to Marcus.

She entered the nursery and discovered the governess sipping whiskey while the children ran wild. The place was a mess and so were the children. She looked at the three children until they stopped their nonsense. "Thank you for your attention. Marcus, may I speak with you, alone."

He made a face, stuck his tongue out, and prepared to toss something at her.

"You are the oldest boy, are you not?"

The child let loose with a curse word.

Taken aback, she cocked her head to one side. "I've never heard such a word. What does that mean?"

The boy shrugged.

"Where did you hear that word?" She was certain she was taking the wind out of Marcus' sails without letting on that she was appalled.

Dill spoke up, "Our last governess used to say it all the time."

"Amazing." She looked at Marcus. "Would you care to walk with me?" Then she turned to Dill. "And while I am with Marcus, do you think you could find some night clothes for you and your sister?"

Dill frowned, lifted both shoulders, and let them drop.

"Marcus, are you ready?"

He followed her out of the room, down the hall, and to a small sitting area.

She took a seat and spoke briefly with him about joining the adults for supper. "I'm sorry that everyone has treated you like a small child. You're really quite a young man." She held her hands out in front of her with her palms up. "You are almost grown. I can tell that you look like your papa, but I think you must have a touch of your mama in you."

The boy gawked at her and raised his eyebrows. "I do?"

She nodded. His hair was closer to the brown color of his father's, but his features didn't really match Marshall's, except for his eyes. They were the same shape and golden-brown color of his father's. Dill's coloring was lighter, but both boys shared the same chin. "You must miss her terribly. Do you have a picture of your mama?"

He shook his head. "Papa took it down when she died."

She placed her elbow on the armrest of the chair and made a frown as she rested her chin in her hand. "I wonder if he still has it?"

"Oh, he had it moved to the attic."

"What a strange place for your mama's picture. Do you think we could look for it?"

The boy nodded with enthusiasm.

She smiled at the young boy. "We'll look

tomorrow while Sophia takes her afternoon nap." She put a finger to her lips. "It'll be our secret."

Her heart went out to Marcus. Not only had he lost his mother, but his memories were being stripped from him. "I think if your mama were here, she'd like to give you a big hug. May I give you one for her?"

The boy crashed into her arms and she hugged him tightly. She kissed the soft curls on the top of his head and realized the boy was sobbing. These children were starving for affection and love.

The following afternoon, she and Marcus silently stole to the attic. It wasn't difficult to find the beautiful, life-sized oil painting of his mother. Her light-brown curls were perfectly coiffed and she wore a cream-colored dress. Marcus stood at her side, Dill played at her feet, and Clara was the infant in her arms.

"Oh, yes. I can see how much of your mother is in you. Look at her chin and her curls. She was beautiful."

"I hate her!"

"You don't really hate her. You hate the fact that she died and left you. She couldn't help that. I'm certain that it broke her heart to leave you. But no one has a choice about dying. It's something that happens."

He sat on the floor and pouted.

"It is natural that you feel all alone. It is called grieving, and you are still grieving her death."

Marcus turned his back to her and the oil painting.

Malene knew the healing process for this boy was going to be long and arduous. She leaned down and tickled the back of his neck. "No one can tell you when the pain of her death will go away. Time helps. You are still young enough to want your mother's love and attention as a little boy, and you're not quite old enough to know how to accept what has happened."

"I'm not a baby."

"You are not. But are you old enough to let go of your anger because she has left?" She hoped she was making progress.

Spending all those months with Alisa Coleman had taught her much about dealing with children. Alisa had total patience with all the children. She never yelled. Malene noticed when Alisa was very upset she tended to whisper. And often, when she did fuss at the children, it was with laughter in her voice.

"Tell your mother goodbye, and we'll go downstairs. You can visit with her another day."

Marcus walked over to the painting and waved, then ran down the stairs.

"Don't forget to dress for supper tonight, young man," Malene called as she closed the attic door. "I'll meet you at five minutes to six."

She didn't have to meet him for he appeared at her door dressed immaculately in a pair of shorts with a matching jacket and tie. His white socks came to his knees and his shoes were neatly buttoned.

"Oh, you are handsome. Are your hands washed?"

He held up hands that looked clean.

"I am thrilled that you will be joining us."

The evening meal went well, other than her coaxing both of the males to talk. Marshall clammed up. Normally, he dominated the conversation.

She wished she could have been a tiny fly and flown into the kitchen to see how that meal was progressing. She looked at Marshall and smiled. "Last night you were telling me about your trip to Bombay and the wonderful markets there. It sounds so colorful and exciting."

"It is."

"Please tell me more."

He said a few things and then became silent. She tried again. "I cannot imagine fabric woven with threads of silver and gold."

"I will send a piece to the house for you."

"I'd love to see it. Thank you."

"Tell me what colors you would like and how much. I leave for Bombay on Friday."

Malene looked at him as what he said registered in her mind. "Y-y-you're leaving?"

"Did you not get my last letter?"

"The last letter I had from you said nothing about you going to Bombay."

He made a little tsking sound and said nothing more.

She turned to Marcus. "Did you know that your papa was leaving?"

The boy shook his head.

"Well, there go our plans for you to dine with your papa. Will you join me for these evening meals?"

"Yes, ma'am." He drank all his milk with a noisy gulp.

She wasn't going to say a word about his lacking table manners because he was sitting quietly and behaving himself.

Marshall looked briefly at his son and then glared at her. "After supper, we'll discuss the paperwork to leave you in charge of the children in my absence. I'll only be gone for a month. When I return, I have no further travel plans for a few months." His facial expression softened almost into a smile. "Maybe you would like to go with me to Las Peñas in Mexico. I have some business to attend while I am there. It has lovely beaches and is a quaint little town known for its pearls, among other things. We can make a holiday out of it."

"I have never heard of such a place."

"It is very small. I shall buy you strings of pearls so that you are the envy of all the women here."

She swallowed. Suddenly she had no desire to eat another bite of food. She had just arrived, yet he was leaving her in a strange house, in an unfamiliar city, with three children who need more attention than she was capable of giving. Turning her attention to

Marcus, she forced a smile. "That will make you the man of the house. Are you ready to step into those shoes?"

Marcus shrugged.

On Thursday, she signed papers that gave her access to some money and put her in charge of the children and the house. Her heart was someplace in her stomach, and the burden rested on her shoulders with such force that the thought of eating that night with him was almost unbearable. As she had suspected, she was nothing more than a live-in employee. He could have stopped her from coming until he returned. Instead, he had her come so that he had someone to watch over his house and children.

She squared her shoulders and prepared to greet him dressed for supper in one of her finer outfits. The blue silk skirt and matching waistcoat brought out the blue in her eyes. She pinched her cheeks to add a bit of color and bit her lips to make them pinker. She brushed her eyelashes with a little warmed beeswax making them more noticeable.

"You look lovely, my dear," Marshall said when she walked into the room. "You make me want to stay home instead of leaving you."

She smiled graciously. "Thank you."

"I have employed extra day servants to help with routine matters. If you have any problems that you cannot handle, send a telegram to my parents. But I'm sure you will do well in my absence."

Instead of feeling good about his compliment, her blood boiled with anger. *If I can survive over four weeks of winter weather in an open wagon in the middle of nowhere and then live on a ranch, I can certainly manage in a house full of servants!* "It is very thoughtful of you to provide me with additional help. But I doubt if any of it will be needed."

Dinner progressed as usual, and after dinner, he offered her a brandy. She'd never had one. She had seen her mother drink such a thing on occasion. Maybe it would calm her quaking insides and take the edge off her anger. She sipped it. The candle-warmed liquid felt like fire on her throat. She took another sip and could feel an odd sensation forming in her head. Setting the glass beside her, she had no desire to touch it again.

Never once did he inquire about her happiness, nor did he seem that interested in her. She was being used and that bothered her. There was not even the slightest attempt to court her. Her mind drifted for a moment to Mark. His love showed in his eyes, but Marshall's were blank and devoid of all feelings. She forced herself to pay attention to what Marshall was saying.

Marshall went over many things with her that night concerning running the household, and when he was finished, she looked him in the eyes and asked, "What would you have done if I were not here?"

"I would have hired someone."

"Then why did you not wait until after you returned to bring me out here?"

He smiled. "This will give you a chance to learn about my life and my house."

She tamped down the desire to jump up and choke him. "Running your house is not a difficult job if everyone does theirs."

His grin widened and he held up one slightly cupped hand as though he was about to hold something in it. "Ah, but while I am away - I have no idea if anyone will actually *do* their job."

***

Mark worked hard harvesting and then driving cattle to market with the Coleman men. Joseph was paying him for his services so Mark had kept careful track of his days on the ranch. When the drive was over, he headed back to the reservation.

About a week later, John and Frank picked

up the plow that Mark had ordered from a store in Sheridan and brought it to the reservation along with quite a few other supplies. Together with Rabbit Hunter's help, the men managed to drill a well, assemble a windmill, build an actual chicken coop, and raise a basic barn with wood the Coleman men had brought with them.

It was a start and Mark beamed with pride. He still had plenty of money and enough to keep him busy all winter. But it was with sorrow that he said goodbye to his friends. He'd stay on the reservation for the winter and he hoped by spring, he'd see Malene.

***

Malene had a baby that required her attention and the three children created such a ruckus that she couldn't get Sophia to take a morning nap. After almost an hour of non-stop screaming coming from the far end of the house, she took Sophia and headed to the nursery. Her own temper flared like a boiling caldron, but she knew not to let it show. She opened the door and stood in total amazement at the mess that had been created. In a whisper, she asked, "Where is your governess?"

Marcus answered with a shrug.

Trying to control her annoyance along with the headache that threatened, she asked in a low voice, "What does that mean?"

Marcus held his palms up. "I don't know. She packed her things and left."

Malene wanted to scream. Instead, she smiled. "Well, it's probably for the best." She looked around the rooms. "We'll take care of this after Sophia is asleep. Come to my room and we'll read a book. Marcus, go into the library and see if you can find a children's book."

It didn't take Marcus long to return with a book called Treasure Island. It was thick and she smiled. She sat in the rocking chair with Sophia and began to read. When Sophia was asleep, she called Ellie to watch over the baby. Taking the book, she went into the backyard and found a seat in the warm sunshine. The children sat at her feet and listened as she read more of the tale to them.

She smiled at the children as she closed the book. "That's enough for now. We must clean up your rooms. You may each show me your room, then tell me what you like about it, and what you dislike. But first, where is the broom closet?"

She helped the children clean up the mess they had made with the feathers from their pillow fight and pick up the toys that were scattered everywhere. As she went into each room, she had the child stand on one side of the bed while she stood on the other. "Just copy what I do."

Each child made his or her bed. But the toys were overwhelming. It was certainly more than any child could manage, and many were broken. She found an ample trash bin and called downstairs for a small crate.

"We've got to sort these toys. You need to find the ones you like, and we'll throw away the ones that are broken. And if you've outgrown them, we'll put them in the attic."

Five times the trash bin was filled with broken toys. The two boys took turns carrying the bin downstairs and out the kitchen door to the big bin. When they were done, there was a small pile the children agreed to give to Sophia, so Malene sent Clara with that pile to the suite where Sophia was sleeping. The rest she let Dill and Marcus carry to the attic.

"Do you boys need help?"

Marcus shook his head.

"Say hello to your mama."

"I will," Marcus called back as he left the nursery.

Her headache remained as a dull throb that eased and then returned, only to mellow before started again. She had never been one to suffer with headaches except when she was feeling the pressure of an important school exam. But ever since she'd had Sophia, she'd had headaches. And they had become worse since she was in San Francisco. She rubbed her fingertips over her brow.

Both boys returned with smiles on their faces and Malene smiled back. Ellie brought Sophia to the nursery, and Malene found a place to sit with the baby. "Ellie, I'm afraid there's been a terrible accident with the pillows. Is it possible to find some needles and thread? The children are going to mend them after their noon meal."

Ellie's face drained of color. "Needles?"

"Yes, please."

She instructed the children on what they should be wearing and soon she had them bathed and dressed in actual clothes instead of nightgowns. She helped them button their shoes and then they all went to the kitchen for their midday meal.

When she saw the bowls of oatmeal for the children, the images of eating it during her wagon trip to the ranch turned her stomach. "Please no oatmeal. I don't think I can bare to look at it." She turned to the children. "Does anyone seriously like oatmeal?"

They all shook their heads.

She handed four plates to Clara. "Please set a plate for each of us at the table." Then she turned to the boys. "Marcus, will you get the silverware and, Dill, we need napkins."

The children did as instructed. She looked in the icebox and found a large wedge of cheese. She cut several thick slices from it and handed Marcus a bunch of grapes. "Will you divide the grapes onto the plates?" She handed Dill the cheese and told him to do the same. A bowl of oranges sat by the window. She took two and sliced them in half. "Clara."

The children behaved themselves as they ate. They remained calm and focused on their meal. When they were finished, she told them to take their plates to the sink.

"Is the watermelon ripe?" Malene asked Mrs. Ellsworth.

"Yes." The woman wiped her hands on her long apron. Her dark brown hair showed silver threads through it, but her face remained youthful and her figure was trim.

"Wonderful. I think we're going to have a seed-spitting contest. Who is going to join us?"

Mrs. Ellsworth laughed. "It's about time someone has fun in the house."

Everyone except for Ellie joined them, and they were having a grand time spitting seeds. The children were laughing instead of having screaming matches. Malene fixed Sophia's basket so she could see all the activity around her. Sophia smiled, kicked her feet, and seemed to enjoy the attention that everyone was giving her when they weren't spitting. Malene wiped watermelon juice from her chin, but realized she had dribbled some down the front of her. *Oh dear!*

Ellie appeared. "You have a friend of Mr. Hamilton's who has come to call."

"How nice. Bring whoever it is back here. Maybe they will join our fun."

Mrs. Annabelle Lippcott introduced herself but kept her nose in the air.

"Would you like a slice was watermelon?" Malene asked. "But I'll warn you, I can out spit most everyone here."

"No thank you. I can see I've come at a bad time."

"Oh, not at all. We're having fun. Are you certain you wouldn't like to join us?"

The woman's face looked terribly pale. "No. I came to ask you to tea tomorrow afternoon at my house. I'm having a little get-together with several of the ladies from society."

It dawned on Malene that she wasn't back at the ranch where such formalities were not observed. "Oh, that sounds lovely, but I cannot leave Sophia." She put her hand to her chest and realized the material clung to her sticky hand. "She depends on me."

"Well, if you must bring the baby… We are doing this in your honor."

"Ellie, will you bring me a wet cloth for my hands. I should have thought about that before we all got started."

Ellie brought a pitcher of water and several towels.

Malene washed up and then turned to Ellie. "Stay with Sophia while I walk Annabelle back inside."

Ellie nodded.

"Please come this way. We had just finished our noon meal. The governess is not here today." Malene held open the kitchen door. "Tea sounds lovely. What time tomorrow?"

"Three o'clock."

Malene walked through the kitchen and into the main part of the house. "That will be perfect. Sophia usually sleeps from about two-thirty until five. It's her longest nap of the day.

Do you have children?"

The woman held up two fingers.

"Thank you for inviting me. Marshall had business to attend. He'll be gone for a few weeks. I'm here by myself and I know no one, other than the staff."

"That's what he told my husband. He was anxious for you to make friends."

"Thank you again, for the invitation. I'll be there at three."

She plastered a big smile on her face and tried not to push the pompous woman out of the house. The minute the door closed with a click, Malene ran through the house to the backyard. "Okay, children. I think your bellies have had enough watermelon. You'll all have tummy aches if you don't stop."

She cleaned up the children, took Sophia, and went back to the nursery. Clara couldn't keep her eyes open, so Malene tucked Clara into her bed. Then realized Dill was rubbing his eyes and yawning, so Malene tucked him into his bed. That left Marcus wandering aimlessly in the nursery.

"What would you like to do, young man?"

The child shrugged. "Can I stay with you?"

Malene sighed. "Can is asking if you are capable. We know you have that ability, therefore you are asking permission. Your question is *may* I stay with you."

Marcus frowned. "May I stay with you?"

"Certainly. I need to get Sophia ready for her nap and I was going to write a letter to a dear friend. Maybe you'd like to write a letter to your grandparents?"

She asked Ellie to sit with the sleeping children. Malene instructed Ellie that as Dill and Clara woke up, they could join their brother, but they had to be quiet in case Sophia was still sleeping.

As Malene got Sophia ready for her nap, Marcus wandered around her rooms, snooping and fingering everything. His every move sent another round of panic through her system. Unable to bear his curiosity, she finally said, "It's not considered polite to touch things that are not yours."

Marcus shrugged and came back to where she was sitting with Sophia. "Ellie said you are going to be our new mother."

"Well, your papa and I would need to get married, and that still wouldn't make me your mother. You only get one mother. I would become a stepmother, because I would step into the role of being your mother."

"Are you going to be married?"

She chewed on her bottom lip. "Your papa and I are trying to get to know each other. Getting married is a big decision, and you, Dill, and Clara, are part of that decision. I think it's very important that we all like each other."

"Do you like me?"

Trick question. "I do, but you are much easier to like when you are being good." She placed Sophia in her crib. "Did I tell you that I have a little sister?"

Marcus shook his head.

"When I was your age, I thought she was very annoying. But when we got older, I realized how much I loved her. Now we are very close, but we are also very different in many ways." She took out some paper and found an extra pen. "Shall we write our letters?"

Marcus dipped the pen to the bottom of the ink well, soaking the nib, part of the wooden pen, and the tips of his fingers.

She inhaled as she grabbed a piece of cloth, took the pen from him, and tried to wipe his fingers and his pen. "Oh, dear. I should have warned you that my ink jar was full. I'm terribly sorry. Let's try again."

Mustering all the patience that she could find, she steadied her own emotions. She assumed he already knew how to use a pen, but he didn't. It wasn't his fault. She smiled as she cupped his hand in hers. Guiding his hand, he managed to put only the tip of the nib into the well. With her other hand, she pointed to the nib. "That's much better. You only need ink in the little hollow area."

She watched as he made a scribbled mess of the paper. "Hmm, I thought you had a tutor to teach you?"

"You mean Mr. Hill?"

Names raced through her head. "That might be the man your father mentioned."

Marcus shrugged and made more squiggles until he'd dug a hole in the paper.

"What does he teach you?"

Marcus shrugged.

"Please talk. Even a simple yes or no is better than you wiggling."

"Nothing."

"And when was he last here?"

"I don't know."

"Well, summer has ended. He should be returning. Until then," she lifted Marcus from his seat, and she took it, then set him on her lap. "We're going to do it together."

Taking her unused sheet of paper, she slipped it in front of the boy. She moved the pen in his hand so that he held it correctly, dipped the nib into the ink and held it poised in the air. "I'm going to help you write. Let's start with Dear…"

It took forever to form the letters for the salutation. "You give me the words you want and I will help you form them."

"Papa is gone and so is governess. I hated her. She was mean."

"Oh, Marcus, can you find something nice to tell your grandmother?"

The child put his left elbow on the table and his chin on his fist. "Humph!"

She bit the insides of her cheeks to keep from laughing at him. "Certainly there is something fun and wonderful to tell them."

He wiggled from her and paced the room a few times. Then he climbed back onto her lap. "Malene let us spit watermelon seeds, and I beat Mrs. Ellsworth and Mr. Titus. We all laughed."

Oh dear. I asked for that one. She wrote his words on the page. "Okay, what else?"

"Malene dribbled watermelon juice all down her shirt. She was as messy as us." His hand and arm relaxed as they formed each letter. "I like her. She's nice."

Tears formed in her eyes. She leaned down and gave him a kiss on the cheek. "I like you, too!"

That night she wrote to Alisa. *Trying to keep a three, five, and seven year old organized and busy, adds a burden that I wasn't expecting. The two boys are most affected by their mother's death. I am certain they aren't doing anything more than acting out their disappointment and grief. I try to watch over them like a mother bird. I put them to bed, then spend a few minutes on myself before going to sleep.*

We take all our meals in the kitchen. I have changed their diets to healthier foods that are not as sweet, except for the delicious sour dough bread that seemed to be a standard part of every meal.

After making the children mend their own pillows, they haven't had another pillow fight. That sentence made Malene laugh. *They're learning.*

Clara was easily excitable, and Dill was reacting to Marcus' constant outbursts, but they seemed to be calming down if she kept them physically busy.

Knowing she'd reached the end of her rope, she needed help. She took a few moments one morning to write two advertisements for the newspaper. She wanted a private teacher and a sports instructor for the boys. Swamped with inquiries, she read each one, chose a handful, and then set up interviews in the afternoon.

"Marcus, I'm going to be interviewing teachers for you. Would you like to join me? I think it's very important that we find the perfect teacher for you and your brother."

Marcus crossed his arms over his chest. "I

want you."

"Oh, don't be that way. I will still be here for you and help you with your letters. But we need a real teacher, and not someone horrible like Mr. Hill."

After much pouting, Marcus joined her in the parlor as she interviewed the various applicants. It was on the third day, that Angelina Cortez came for her interview. She had dark chocolate-brown hair that was tied at the nape of her neck. She wore a black riding skirt and waistcoat, and a vibrant red blouse. She spoke perfect English and her credentials showed that she had graduated top in her class. But what struck Malene more than anything was that Angelina had been orphaned. She would understand the pain these children had suffered.

Malene said nothing to Marcus about it, but Angelina had put it in her résumé. The child had been raised and educated by the Catholic nuns. Saving this interview for last meant all those before had a fair chance at being accepted.

Malene looked at Marcus, "Is there anything you'd like to ask Miz Angelina?"

"No, ma'am."

Malene almost fell out of her seat. For once, she had a real answer out of Marcus. "I do believe that Miz Angelina seems like the perfect teacher. Do you agree with that, Marcus?"

"Yes, ma'am."

She turned from Marcus and asked, "Miz Angelina, when would you be able to start?"

"I will need to purchase supplies. Would the day after tomorrow be soon enough?"

Malene looked at Marcus and then back at the dark-haired beauty. "Why don't I let Marcus show you the nursery, just to make certain there's nothing else that might be needed. Although they've had a tutor, they've had no education. I do believe they need desks. And will you need a slate?"

Marcus jumped from his seat and stood beside Angelina.

He took the woman's hand and led her up the stairs. "We have to be quiet. My brother and sister are sleeping."

Once the two were out of earshot, Malene dissolved into giggles. Marcus was smitten with the young woman, but Malene was thrilled with the energetic Spaniard. When the two returned, she suggested that Marcus ask Mrs. Ellsworth to prepare tea.

"I won't lie to you. These children need love and patience. Their mother has died, their papa is frequently gone from home on business, and when he is here, he does not know how to be a parent. They are spoilt and hurting on the inside."

Angelina nodded. "I will do my best."

They discussed supplies, living arrangements, and pay. Angelina left and Malene's insides relaxed for the first time in almost three weeks. She still needed to find a sports instructor.

Marcus was now glued to her side in the afternoons while his siblings slept, so she took him with her while she shopped for desks. Next to the furniture store was a bookstore. She stopped in and bought several books for the children and two for herself. "Will you mail books?"

"Yes. We'll mail anywhere in the world."

"Wonderful." Her heart soared. She picked up three books she knew Mark would like. He was always asking for the great tales of the white man. She hoped these would do. After giving the address, she paid for their purchases. Marcus wanted more books, and she feared a temper tantrum, but convinced him that they would come for more at another time.

She returned to the house in time to hear Sophia wailing. She ran up the stairs to her suite. "I'm so sorry we are late."

"Tell that to your daughter." Ellie handed

over the tearful child.

Malene's head pounded as she took her daughter to the porch near the rose garden. It had been a beautiful day with just a bit of nip to the air. She needed fifteen minutes alone with Sophia. Sitting on that lovely porch and inhaling the sweet scent of the roses wafting on the light breeze, was the perfect way to refresh.

Marshall said thirty-two days. I have eleven to go and I still don't have a sports instructor for the boys. Then it hit her. *Annabelle Lippcott's little brother. What young teen wouldn't like a little spending money?* She didn't need to employee someone full time. She needed someone who could provide the boys with some physical activity in an organized fashion.

She wrote a note to Annabelle and the following day a courier brought Malene an answer. Reggie Hazelwood finished his own classes around three each afternoon and would be available between three thirty and five, and he was available on Saturday mornings.

Malene wanted to dance with joy. Just having someone with whom the boys could play and tumble would be wonderful. They needed to burn off the extra energy.

Angelina started as planned and Malene kept Clara with her. Clara's speech improved and so did her toilet habits. Things were still far from perfect, but compared to what Malene had seen when she arrived, there was a vast improvement.

To try and stop the boys from wetting their beds at night, she had Ellie wake them and take them to the bathroom before she retired. It didn't always work, but as Malene counted down the days until Marshall arrived, the soaked sheets happened less often.

She watched Reggie playing with Marcus and Dill. Reggie had set up a badminton net and brought rackets for the boys. Marcus and Dill looked forward to their playtime.

Everything was running smoother and she had two days left before Marshall was due to arrive. Surprised at her anticipation, her mood lifted. She actually looked forward to seeing Marshall.

The chimney sweep arrived, and when he left, the house staff went to work cleaning every nook and cranny. She took Clara and Sophia for a long walk around the pretty neighborhood to get away from the dust in the house. Leaves crunched under her feet.

Fall wasn't what she had expected. A few leaves turned colors but most just browned and fell. When she thought about it, it hadn't been that cold. The majority of the time she was fine with a shawl, for some days were still quite warm.

The neighborhood was quiet and filled with beautiful homes. Every mansion looked as though it tried to outdo the one next to it. Manicured lawns, and fancy statuary abounded. Having never seen such wealth in her life, she wondered how these people had made so much money.

She looked towards the bay, but a fog had rolled in, obscuring the view.

Mentally she ticked off the list of things that still needed to be done and what she had accomplished. Certainly she had proven herself capable of running a household and caring for the children. Had not life settled into a manageable routine? The children had a normal sleep schedule. They got up, bathed, dressed, ate breakfast, and started their day. They played in the afternoons, had a good meal, and after supper, Marcus and Dill would show her what they had learned. Then everyone would get ready for bed, and she'd read to them. *Yes, things are much smoother.*

Several times during their walk, she stopped to point something out to Clara. When a pretty calico kitten ran to them, she allowed Clara to pet it. The child seemed genuinely thrilled over the small furry creature with a rather large meow for its tiny size.

There were new clothes on order for the Hamilton children, as they were growing like stalks of corn in a field. That thought sent her back to the Coleman ranch. Had she not arrived on the ranch without being prepared? She didn't even understand why her bed was not made daily. Alisa had to show her how to change her sheets and make them tight. Never had she washed a dish until she moved there. With child and uncomfortable, she had never worked so hard in her life, but somehow it all seemed wonderful.

San Francisco was a lovely city. The elegant house was truly a mansion. *So why am I so unhappy here? Why is everything such a chore?*

Just as the fog cloaked the harbor, a fog cloaked her. It weighed on her every step. She rubbed her forehead. Her head pounded on a daily basis, and by nightfall, she was exhausted. Yet, she did less physical work here, and she adored the children. She pondered the situation, then let those thoughts go.

"Come, Clara. Leave the kitten so it can go back to its mother. We mustn't linger too long."

She rounded the bend and the Hamilton house came into view. Yellow, green, and brown leaves carpeted the lawn. The last blooms of the season were fading to brown.

She wished she could sit on the Coleman porch swing and rest her head against Mark's shoulder. She wanted to enjoy living in the lap of luxury in a mansion overlooking the bay. Instead, she was listening to Clara's babbling that only contained a few actual words, and trying to be a calming oasis for two boys who still grieved for their mother.

She thought about Marshall returning. She wasn't at all concerned what he would think of the changes she had made, for she was certain he didn't care. But that led her to another thought. Would he attempt to actually court her? He had mentioned taking her to some little town in Mexico.

Life had changed, and it wasn't for the better. She missed Adie, Alisa, and most of all, she missed Mark.

8

The agent stopped by Mark's ranch and looked around. Mark took him to see the chicken coop, then showed off the barn with its little living area. Mark handed the agent the plans for the house. The agent looked at the windmill and gave his approval. Then the agent did one more thing. He gave Mark a pass that didn't have to be renewed except once a year. It gave Mark free travel on and off the reservation for business purposes.

Pride swelled until Mark thought his chest might burst. The agent considered Mark civilized and making formidable progress to live in a white man's world. But it all came at a price, as the Crow tribe almost considered Mark to be a traitor.

The agent handed over a package that had come by mail and Mark expressed his thanks as it saved him the trip. But the real purpose of the visit was that all the Indians needed to have English names. So when he asked Rabbit Hunter if he was Mark's brother, the young man said yes, meaning they were all brothers on the reservation. Rabbit Hunter was given the name Robert Hunter and Rabbit Hunter's wife became Rose Hunter.

Mark didn't mean to laugh when Rabbit Hunter told him what transpired. Neither man shared the same mother or father. The friendship had bonded them as if they were siblings, but they both agreed that Rose was the perfect name for Rabbit Hunter's wife, as she had a bright smile and a petal soft look to her.

It was the package from Malene that warmed Mark. Three books. He opened each one and looked at the pretty colored paper inside the cover. She had given him books with tales about great American men.

He missed her. He missed her quiet company, her eyes that were the color of a cloudless sky, the way she blushed pink, and the look on her face when she first saw him naked. She was hungry for him and he knew it. It showed when he kissed her.

Winter was not that far away. Rabbit Hunter and Mark worked hard on the ranch. Mark had made friends with a rancher south of him. The rancher gave Mark permission to cut some timber in one wooded section of his land. For every three trees Mark cut, he had to return one in lumber. To Mark, that meant free wood. It was also hard work, but the windmill helped, as it ran his saw that he had bought.

The real problem was getting enough lumber cut to build the house he had envisioned. For five weeks, he felled trees. Then he dragged them to the edge of his property, from there Rabbit Hunter dragged them to where the house would be built. On his final day, he cut six more cedars. They weren't as large as the other trees he had felled, but he was pleased he had found them near a tiny stream. As he was lashing the trees together for transport, three men approached him.

"What are you doing off the reservation, injun?"

"I have permission from the Bureau and from the land owner."

One man raised his rifle and fired a shot into the air. "I don't believe you."

Mark casually moved from the back of the sled towards his horse where a holster containing his gun hung from his saddle.

The man fired another shot into the air. "Looks to me like you're stealing firewood."

Mark bit his tongue. Silence would serve him better than angry words.

Two more men rode up. "What's the problem?"

Mark breathed a sigh of relief. Ernest McLaughlin was the landowner and his grown son, E.J., was with him.

"I asked, what's the problem?" Ernest McLaughlin put his hand near his hip and exposed the pistol he wore.

"Seems we found an injun stealing trees," the younger of the three men said.

"He ain't stealin' nothin'. Seems to me the three of you are trespassin' on my land. I'm gonna suggest you get off before I shoot you."

The men turned their horses around and headed towards the Bozeman Trail.

Ernest turned to his son. "Follow them, E.J. and make certain they don't come back. I'm goin' with Mark to the reservation."

Ernest dismounted and stood beside Mark and pointed to the cedars. "What are you goin' to do with these?"

"These will shingle the outside of the house. I have more like them for the base. This wood lasts forever."

"It's mighty red."

Mark nodded. "Unless I run out before I'm finished, I think this will be the last trees I'll be taking."

"Well, let's see what you got."

Mark smiled at the older man. Six horses pulled the heavy load and he dropped the logs inside of his property line, then rode to the barn. Within the barn, neatly stacked, were all the trees he'd recently cut and the lumber he'd put to one side for the McLaughlins. "Any time you want to get it, I'll help you load it."

The man looked the pile over. "Why you got those pieces of wood between them?"

"They dry better. You don't want them warping."

"That's quite a bit of pipe." Ernest jerked his thumb at a large pile standing in the corner of the barn.

"It goes into the house. The house will have water running through it."

"Water in the house. Ain't you fancy."

Mark grinned. "I need to impress my woman, and I want to set a good example."

The man looked around the barn. "You built this yourself?"

"I had some help from friends."

Ernest walked over to the saw. "How you supposed to run this thing without any treadle?"

"Windmill. For a few hours I have my choice of running a saw or having water. Rain, snow, or shine, I can cut wood." He showed his southern neighbor how it worked.

"I'm mighty impressed. You got yourself a real sawmill goin' in here."

Mark nodded. "I still do a lot by hand."

They chatted a little while longer and then Ernest left. Mark pulled out his plans for the house and looked very carefully at them. He was the one risking everything, but he couldn't have done any of it without Rabbit Hunter's help. One large house would be cheaper to build than two smaller ones.

He picked up a piece of scrap wood, found his pen, and began to draw. There were two families, plus Malene and her sister, living in the Coleman house when he was there, and the women all shared the chores. Why wouldn't Malene be willing to share with Rose?

***

Word reached Malene that the ship was being quarantined outside the harbor. The next day she asked Mr. Titus to take her to the harbormaster's office. The trip didn't take long, but once at the office, she had a long wait.

The room was filled with men both young and old, dressed in everything from rags to starched uniforms. They gawked at her. She pulled her shawl over her chest while trying to avoid all eye contact. Fear choked her and she stifled a cough. It was not a good idea to be a woman alone in such a place.

When her name was called, she stood. "Please, I'm here for Marshall Hamilton. He's on the quarantined ship. I only need to know when he'll be allowed on shore."

The harbormaster motioned for her to follow

him into a tiny office. "Have a seat, ma'am."

She took a seat but found it was difficult to see the man's face, for he was backlit with bright light from all the windows facing the harbor.

"Hmm." The man mumbled several words as he pulled out a listing. "They were to have docked in Bombay. They dropped their anchor in the port, but they didn't pick up any cargo. It's the Black Plague, ma'am. It's in Bombay. Three people aboard the ship came down with it. Mr. Hamilton died."

"What? He's d-dead? Are you absolutely certain?" The room spun, and she clung to the arms of the wooden chair.

"Yes, ma'am. He was with the Hamilton Wholesalers & Importers Trading Company out of New York, correct?"

She nodded.

"According to the notes we were given, he died October fifth."

She wanted to stand, but she wasn't ready.

"His body?"

"Buried at sea. Nothing of his was kept."

The children.

"I'm sorry, ma'am. We informed the local office of the trading company yesterday."

"Thank you for your time, sir." She stood slowly and tried to square her shoulders.

How was she going to tell his children? Hadn't they been through enough? Her insides trembled. Goose bumps covered her arms as ice water rushed through her veins, yet her forehead beaded with perspiration. She needed fresh air.

She had Mr. Titus take her to the telegraph office where she sent a telegram and inquired as to when she should expect his parents to arrive.

By the time she returned to the Hamilton house, her hands were shaking and her head pounded. She asked Ellie to take care of the three older children and informed her that everyone was to meet after dinner, including

Miz Angelina.

She needed time to think, time to pull her thoughts together, and make a few plans. In her room, she went over the papers Marshall had left her. One of the clauses spelled everything out if some unforeseen circumstances prevented him from returning or upon his death. She read the papers three times, each time wishing Adie was in San Francisco to help.

He had left her with an ample supply of cash and she hadn't used hardly any of it. Now she'd have bills to pay. Her insides twisted into knots.

A tiny little piece of her mourned Marshall's loss, for it was a tragic death. She imagined him being alone in his room aboard the ship as the plague consumed him. *What a horrible way to die.*

But the weight of her responsibilities depressed her far more. *Certainly someone within his family will claim these children*

That left her with another worry. Would whoever took them be kind to them? Would they love them and truly care for them?

She went over the papers one more time. The children were financially provided for beyond anything she could have ever imagined, and a sum of money would be given to her every month for their care. There was money for formal schooling, and for household expenses. In a way, it amazed her, as Marshall seemed oblivious to them. Everything was there for her to keep the children as her own. There was no mention of anyone taking them.

She rubbed her forehead as if she could loosen the nonexistent band that wrapped her head and threatened to crush her skull. She rang the bell and requested a cup of tea and a slice of bread be sent to her room. "I have a wicked headache. I will not be down for dinner, but I will meet with everyone after their meal."

A few minutes later, Ellie appeared with a pot of tea under a cozy, several slices of sourdough bread, and orange marmalade.

"Thank you." Malene turned her attention back to the paperwork.

This was a blow that these children didn't need. But it also left Malene in a precarious position of being permanently employed as a substitute mother for the children. *What am I going to do?*

***

Mark spoke to Rabbit Hunter and his wife about his plans to expand the house. Rose could not imagine living in a house, for she had never seen one. To her, the barn was a huge change from living in a tipi. She seemed content to share a house with Malene.

"Adie had sent me several house plans. I had chosen this one for Malene, but..." He handed Rabbit Hunter another piece of paper on which he had drawn new plans. "I can make it look like this. We both would have plenty of space, but this will be less lumber than two houses."

Rabbit Hunter raised his eyebrows as he looked the plans over carefully. "One room for cooking. What is a parlor?"

"A room for the adults to sit and talk. We will have comfortable chairs so no one sits on the floor."

Rabbit Hunter stared at the plans. "I cannot imagine. I trust your judgment."

Mark found another page from a magazine that showed a picture of a woman sewing. "Here. Like this."

Rabbit Hunter agreed to the changes in the house. "I think my lovely Rose will like this. I will tell her of our new plans. Together but separate. It is good."

Mark had plans to fill the house with children. He wanted a son. He'd teach him to hunt, and he'd teach him the ways of the

Apsáalooke. He may have adopted the white man's ways, but he was still proud of the fact that he was a Crow. He had to prove he could live in both worlds. *Come home to me, Malene. Come home. I am waiting for you.*

***

The children and staff met in the main parlor. Malene called the children to gather around her. With one arm around Marcus' waist as he stood beside her chair and Dill on her lap, she broke the news to everyone. She waited for the wails and tears from the boys, but there were none.

Their papa had never been a part of their lives. He was a man who came and went. There was also no excitement at the mention of seeing their grandmamma. Marcus was only concerned that Malene might leave, too.

"No, my sweet Marcus, I will never purposely leave you. I am hoping that I grow to be a very old lady."

Dill wiggled from her lap. "I want a dog."

"Now is not a good time, but maybe in the future we can discuss it."

Mr. Titus and Mrs. Ellsworth were stunned. Both agreed to stay as long as needed and Malene promised to give both of them recommendation letters. It was Ellie that fidgeted and finally blurted out that she was getting married in the spring.

"Then we shall make plans around yours." She turned the children loose and allowed them go to their rooms to play with their toys. "Marcus, hold your sister's hand on the stairs, and be nice. We'll be up in a little while. The adults have much to discuss."

She didn't totally trust Marcus to behave without supervision, but he was doing much better. She turned her attention back to Ellie. "I will not travel with children in the winter. I will stay here until spring. Then I will make some decisions. I am a long way from my sister and my parents. I do not want to stay here forever." She gazed at Angelina who appeared to be just as stunned. "No matter where I go, these children will need a teacher. I am hoping you will consider going with me."

Angelina smiled. "I have no ties in San Francisco, and I understand being orphaned. Had it not been for the Church, I would be on the streets begging for the next meal. I will stay with you wherever you go."

Malene dismissed everyone and put her coat on before stepping onto the porch with Sophia. Alone with her baby sent a calming peace through her. Her headache had subsided, but she had no idea what was in store for her.

She couldn't seriously plan that far ahead, but if she could stay with Adie... Several possibilities floated through her mind, including going back to her parents in Montana and settling there.

Malene considered building her own home,

if she could claim land by Frank Coleman. It would give Frank more land, and he could increase the size of his herd. *Too many unknowns with no answers.* She wished she were as good as Adie was at planning and handling money.

With Sophia asleep for the night, Malene sat at the small table in her room. Her intention was to write to her sister, but instead, she wrote to Mark.

Malene realized that her grief was not over losing Marshall. She wished the man no harm, but she had no feelings for him. It was his children who had captured her heart. Now they were alone in the world. She was all they had left, except for some grandparents that the children did not know.

As she wrote to Mark, she started to cry, not tears of grief for Marshall, but tears of loneliness. She, too, had been abandoned. Except instead of one child, she had four.

Ten days later, the elder Mrs. Hamilton

arrived. Foxes draped the shoulders of her coat. Before her hat had been unpinned from pure white hair, she was barking orders to anyone who would listen. Malene wondered if she would have been better off without the woman's presence.

"Where are these children?" The woman tapped her foot on the floor.

"In the nursery."

The woman curled her lips towards her nose. "Bring them to me."

Malene made a snap decision that she would hold her ground. She was not going to allow anyone to treat her as a personal servant. She called Ellie.

The boys did not even recognize their grandmamma. And it wasn't until later that Malene discovered that the woman had only been to San Francisco once, and that was to bury the horrid woman that her darling son, Marshall, had married.

It was as though a tornado had blown into

the house. The woman refused to eat in the kitchen and only wanted to eat in the dining room. So Malene took her meals with the children and then drank coffee while Mrs. Hamilton ate her meals, which had been kept warm. Mrs. Hamilton complained the entire time. Malene's head pounded.

Malene finally collected a breath and cut the woman's diatribe off. "Mrs. Hamilton, is there anyone who will claim these children? Did Marshall have a sister?"

"Marshall was an only child. Then he married that trollop and tried to pass her as society. Pfft! He found her in Hong Kong and claimed her father was a buyer for some company in England. Oh, the story Charlotte spun about her father dying and leaving her to fend for herself."

Charlotte. So that was her name. It suits her.
"And you have no intention of taking them?"

"Never! Why would I want them?"

"Because they are your grandchildren?"

"Keep them or put them in a boarding school. I have no use for the children of my son's whore."

Malene swallowed. "I will keep them."

The woman reached in her ample bosom and withdrew a folded letter. "I was told to give you this, if you were still here when I got here. You are capable of reading, are you not?"

Malene reached across the table and took the letter. Since the woman acted as if it were an afterthought, Malene decided to pocket it for later reading. "Your son left me with several papers. Would you care to read them?"

"Anything he left with you, he also sent to his father."

Malene nodded. "Very well. It is time for me to read to the children. They are enjoying Treasure Island."

She excused herself and went to the nursery. An hour later, she returned and found Mrs. Hamilton in the parlor doing nothing other than tapping her nails against the arm of the chair where she sat. Malene forced a smile as she entered the room. "I pray you've had a pleasant evening."

The woman looked at Malene as if she were a rat that needed to be disposed of quickly.

Malene took a seat across from the woman. "I usually spend this last hour in my room writing letters to family and friends. I find it a pleasant way to unwind from my busy day."

The woman waved her hand through the air as if she didn't care. "You brought me out here for what reason?"

"I needed to know what would become of the children, and was there anything of your son's that you wanted."

Mrs. Hamilton shook her head. Malene found it strange that the woman didn't really seem to care that much about her son, and didn't appear to be grieving his loss. "I thought I should have a service for Marshall, but I do not know to what church he belonged. Do you know if he had a preference?"

"I have no idea."

"Then I shall send notice and invite his friends here to remember him." She found Marshall's stationery and withdrew several sheets and envelopes. "We'll do it the day after tomorrow."

She wrote one to Mrs. Annabelle Lippcott, one to the local Hamilton Wholesalers & Importers Trading Company office, and another to the newspaper.

The following day was busy for Mrs. Ellsworth and Mr. Titus, but by late evening, they had plenty of food for everyone who might attend. Mr. Titus had a new suit and Mrs. Ellsworth had a pretty apron to wear over a new dress. Everyone tumbled into bed exhausted, including Malene, who had worked in the kitchen preparing several dishes.

Malene got up extra early and went into the kitchen to put the finishing touches on the food and to handle any last minute preparations. When she was done, she bathed and dressed to greet the guests. Annabelle was one of the first and Malene breathed a sigh of relief.

"What can I do to help?" Annabelle asked, as she kissed Malene's cheeks.

"Help me greet people. I know no one."

The house filled with people. Most were from the local office of Hamilton Wholesalers & Importers Trading Company. Others were from the railroad, several were members of society, or neighbors. Annabelle was wonderful as she seemed to know most everyone who came.

Quite a few claimed they were from a men's club in the downtown. That sent flags of caution through Malene, as they didn't seem to be of the same ilk of Marshall. But she really didn't know him, and she'd only heard stories of such places. Had he meet Charlotte in such a place in Hong Kong? Was that why his mother had washed her hands of her son and his children?

The entire affair went very smoothly, and when the last visitor left, Malene collapsed in a parlor chair.

Mrs. Hamilton appeared and announced, "I'm going home tomorrow."

Another wave of relief went through Malene. *Thank goodness!* A smile tugged the corners of her lips upward. "I'm so glad that you came and that you could be here for your son's memorial."

"Surprisingly, it was very nice."

The backhanded compliment wasn't sitting well with Malene, but at that point she was too tired to cope with her own anger. She had all she needed from the woman, the knowledge that the house and everything in it, along with the children, belonged to Malene. According to the letter from the Hamilton family lawyer, the children would have plenty of money. She was going to be paid a very generous sum for keeping them. Each child had income and there was an additional amount for running a household.

Malene looked at Marshall's mother. "Thank you, and again, thank you for coming."

The next day, Mrs. Hamilton went to the train station. The children stood and watched the white-haired woman board the private car.

"Wave and say goodbye to your grandmamma," Malene instructed.

Marcus shrugged and did as instructed.

Malene had requested a picnic basket before they had left the house. As soon as the train began to move, Malene and the children went back to the house. She picked up the basket and everyone else from the house rode in the carriage to an open meadow near the mountains that surrounded the city. Malene spread blankets on the ground and let the children run and play.

Miz Angelina soon had the children looking for things in the meadow. Mrs. Ellsworth and Mr. Titus sat on one blanket chatting and Ellie had joined Angelina's scavenger hunt.

Malene sat on a blanket, stretched her legs out, then leaned her elbows back, and rested on them. The air was clean and crisp, and the sun beat down on Malene's face as she watched the children scamper about.

Her mind wandered to the painting in the attic. She would never know the truth about the young woman in the portrait, but judging by Marcus' grief, the woman adored her children. *Charlotte. I must remember that name. The children have the right to know their mother's name.*

For a welcomed change, she totally relaxed. She wanted to rest her head in Mark's lap and have him tell her of the world around her. The thought of the soft rumble of his voice in her ear sent a warm pulse through her.

Sophia rolled over several times as if she were attempting to escape from the blanket.

"Come back here. Where do you think you are going?"

Sophia giggled.

Malene tickled the baby's tummy as she rolled Sophia onto her back. "Let's fix your bonnet."

Sophia kicked her feet, then grabbed them with her tiny hands, and pulled her booties off.

"I fix your bonnet so now you pull your booties off. If it's not one end, it's the other." Malene laughed at her child's antics, then moved the pillow in the travel basket so that Sophia could sit up and watch everyone.

The cry of a bird overhead caught Malene's attention. She shielded her eyes from the bright autumn sun and saw an extremely large bird. As it flew away, a feather floated down not far from where she was sitting. She retrieved it and ran it through her fingers. *My darling Many Feathers, I miss you so much, Mark. So very much.*

***

Mark jumped when he saw the agent standing in the barn. The noise from the saw had drowned out all the other sounds.

"Didn't mean to surprise you. I called your name," the agent said with a grin. "What are you working on now?"

"A house."

"Looks like you've cut enough for three houses."

"Made a deal with a rancher. He traded trees for some lumber."

The agent nodded and jerked his thumb over his shoulder. "What's that stone you've laid out there?"

"The base of the house."

"It's going to be a big one."

Mark shrugged. He didn't like the agent poking into his business, yet he knew the man was trying to make an example out of him. He had laid out the stone according to the measurements that had been provided with the house plans but it looked much too small.

He increased them.

The man put a handful of mail on a stack of wood and left.

Mark opened the letter on top of the pile. It was confirmation that his orchard trees and other plants that had been ordered would be shipped directly to him in the early spring. He leafed through the two catalogs, one for stoves, and another for farm equipment. He'd study them in more detail later. The second letter was from Adie and Frank. He smiled as he read it. The third one he pocketed and would read later, when he was completely alone. It was from Malene.

After supper, Mark took his letter to his room in the tiny living quarters of the barn. His heart screamed with joy, but he uttered not one sound. The man she was supposed to marry had died, but she went on to tell him how she had become the parent to Marshall Hamilton's three children. After traveling last winter, she never wanted to repeat such an experience. She intended to return to the Coleman ranch and specifically to her sister, Adie, during the coming spring. She had enough money to build a house for her and the children. *You won't get that far and you don't need to build a house. I'm building one for you.*

His entire body ached for Malene. He wanted to wrap her into his arms and tell her how much he loved her. His hand traveled over the blue stationary as though he could touch and caress her as a man does when he loves a woman. He listened to marital sounds coming from the other room. The sounds stirred the fire that Malene had lit within him. It was too much. Maybe the night air would provide some relief.

He stepped outside of the barn. The cool temperature felt good on his heated body. He imagined wrapping Malene in his arms and the feel of her breast in his hand. She didn't fear his touch. She wanted him as much as he wanted her. He leaned against the side of the barn and inhaled deeply.

Images of Malene flashed before him in rapid succession. He loved his wife, but he had never been in love with her the way he loved Malene. Was it because he had matured, or had his wife taught him how to love? He leaned his head against the barn, closed his eyes, and pondered that thought.

A gunshot rang out and then another. Plaintive sounds and erratic hoof beats followed each shot. He slipped back into the barn and called for Rabbit Hunter. Someone was killing his herd. He grabbed his rifle and jumped on his horse. Rabbit Hunter was not far behind him. There were three of them, and they had painted their faces to look like Indians, but it didn't fool Mark. He knew exactly who they were. By the time they chased the men off, three of his cows and four of the young calves lay dead or dying. He screamed his frustration into the night.

"We'll buy more." Rabbit Hunter said when

they were finished putting the dying animals out of their pain.

They dragged the dead animals back and hung them in the barn.

Deep sadness filled Mark. "They'll be back. They're after me."

"Why?"

"Because I am not white like them. They have evil hearts."

Both men stayed awake and listened to the sounds of the night. There was no sleep in Mark, as his anger continued to burn. He sent Rabbit Hunter back inside. Mark wanted to track those white men as if they were animals, but he knew not to do it. He wasn't about to let everything for which he had worked so hard to vanish over a fit of rage. The white man didn't take kindly to an Indian killing a white man, but they did nothing if a white man killed an Indian.

Later that day, Rabbit Hunter went to the main encampment and told his people to come get meat. Then he went to the agent's office and told the agent what had transpired. "Mark said it was the same three men who had given him a problem when he was cutting wood."

"Have Mark come look at my Wanted posters. Maybe he will recognize them. Tell him I said it's important."

"Can we get protection?"

The agent shrugged. "I'll notify the Army."

Mark and Rabbit Hunter decided they would spend the next few weeks watching over their land at night by splitting the shifts.

Mark posted several letters at the agent's office and looked through the Wanted posters. He picked out two men instantly and then stared at a third poster. *If he...*"Him." He shoved his finger at the drawing's face. "The mustache is gone and his hair is darker, not red. It is this man, his nose, eyes, and chin. That long chin. Albert Goo dard?"

"Albert Godd-ard. Slur it together."

"Goddard."

E. Ayers

"Yes. You do well. You've become a model Indian. I have written many times of your progress to the Bureau. They are very pleased. I am going to ask them to help you replace your animals. Don't know if they will do it, but it won't hurt to ask."

"Thank you." *Albert Goddard. I know that name. How do I know that name?*

9

The house in San Francisco ran efficiently and the children were doing better. It was still far from perfect, but if the noise level escalated in the nursery, it was usually because the children were laughing and playing.

Malene went through Marshall's things and gave most of his clothes to a local charity. She found a big open box of cigars and two unopened boxes. She kept the one box, knowing she could use it as a gift. The opened box she sent to her father, but the other she struggled with before deciding to send it by way of Mark for the chief and tribal leaders. She knew the men put tobacco in a pipe and smoked it - maybe they would like cigars. She asked Mark to take it to the encampment as her Christmas gift to them.

Marshall's jewelry she boxed up to keep for his sons. She also found a huge amount of jewelry that had belonged to his wife. Malene set the pearl jewelry to one side for herself. The beautiful diamond set that was worn for the portrait, she would keep that for Clara. The rest she probably needed to sell.

Tuesday afternoons, she spent with Annabelle and her friends. Their gossip drove Malene insane, but it was the one chance she had to get away from the house and spend it with other women. The pattern for living was well established. She baked on Mondays and Thursdays, and ran errands on Wednesdays. Her favorite thing on Wednesday was to stop at the bookstore.

Every month, money went into her bank account and every month she sent money to the bank in Montana. She'd take some cash for spending money and pay the staff.

As Christmas drew near, she bought a Christmas tree and decorated the house. The flower shop had a wonderful array of things from which to choose. Never had she seen such elaborate decorations. They were so different from the simple ones her mother and Alisa Coleman used. Not only did the front door have a wreath, she also purchased arrangements for the transom, both inside and out. Swags of greenery decorated the mantels, staircases, and chandeliers. It lifted her spirits, and Marcus appeared to be thrilled, for Christmas had not been observed since his mother had died.

She had bought gifts for everyone in the house and enough candies and little sweet oranges to fill their stockings. Christmas cards were sent to everyone she knew and she had added a short special wish with each one. She had never been so excited about a Christmas, for she had done this one by herself, yet under all of it was a loneliness that would not go away. She kept telling herself that she missed her family, but the emptiness was deeper than that and she knew why.

The closer to Christmas they got, she discovered that Marcus had begun to wet the bed again. She took him with her when she ran errands. Alone, he talked about how much he had missed his mother.

"I think you will always miss her. She must have been very special. But I think you are special. So much has happened since I arrived, and now I have you, your brother, and Clara. I think I'm the luckiest woman on earth."

"You do?"

"Oh, yes. Don't you see what occurred?" She smiled at Marcus. "I think your mother is the angel who sent me to your father so that I would be the one to raise you."

He scrunched up his face. "You think my mother did all that?"

She nodded. "I do believe your mother sent me."

He squeezed her hand. "I'm glad you are here."

"So am I."

Christmas Eve, Angelina took the children to church with her. While they were gone,

Malene helped prepare the feast with Mrs. Ellsworth. She had given everyone off for Christmas Day, but she had an idea. San Francisco was cold, windy, and damp; however, the mountains behind the city were covered in snow.

When Mr. Titus walked into the kitchen, she asked, "I was wondering what your plans were for tomorrow?"

He smiled widely showing off his beautiful pearl-white teeth "I'll be spending it with my daughter and my two grandsons."

"Aren't your grandchildren about the same age as Marcus and Dill?"

"Six and nine, just slightly older than your boys."

She smiled at Mr. Titus referring to the Hamilton boys as hers. "That's what I thought, but I wasn't certain." She chomped on her bottom lip. "Remember that meadow?"

"Yes, ma'am."

"Do you think there is snow in the

meadow?"

"I'm certain there is snow there, but I'm not certain we can reach it with the carriage if there is."

She sighed as she mashed the potatoes. "I thought it would be fun if all the children could play in the snow on Christmas Day."

"That's a wonderful idea. I know another spot where we might find some snow." Mr. Titus laughed. "And I'm sure my daughter would love to have the children out from under her feet while she fixes a big meal."

"Then the children and I will be ready and waiting for you."

Morning seemed to come extra early. The children usually wanted to sleep in, but not Christmas morning. Marcus had to take a quick bath, so Malene made them all get dressed before going downstairs.

The excitement had reached a feverish pitch by the time Marcus was ready. Clara was dancing with expectation, for this would truly be her first Christmas, and although Dill's memories were faint, he remembered enough to make him anxiously enthused. It was Marcus, with his mixed emotions of missing his mother and being denied a normal childhood pleasure of Christmas his father had failed to provide, who tugged at Malene's soul.

Malene wrapped her arm around the boy. His smile beamed so bright that she had to hide her tears of joy. As the children entered the front parlor, they each screamed with delight. Clara grabbed the doll and hugged it tight. She didn't even realize that she had a carriage to go with it. Dill looked at the miniature train and began to push it around on its tracks. Marcus' excitement over his bicycle soon turned to puzzlement, as he looked at his other gifts. "What are they?"

She showed him how to build with his Lincoln Logs, then showed him how he could play with his brother using the bag full of marbles.

The children didn't even notice they had stockings filled with more things until Clara said, "Look! Up there!"

The children rushed to their stockings and emptied the contents onto the floor. She allowed them to choose one piece of candy that they could eat before breakfast.

But when the doorbell rang, Malene smiled. "Marcus, go see who is at the door."

She listened as the boy ran to the foyer and opened the door. His squeal probably penetrated the entire block. Her smile broadened and filled her whole being with bliss. "Well, don't just stand there. Bring him in!"

A moment later, Marcus entered the room holding a leash attached to a six-month-old Pit Bull mix. White faced with a brown ear, he was a funny-looking thing with legs that appeared too short to support his stocky body. But the pup seemed ready to adopt his new family. Thanks to Mr. Titus' connections, she had a trained puppy. She swiped at tears of happiness to see the children this ecstatic.

She wasn't too certain how she'd manage to take a dog with her when she went home, and she really wasn't certain where home was anymore. She only knew that home was not in San Francisco.

The puppy stood on his hind legs and sniffed at Sophia, so Malene put the baby on the floor. Immediately, the dog began to lick the baby's face. Sophia giggled and tried to grab the pup.

Malene sucked in a deep breath and scolded no when Clara latched into the puppy's tail. But the puppy merely responded by licking Clara.

Getting everyone into the kitchen for a meal wasn't going to be easy. With a little cajoling, she managed to convince the children to leave their new toys long enough to eat breakfast. But deep inside, she was pleased that they were enjoying their new things and playing nicely.

Angelina appeared in time for the late breakfast.

"There are presents for you under the tree," Malene said as she added a few more eggs to the bowl. Even making breakfast for the family, added to the intimacy of the occasion.

Angelina's mouth opened slightly and her eyes grew wide. "For me?"

"Yes. You are family."

Marcus had chosen a book from the bookstore for his favorite teacher. And from the jeweler, Malene had chosen a pretty timekeeping piece the woman could wear.

Angelina returned to the kitchen with tears in her eyes as she kissed Malene and Marcus. "I have never had such wonderful gifts."

About eleven o'clock, Mr. Titus appeared with his two grandsons and everyone bundled up for the wonderful ride. Malene grabbed several small pieces of coal and a carrot.

Angelina looked at Malene as if she had lost her mind. Mr. Titus grinned with a knowing smile.

By three o'clock, she was pushing coal into the top snowball and shoving a carrot into the center of it. The children danced around their snowman, and the puppy promptly lifted its leg, creating a yellow streak down the side of the lowest tier of snow.

Snow angels seemed to be everywhere. Mr. Titus' grandchildren were wonderful companions to the Hamilton boys. Everyone complained as Mr. Titus called for an end to the festivities in the snow, but it was important go home before the sun settled for the evening. It was all Malene could do to stay awake on the ride home.

Once home, she fed the children leftover ham and potato salad from the previous night's dinner. And before chasing them to bed, she made the warm milk that Alisa used to make on special occasions for the children.

The children guzzled the unusual treat that had been sweetened with sugar and flavored with specks of vanilla.

She tucked the children into bed and listened to their prayers. Clara was fast asleep before she had finished. Dill managed to say amen before falling asleep, and Marcus thanked her for the most wonderful day he could remember.

With tears in her eyes, she left the nursery. She had letters to write telling her family and Mark of her day. But in the back of her mind, she knew this would be her only Christmas in San Francisco.

With the children tucked into bed and sound asleep, she sat at her desk and began to write. Holding her pen mid-air as she daydreamed, she looked forward to homesteading near Adie. There was no need for a grand house, just something that would hold her, Angelina, and the children. Maybe a little garden with rosebushes and some vegetables, a place she could call her own. It was her dream and no one would keep her from it.

***

Mark and his friend Rabbit Hunter, now known as and accepting his new name of Robert, worked hard. The Bureau of Indian Affairs refused to replace the lost animals, but Mark and Robert managed. Between the two of them working as liaisons, they were selling horses to Adelwulf Reiner. It gave the tribe a small income. Chickens kept the tribe in meat that winter.

Adelwulf Reiner brought a big box of candy canes to the tribe a few days before Christmas. The tribe knew there was a Coleman behind the gift. The women and children of the tribe enjoyed the sweet red and white candy sticks. But the package from Malene Reiner, sent to Mark but addressed to the Chief, impressed the men. They all remembered the Children of the Sun.

The scent of tobacco was strong that night in the chief's tipi. Mark had seen white men smoking the cigars and knew what to do with them. The council enjoyed the gift. In a small way, it helped Mark and Robert's status with the tribe. At least for a little while, the two men were not considered outcasts. The tobacco was considered a very valuable and revered gift. The men didn't smoke it often, as it was reserved for special occasions.

Mark and Robert spent their days cutting wood and stacking it. Rose fixed meals on a cast iron stove and seemed to enjoy living in a barn. It was all new to her, but she adjusted to it and looked forward to the house that the men planned to build.

While Rose's family and friends lived in tipis, she stayed warm. It was different, yet the same. Instead of round, the rooms were square and separate. But for the first time in her entire life, she never felt the pangs of hunger. That pleased Mark. The meals were still far from what the Coleman's served, but it was food.

Many a night, he and Robert talked about what they would plant and how much. He had put some money aside for the house and he didn't want to touch it, but he didn't have much money left. If he went back to work for the Coleman's, it would take him away from his house and planting his own fields. It was too much for Robert to do alone.

Robert leaned against a post in the barn. "What if we ask Little Cloud or Iron Tail to help in the fields?"

"And do what, pay them in…food?"

"It's all we've got."

Mark let out a sigh. "We're in too deep to stop." He got up, removed a small board from the floor near a wall, and retrieved a tin. "It's my house money. It's all I have."

Robert counted it. "We're going to need all of this for the house." He handed the money back and looked at the saw. "I'm thinking--"

"Oh, no. I'm not selling the saw."

Robert shook his head. "Where's the nearest sawmill?"

"Billings."

"South of here?"

"Fort McKinney area, then Creed's Crossing."

"And E.J. McLaughlin wants to build a house? Where's he going to get the rest of his lumber?"

"You're saying I should run a sawmill this winter and cut wood for other people."

Robert nodded. "Let them bring you the timber. We get wood for our stoves with the odd pieces." He looked at the pile. "Too much. You said white men's children play with blocks of wood. We buy smaller saw and make perfect blocks. We show Little Cloud how to make them smooth. His wife can sew bags to put them in. Then he can sell them to stores."

"And what will she use for bags?"

"The material from the bags of sugar and flour."

What his friend was saying made perfect sense. The more Mark turned it over in his mind, the better he liked it. "I will ask Ernest McLaughlin about the wood and tell him that we are looking for more work. I will also ask Broken Spear to help us with the sawmill. We operate the sawmill in the winter and make money."

"Broken Spear will not want white man's money."

"Every man wants something. No one is ever satisfied. We need to find his need."

***

Malene made plans to leave San Francisco. Each piece of furniture was being scrutinized. What would she take? What would she leave behind? There were so many beautiful things in Marshall's house that she wanted them all, but she would never again have such a grand house. She needed to simplify.

"What are you doing?" Marcus asked Malene.

"Writing a letter to my papa. Would you like to write a letter?"

He nodded and climbed into the seat across from her.

She retrieved a pen and paper for him. "To whom would you like to write?"

"Your papa."

"That would be lovely. He would like that. He never had a little boy."

"Why not?"

Malene shrugged. "He only had two girls."

The answer seemed to be enough for Marcus. She watched him work hard to form his letters and this time, he was very careful with the ink. He was still behind for his age in his schoolwork, but he was catching up with Angelina's tutoring. He was making great strides and that warmed Malene's heart. She looked at her own letter and read it.

I want to sell the house. I will keep some furniture, but the rest will stay with the house, if you think that is the right thing to do. Hamilton Wholesalers & Importers Trading Company filled this place with beautiful things from all over the world. Marshall only bought the best.

I will begin to ship home little things that I want to keep. The local officer of Hamilton Wholesalers & Importers Trading Company has told me I may use a company railroad car. Then you or Dan can retrieve them when the train stops at the stockyard. They are making a key for each of us so that we can lock the car. HW&ITC is providing me with crates from their warehouse.

She finished her letter and added Marcus' to it. Mail traveled quickly between her and her parents, but not between her and Adie. Since Adie did not live near a railroad and the Coleman's usually only went to town once a week, their letters took weeks to reach their destination. But they both wrote almost daily.

Excitement began to build within her. She couldn't wait to see her parents and Adie, who was now with child. Malene laughed to herself. Adie was thrilled with marriage and the marital bed. Maybe what Mark had said about being with the right man was true?

***

Mark sat one evening and wrote a letter to Malene. He wanted to tell her about his new venture with the sawmill. He wrote on packaging paper, as he had no more stationery and didn't want to spend the money to buy any. Even stamps cost pennies, and he was watching his money very closely.

The sound of the saw is constant. We have much work. Broken Spear and his son Jumping Buck do much of the work. Robert and I have decided to move the saw from the barn and make a building for it. There is sawdust on the floor and in the air. I worry about fire.

***

Malene took the letters from the courier and thanked the man. Anything concerning the house, she opened first. Hamilton Wholesalers & Importers Trading Company was sending several crates on Thursday.

Then she sorted through the private correspondence and smiled. Anxious to know the latest news from the ranch, it was the letter from Alisa Coleman that she ripped open first.

My dearest friend,

It is with sadness that I tell you that on December 27, I gave birth to a son who never took a breath. Joseph made a box and I dressed the baby in a pretty gown. John dug a deep grave by the orchard and I will plant an apple tree there this spring. Nine months for naught, my heart is heavy.

Malene burst into tears. She could barely imagine Alisa's pain. What if Sophia had not lived? The letter from Adie, she stuffed in her pocket. Malene knew her sister would tell her more. But Malene couldn't stop the tears that flowed. She wiped them away only to have them return and roll down her cheeks. Her heart was heavy, too.

That evening she opened the letter from Adie, and then the one from her father. There would not be a problem with her shipping things home. Her father would store her furniture in the attic until she had decided where she would build a house. He thanked her for the cigars and the beautiful pen and ink set that had once belonged to Marshall. But it was Marcus' letter that impressed him. Her papa looked forward to her visit and to meeting all the children. He had included a note to Marcus.

The letter from Mark, she savored as if it were the finest confectionary. She wanted to nuzzle into his neck and feel his arms around her. No matter how hard she tried to convince herself that he was not the man for her, she couldn't. He was funny, brazen, fierce, protective, and tender. She loved him.

Malene stayed busy emptying the house of things that truly were not needed. Four heavy boxes of pale blue stationery and two boxes of envelopes, with the Hamilton crest and Marshall's name, sat in the man's office. She took the boxes to the printing office when she ran her errands.

"Is there anyway to salvage this stationery?"

"I can cut the header from the pages and you will have shorter paper, but the envelopes..." The man frowned. "I can block it with more ink and create a solid blue box. Do you wish me to print your name there instead?"

"Will I be able to write on the blue box with black ink?"

"Certainly."

"Then just block it out and cut the paper. There's no point in wasting so many envelopes."

"Excellent decision. I'll send them to the house when they are done."

She thanked the man, left the boxes, and headed to the bookstore. Books had become her friends on lonely nights, which meant every night. When she was done reading them, she'd ship them to Alisa. Buying books was a luxury that Malene loved. The little bookstore knew her and usually had several in a pile waiting for her. She chose several books and bought them.

She stopped at the dry goods store and bought several lengths of material for Adie and Alisa, along with several patterns. She would ship them immediately, knowing that both would be thrilled with the beautiful imported fabrics.

Life was different in San Francisco. It wasn't like Chicago or the small towns that she had grown to love. There were more stores like Chicago, but San Francisco was smaller and friendlier. There was also a wide array of imported items that were not seen elsewhere. She would miss that aspect of the seaport that she presently called home.

Those were things about San Francisco that she would miss, but she wouldn't miss the saloons and the prostitution. Mr. Titus never left her out of his sight for two seconds. She appreciated his constant companionship, but she wasn't certain he was capable of protecting her.

She stopped by the market and picked up lemons. Holding one to her nose, she sniffed. The fresh citrus scent filled her lungs. *Lemonade.*

Snow swirled through the air and melted the minute it touched the ground. It looked pretty. As Mr. Titus took her home, her mind drifted back to the snows that had delayed her trip from home to Creed's Crossing. San Francisco wasn't anywhere near as cold, but it could get blustery. The ride to the fancy Georgian mansion high above the city was never direct, for the streets were so steep. Mr. Titus often took a route that was easier on the horses. She never minded, for she enjoyed seeing the neighborhoods and the colorful houses that were springing up.

She spent the rest of the day boxing things to send home. Slowly, the house was being emptied. Angelina often talked about the orphanage, so Malene sent the children's outgrown clothes there. She offered several household items to Ellie, since she would be marrying and in need of everything.

Ellie had sent the date for her wedding as the first of May. Malene would attend the wedding and planned to leave on May third.

Mr. Titus was looking forward to spending time with his daughter and grandchildren, for Malene had offered a substantial sum to him when he left. She didn't want him being a burden to his daughter, or for the Hamilton horses to go without food. Rather than sell the horses and carriage, she gave them to Mr. Titus. With luck, he'd pick up a few taxi jobs.

There were other staff members that only

came one day a week or only for a few hours daily. Most were young and would find other work with a letter of recommendation. It was Mrs. Ellsworth's future that concerned Malene.

Malene peeled potatoes and glanced over at Mrs. Ellsworth. "If you would like to come with me, that would be fine."

"Oh, no. My son is on a ship and my daughter would never forgive me for running away from her."

"Then I must work harder at finding you another position."

It was a Tuesday afternoon tea that gave Malene the opportunity to suggest Mrs. Ellsworth to one of the women who complained bitterly of her staff. "She's very good. I wanted her to come with me, but she wants to stay here in San Francisco."

"You're leaving us?" Annabelle asked.

"Yes. I do not belong here. I miss my friends and family, especially my younger sister." Malene smiled. "I will be an aunt this coming

June, and I want to be there for the baby's birthing."

Annabelle's face registered horror. "You can't leave!"

"The dates are set. Ellie will leave to get married, and I will depart behind her."

Annabelle put her hands to her chest. "What will I do without my new best friend?"

Gossip without me? "I am only a letter away." She giggled. Yes, she would miss the women in the group, and she realized that. But home was not here, and she wanted to go home. *If only I knew where home really is.*

***

Mark and Robert managed to construct another building for the sawmill in spite of the snow that fell as they worked. It was primitive compared to the barn because it was made of sod and bits of wood, but it was a better place with more airflow. The amount of sawdust in the barn's air had become a serious fire hazard, and it worried Mark.

He'd seen what happened when sawdust was burned. Yet members of the tribe would collect bucketfuls of it for burning. Several people had experienced it igniting before the little chips hit the hot coals from the previous night, but he couldn't be responsible for all his people. He could only warn them.

It took three days to remove all the sawdust from the barn and get it aired out. It was still stacked with lumber for his house and E.J. McLaughlin's. But once the barn was cleared, he spent time splitting small logs to make cedar shakes for his house. He stacked and counted, hoping he would have enough.

It passed the days away, but inside, he knew he was running out of time. Malene was leaving San Francisco the third of May. She would stay with her parents until June, and then she intended to go to Adie. He had to catch her before she went to Creed's Crossing in Wyoming, and he had to have the house done by then.

He needed a lathe similar to the one Frank had used. After counting the money he had for the house, he figured what it would take to buy a lathe. If the sawmill could find work to be lathed, he would be able to pay himself back. Except lathes were expensive. It was possible that it might take a year or more to replace the money that he took for the lathe. It was a chance he didn't want to take.

The sawmill was doing well, and he tried to stay away as much as possible. Broken Spear and his son, Jumping Buck, worked well together, and kept the saw going almost non-stop. Mark paid the men and took a tiny cut for Robert and himself.

He pondered the lathe purchase. A lathe was nothing more than something that would turn wood. He looked at the saw and how the belts turned a rod that turned the saw. He'd make a lathe and use it at night when the belts didn't have to run the saw. He only needed something that would spin the wood.

The winter was bitter cold and what snow fell, remained. To some extent, he felt safer with the snow, for any tracks from man or animal were visible. And several times there were tracks. Whoever it was, watched from afar, and he wasn't alone.

A trip to the agent's office yielded him several packages. One contained several hand tools in a paper box. Another large parcel had things he had ordered for his house. Malene had sent him a package wrapped in heavy brown paper.

He saved Malene's and opened the other items first. Pleased with the quality of the hand tools, he showed Robert the contents of the box.

Robert picked up one of the tools but poked at the paper box. "This is good. Less weight." He fingered the tool and ran his thumb over the blade. "It is not sharp enough for a knife."

"It's a white man's chisel. It's for working wood on the lathe."

"Ready to try out the lathe?" Robert asked, as he felt the edges of the other woodworking tools. "I am anxious to learn new tricks."

Mark could feel the grin as it spread across his cheeks. "Tonight after supper? I'm ready."

He opened the package from Malene, expecting it to be books. Instead, he found a box of stationery and matching envelopes. He laughed when he saw it. *You don't like my paper?*

Also in the box was a handful of pencils and a pen, a fancy pen that could be refilled and would hold enough ink for several letters. It was gold and blue. He knew it was expensive. Never had he met anyone important enough to have such a beautiful pen.

He held the pen between his fingers. Light glinted off its polished surface. The contrast against his callused hands made him inhale and hold that breath. His chest swelled with pride, for Malene thought he was worthy of such a magnificent gift.

Supper was fried corncakes, winter squash, and bits of chicken. No one on his ranch felt the pangs of hunger, and no one was cold. He had bought plain plates and cups for Rose to use, and had made a table and several stools from odd pieces of wood so they did not sit on the floor to eat. Each step forward sent a feeling of accomplishment through him.

Success was measured in tiny increments and he took pride in each one. He listened to Robert and Rose converse. Laughter was rarely heard among his people, for they were too busy trying to survive on nothing. On his ranch, laughter often filled the air.

Already in a good mood from his packages and with filled bellies, he and Robert rigged the handmade lathe to the saw. They attached a piece of wood for the staircase spindles and started the lathe. It worked!

Excitement mixed with joy flew from deep

within him and came out in a loud whoop. But they couldn't talk over the screeching sound it made. The high-pitched squeal seemed almost deafening.

It didn't take long for Mark to create a round spindle. His spirit soared as he ran his hand over the smooth wood. He grabbed a piece of leather, and while it was still spinning, he buffed the wood to a shine. Each one took time. There was no way to speed up the process, and setting up each piece of wood took longer than it would on a store-bought lathe. But his design worked.

As they set another piece in place, they decided it would be the last one for the night. They would do more tomorrow. Robert couldn't envision a staircase or what these small round lengths of wood would do, but his smile, as they worked together, grew. Each piece put them closer to building their house.

Mark kept his attention on the chisel, for one wrong move would ruin what he had done, but in the corner of his sight, he spotted a flash and Robert's movement. He turned the lathe off and a split second later, heard the shattering of glass. There were horses outside and voices of white men. A fire raged on the sawdust-covered floor. He shouted to Robert, "Leave it."

Between them, they had one rifle. He passed it to Robert, as the small sawmill became choked in smoke. The doors had been barricaded. In an unspoken decision, the two men pushed through the blocks of sod. Near their escape hole was a coil of rope used for hauling wood. Mark grabbed it as he slipped into the yard. Broken Spear was shooting a pistol. Robert ran around the flaming side of the sawmill with the buckshot-loaded rifle. Through the sounds of gunshots, Mark heard a scream as he turned his rope into a lasso.

He pulled himself onto the snow-covered metal roof. The snow was melting, the metal hot, and his footing precarious at best, but no one was looking upwards. He took aim and dropped the rope over one of the men. Pulling it tight, he yanked the man from his horse. The other turned to shoot. He reached in his waist overalls' pocket and tossed the chisel. He hit the man in the cheek and the sharp chisel did not fall. The man yelped, turned his horse, and rode hard.

Robert and Jumping Buck tied the fallen man in such a way that he could not escape. The first man was dying a slow death as a small stream of blood spurted from a neck wound. Broken Spear's wife appeared with another gun and kept a watchful eye over the two white men, while the rest of them worked to put out the fires.

They threw snow at the barn where the white men had attempted to burn it. The scent of kerosene was strong, and there were shards of glass everywhere. Mark took a shovel and began shoveling snow into the sawmill. When they were certain the fire was choked with snow, Mark took a lantern from the barn and accessed the damage. The building was ruined, but the saw appeared to be salvable. It would need new belts and that would take a few weeks. The spares that had come with the saw had been hanging on the sod wall. Now they were burnt to a crisp.

Jumping Buck offered to get the agent and Mark approved.

"Two out of three," Robert said, looking at the men lying in the snow.

"Albert Goddard got away. He'll be back. I'm glad it was not our house or the lumber for our house that he burned. The only thing we lost were the pieces for the staircase." It was still a heavy loss and it pricked at his pride. "Malene will be here in June. We're running out of time."

It was then that the name registered. Albert Goddard was Malene's former husband. Mark's heart fell into his guts. *Does he know who I am, or am I an easy target because I don't hide on the reservation?*

Was a lone wolf more dangerous than a pack? He was the great hunter, yet he was the one being hunted. Pressing his lips together, he tried to let go of his anger, but it boiled inside him. He remembered too well the danger of his rage. Apsáalooke were known as peaceful people, but they were also known for their fearless ability to fight to their death. It was that part of him, the Apsáalooke part, that made him realize the consequences of his emotions.

Hours later, the agent rode to the barn. "I sent your messenger to the fort for help. I hope he returns."

Broken Spear nodded. "He is my son. He will return."

If he doesn't find himself face to face with Albert Goddard. Mark looked at the agent. "It was the same three, except Albert Goddard got away. We want the reward money. They set fire to our sawmill and trapped us inside. They tried to set fire to the barn, too."

"Don't take it personally, Mark. These three have been spotted several times along the Bozeman Trail. They robbed a bank in Buffalo and a Wells Fargo stagecoach near Billings. You're going to be wealthy men. There's a reward for them."

The same way we were compensated when they killed my cattle?

***

Malene had men at her house every Monday in February and March, packing furniture into wooden crates and then transporting those crates to the railroad car. On Sunday, her papa would meet the train and take the crates to his house. She giggled when she read his letter. He wondered just how many houses was she robbing of furniture. *Oh, Papa, there is much more. I have only sent a small amount.*

She took the best, but carefully chose what

she was certain she would use. Bookcases once laden in books, now sat empty. Closets, cupboards, and drawers were bare. By mid-April, the house was almost stripped of what she was taking and she was leaving two-thirds of it behind.

When Angelina finished with the children's schooling for the day, she'd help Malene. Ellie often helped sort and pack items. Having their help was invaluable, especially when it came to items that caused Malene to hesitate.

Malene gave Ellie several pieces of furniture, including the bedroom furniture and linens that Ellie used, as a wedding gift, and that thrilled Ellie. With china and silver packed and ready to go, it was only a matter of days before Malene and the children would move.

Malene, the children, Mr. Titus, and Mrs. Ellsworth attended Ellie's wedding. She looked lovely in her long white gown and even longer train.

Malene reflected back on her sister's

wedding and on her own. Ellie's was a simple church wedding, but everyone was dressed in their finest. Marrying the bank's junior account executive must have been a bigger event than Malene had realized. The groom looked handsome in his black suit. Tall and slender, with wire-rim glasses, he looked the part of the young employee at San Francisco's largest bank. But it was the way he looked at Ellie that melted Malene's heart.

There was no question that this man loved Ellie and was proud to have her as his wife. Ellie looked up at him adoringly. Malene was pleased that she had given this young couple a start for Ellie's family had no money to spare. Nothing in Marshall's house was less than perfect. Malene had given them enough to fully furnish their little row house they had bought on one of the hills surrounding the city.

The reception was held at the church hall and consisted of tea sandwiches, little balls of fish on toothpicks, and the fanciest cake Malene had ever seen. Mrs. Ellsworth had made all those tiny sandwiches and fish balls for Ellie so that she could spend her money on a cake from a local bakery.

Mr. Titus wouldn't join them in the pew at the church. Instead, he stood in the very back of the room. Then during the reception, he, again, stood in the back of the room with his hat tucked under his arm. But Ellie took him a plate of food and a piece of cake.

Malene knew she'd miss the staff at the house. In less than eight months, she had become friends with them. Mr. Titus couldn't read but his daughter could. She promised she'd write and keep in touch with all of them.

In an attempt to stay positive around the children, she told them moving was going to be a great adventure. She had written the Hamilton parents and let them know where she and the children could be found, but they never replied. Her own excitement built as the moving day grew near. Having not seen her own parents in over eight months, and that visit was too brief, she was overjoyed at the thought of going home. Except, she didn't have a home, not yet.

She filled the boxcar with all the final things that they would be taking, and she'd be with the children, a dog, and Angelina in the private passenger railcar for days.

Starting in the attic, she walked through the entire house alone. She checked each drawer and behind every door. Stepping onto the side porch, she looked at the gardens. Only a few roses bloomed. They too looked as isolated as she felt. Her footfalls echoed through the rooms, reverberating her loneliness and the pall of death that this house had seen. Money didn't guarantee happiness.

For a moment, she stood with her hand on the latch of the front door. The sadness that had seeped into her bones kept her standing there. Silently she said goodbye to Marshall and Charlotte. *I will love your children as my own.*

She closed and locked the front door. Turning, she looked past the carriage where everyone was waiting. The view of the harbor almost took her breath away. The day was clear and the harbor was busy. With the city below her, she thought about the bookstore and the friends she had made. Then she turned her gaze to the beautiful house and remembered her evenings with Marshall on the side porch. She'd only really known him for a little over a week, and he had left her with so much.

Her mind did not question why she had come. She knew the answer. It had very little to do with Marshall and everything to do with three children who needed to be loved.

It was the end of this chapter of her life and it had been a long and lonely one. From this moment forward, she was in charge of her life. She would build her own life with her not so little family. *Yes, this will be an adventure and I shall chart my own course. No one is going to interfere this time. No one!*

Part Three

10

Malene let out a sigh of relief when she saw Juanita in the Hamilton railcar.

"Your family has grown!" Juanita held the back of her hand to her forehead as she looked at the children.

"Yes. It has." Malene introduced Juanita to Angelina, Marcus, Dill, and Clara. "Hush, Brownie. Do not growl at her. She will feed you."

The dog wasn't convinced.

Malene turned to Marcus. "Please, talk to Brownie."

The boy sat next to the dog and petted him, but the dog continued to keep a watchful eye over the children.

"I am sorry." She returned her gaze to Juanita. "He's never acted this way, except when strangers have come to the house. He's very protective of the children."

"Keep him away from me, and we'll be fine."

Juanita began to back out of the car. "I'll bring you tea and biscuits."

"Maybe it is best if we keep his leash on him and keep him tied to that end of the car." Malene watched as Marcus tied the dog to a metal handle near the far door. *Some adventure!* A headache threatened.

They'd ridden about an hour, when Angelina made a dash for the small bathroom. Malene had heard of motion sickness, but had never experienced it. Angelina's normal glowing complexion had taken on a greenish-gray cast. Then Brownie began to whine, and Malene knew he wanted to go out. *It's going to be a very, very long trip.*

By the end of the first day, Malene realized what she was facing. The boys had begun to bicker and Clara dissolved into tears over the tiniest disturbances. Trying to get the children to sleep that night was almost impossible, and with every whistle blow, they were wide-awake wondering where they were and what was happening.

If Angelina wasn't in the toilet, she was curled into a ball on a bench seat. Malene felt sorry for the young woman, but it also positioned all the responsibility for the children onto Malene's shoulders, and she wasn't completely certain what she should be doing with the children to keep them occupied.

Their books were packed, along with their slates, and so were their toys. She attempted to make a game of things they might see out the window, but the children soon tired of that. Brownie rested his head on his front paws but continued to whimper. Her own head pounded. Why couldn't the children keep their hands off each other and occupy themselves by looking out the windows?

The train noises that had lulled her on her way to San Francisco, now grated on her nerves and intensified her headache. Any positive feelings of adventure had left her.

This time, she had to endure it.

Each little stop along the way, she'd take Brownie out of the car so that he could handle his business. Then she'd quickly scurry back to the train half panicked that the train would leave her and half panicked over what the children were doing when she stepped away from them.

The following day, the train pulled into a not so small town. The conductor tapped on her door. "Excuse me, ma'am. We're going to be here for two hours. Thought the children might like to stretch their legs."

Malene breathed out a sigh of relief. "Thank you, sir. I think they would love some fresh air." She smiled at the man. "And so would I."

Juanita managed to find some books, crayons, and paper at the little general store and brought them back to Malene.

"Oh, Juanita, you are wonderful!" She paid the woman for her purchase and added a wee bit more to it as a way of saying thank you.

The train's whistle blew.

"Children, look what Juanita brought you!" She hurried the children back onto the train and retied Brownie to the handle at the far end of the car.

Marcus immediately sat with the new books and began to read. At the end of the day, the thrill was gone.

The only reprieve Malene had was when they stopped in a town for she had learned that she could leave the train for a few minutes. Marcus would take Brownie for a walk and the children would run and play until the whistle blew. But each stop also brought a new round of fear. She worried she would lose the children and not get them back on the train.

Juanita laughed. "That will not happen. Companies like Hamilton are what keep these trains profitable. They wouldn't dare leave you or the children behind. They want the Hamilton business."

"Thanks, but I also would not want to hold up the train because we've lost one. I'm still learning to be a parent."

"And you are doing very well. No one has an easy time with children when they are confined. Some children travel better than others."

Malene rubbed her forehead. "Angelina is wonderful with the children, but--"

"She has been too ill. Not everyone travels well." Juanita shook her head as she looked in the young woman's direction.

"I don't travel well," Malene said.

Juanita laughed. "I'll bring your afternoon tea. You will like tonight's supper. Our chef picked up freshly caught trout at our last stop."

By the time they reached the Reiner stockyard, Malene was certain every nerve she had was frazzled. Angelina would take two sips of tea and toss it all up - she hadn't eaten in days. The children were bored and had whined almost non-stop for the last three days. Even Brownie acted strangely.

Malene rushed off the railcar and into her mama's waiting arms. "Oh, Mama, I think I hate traveling!"

It took several minutes to unhitch the boxcar that was filled with items from the house and for Malene to collect everything from the railcar including the children, dog, and Angelina.

Angelina went to her appointed room and stayed there. Cook would take her meals and watch over her.

Malene realized that she, too, was failing the children, for she turned over their care to her mama and Cook. She'd been home almost a full twenty-four hours when it dawned on her that she hadn't seen Brownie since they stepped off the train. Her breath hitched and panic ran through her like ice-cold water.

"Brownie! Come here, boy. Where are you? Come, Brownie!"

Dan walked out of the barn, and Brownie followed wagging his tail as he greeted his mistress.

"Where were you?" She squatted down to the animal and Brownie happily licked her face.

Dan scuffed his toe in the dirt. "He's been with me. Wasn't too sure at first." Dan reached into his shirt pocket and retrieved some pieces of beef jerky. "As long as I have this in my pocket, he's stayed at my side. I've even taught him some tricks."

Malene laughed as Brownie showed off his ability to roll over on command. He'd also learned to play dead, and even shake hands. After each trick, Dan rewarded the dog with a treat.

Her papa had kept Marcus and Dill with him. For the first time in the boys' lives, they had a man who paid attention to them, and they both lapped it up like honey.

Cook was having tea parties with Clara. It

reminded Malene of the parties she and Adie would have. Malene couldn't help but giggle at the sight.

From somewhere the small table with child-sized chairs had appeared in the kitchen and so did the miniature-sized set of dishes. Real tea was served from a small fancy teapot and poured into tiny cups. The cookies were leftover bits of piecrust that had been dusted with cinnamon and sugar.

Clara was draped in Fredericka's pearls and wore a hat that was much too big. But the child was content and happy in the bright kitchen with Cook's almost constant attention.

After a few days, Malene relaxed and got the children back onto a schedule and Angelina resumed her role as a teacher. That's also when Malene realized that the barn cats had vanished.

"They're fine, Malene." Dan grinned. "Seems Brownie made sure they knew he was boss. The minute they see him, they scamper up to the loft."

Brownie sat at Dan's side and stared up at her with what appeared to be a smile, as his tail swept the dirt behind him. He'd more than doubled in size since he'd come to live with them on Christmas. His body was stocky and his legs still looked too short for his powerful body. One ear flopped and the brown one stuck up, except for the very tip, which drooped.

She reached down and scratched him behind his ears.

"And the chickens?" she asked.

Dan laughed. "They showed Brownie who was really in charge of the yard. Brownie didn't take too kindly to getting pecked. He put that tail between his legs and ran to me for protection." Dan took his hat off, wiped his brow, and deposited his wide-brimmed hat on his head. "But if the children are out here, your papa is the only person he'll allow near them. That dog even growls at me if I get near the children."

"That's his job, Dan. He's their nanny."

As she walked back inside, she pondered why Brownie would allow her papa near the children but not Dan. Was it possible that the dog could somehow tell that her papa was family?

Malene stopped in the kitchen with the hopes of having a cup of tea and maybe a chance to chat with Cook. The familiar look of the kitchen warmed her. Bright and cheery with big windows that let in plenty of light, it was where Cook ruled, a lesson Malene learned as a small child. The aroma of bread baking and delicious scent of onions and corned beef made her crave the noon meal.

She glanced around the room. The big eight door cupboards held cooking supplies and pantry items. And two large tables were made for food preparation. Alisa would have been thrilled to have such a kitchen for her large family.

She poured a cup of tea and leaned against a large butcher-block table. "I want a kitchen like this for my house so that I have ample room to bake and cook."

The woman's red curls bobbed as she tittered. "Since when did you learn to actually cook?"

"Since I've stayed with the Colemans. Alisa taught Adie and me to cook. We weren't just peeling potatoes in her kitchen. I've learned to make delicious bread and rolls, and I can fix potatoes and other simple things, but there are so many more recipes that I wish to have. Alisa's cooking was simple. I want to learn to make your fat noodles and your spicy meats."

"Join me in the afternoons, for I promise I will teach you to make all of your favorite foods."

"Oh, Cook, that would be wonderful. I've missed your cooking and your company." She went to the woman, threw her arms around her, and hugged her tight.

"Ah, *bairn*, I've missed you, too. You've brought me four little ones to spoil, but you are taking them away too soon."

"*Nein*. I'm going to see Adie. I have much to do, but I will be back." She looked over her shoulder at the service door. "I think my papa would not forgive me if I failed to bring the boys back to him. I'm not sure who is having the most fun, him or the boys."

Cook laughed with her high-pitched bird sound. "It's been very quiet with you and Adie gone from the house. It is good to have noise again."

"I'm not so sure Mama likes all the noise."

Cook waved her hand through the air as if she were shooing a fly. "Your mama might be overwhelmed, but she is enjoying every minute of the children being here. She misses having children around."

Malene looked again at the service door. "I was expecting Papa to help me this morning. I had something shipped for Mama and I want to find it."

Cook nodded. "He was with Dan. Seems he can't get much done, except while the children are taking their lessons."

"I believe you are right. He and Marcus have grown very close, very quickly. The boys need a man in their lives. "

Malene wandered up to the attic, but only a few of her crates were there. Had her other things somehow been lost? Her heart fell into her stomach. Images of her boxes going to New York and becoming permanently lost made her head spin. She grabbed onto a tall crate as the room swam, and then steadied itself. Only when she was certain that she wasn't going to faint did she attempt to leave the attic and find her father.

Reaching the first floor, she found her papa sitting at his desk. His office looked exactly the same, except he now had a very fancy pen and ink set sitting between piles of papers.

At that moment, it struck her that her father

was not rich. He had money, enough to provide for his family and to spoil them, but nothing compared to Marshall Hamilton or her friend Annabelle Lippcott. Yet her papa had tried hard to make certain that she never lacked for anything. Marrying Marshall would have assured that.

She stepped back into the hallway and hoped he'd not noticed her. Her father had tried hard to give her more. Guilt crawled up her back.

She had only known Marshall for a short time when he'd left her for Bombay. She leaned against the wall as their days together played through her mind. It's not that she hadn't given the man a chance - fate had separated them. Maybe he had remained aloof because he was still grieving his wife's death. She would never know.

She stepped around the corner, into her papa's office, and noticed the silver strands that had begun to mix with his golden brown hair. Her father wasn't much older than Marshall, yet in many ways, he appeared to be. "Papa, may I have a word with you?"

***

Mark left to pick up supplies in Sheridan. He cut across the McLaughlin's land and noticed a set of tracks in the wet earth from a single horse. He followed the tracks for quite a ways until they ended by a stream. It might take hours to pick up the trail again, and he didn't have the time to spare. He needed to get his supplies and get back. There was no way to tell if it was Albert Goddard or a hunter. It was also possible that it was one of the McLaughlin men checking their own property.

It had been several months since the fire. There had been with no signs of Albert Goddard returning, yet a feeling lingered within Mark. It was as if he were being watched from afar. *The hunter becomes the hunted.*

***

"Yes, my daughter, what is on your mind?" Adelwulf Reiner moved several papers to one side.

Malene tried to push her worry away. "I went to the attic for my things, but most of them are missing."

"There wasn't enough room, my dear child," her papa told her as a smile played across his face. "The floor would have collapsed under all the weight."

"You mean you have everything and the rest is not lost?" Relief flooded her.

"Come with me." He stood and offered his arm to her. "There are crates upon crates in the barn waiting for you."

With help from Dan and her father, she opened several until she found the one she wanted and retrieved quite a few things for her parents, including a fat rounded piece of furniture for her mother. Malene carried the chubby piece into her mother's parlor. "For you. Mama. For your sewing."

Fredericka Reiner's eyes grew wide, and she squealed with delight. "I have never seen such a thing."

"Nor I, until I was in San Francisco. It is from India. Apparently Marshall went to India often and brought back things for his wife. The house was loaded in beautiful furniture. I only brought a small amount. His house was ten times larger than yours, with tall columns, big windows, and lots of wrought iron. I could look down over the city and see the bay. It was beautiful, but it was not home."

"With all that money, why are the children with you?" her mama asked. "I do not understand."

"Nor I." She bit her lip for a moment. "Marshall's parents truly did not like his wife, and they didn't want the children. I had the option of keeping them or putting them in boarding school." She smiled. "I kept them.

They needed a mother."

"I know you will make a fine mother for them." Malene's mother opened the cabinet doors on the small piece of furniture and fingered all the small compartments that were meant to hold sewing supplies.

"There are moments when I wonder if I am a good mother. Alisa Coleman is a wonderful mother to all her children." She plopped into a soft chair near her mama.

Fredericka turned to her daughter. "But she has had them one at a time. You had an infant and gained three instantly. And from what you have said, they have had problems that normal children do not have."

"Yes, you are right, and I've grown to love them dearly."

"Adie is excited about meeting the children and is busy counting down the days until you come. She misses you so much."

She watched her mother begin to gather her sewing things together and arrange them in the new cabinet. "*Ja*, but I don't want to waste precious days with you wishing I was with my sister."

Everything about her parents' house was the same as it always had been. Nothing had changed and that made it feel even more like home. It enveloped her in a comfortable cocoon, yet she was no longer a little girl. The need to have her own place grew inside her.

She spent time with Cook and wrote all of her favorite recipes in a book. Cook even showed her a few tricks for handling dough, which made it much easier for Malene to make piecrusts as well as fat noodles. She gave Cook the recipe for fish balls and several other things that Mrs. Ellsworth made.

Cook laid a dead rabbit on a butcher's block. "You might as well learn to do this, too!"

Malene's stomach rolled as Cook talked Malene through the process of removing the skin and preparing the rabbit for cooking. But the end result was delicious.

"Malene, you must come more often for I don't think we've had this many variations of food since you and your sister left." Adelwulf rubbed his stomach. "Every night has been a feast."

"*Ja*, it has. Cook has taught me so much."

"Don't you want to hire a cook?" Fredericka furrowed her brow.

"Having Mrs. Ellsworth was wonderful, but I also enjoy being in the kitchen."

Fredericka put her hand to her chest. "I don't know what I would do without Cook.'

Malene giggled. *Starve?* "Papa does not want you in the kitchen. Your needlework is where you excel."

Adelwulf looked at his wife and smiled. "That is true. I enjoy knowing my wife is pampered and she can relax and take pleasure in her life and friends when they visit."

"Mama, are you still giving needlework classes?"

"Oh, yes. I have a new little girl who will be

coming next month. And once a month the women from town come here for a special afternoon of sewing." Fredericka grinned. "And a little gossip."

It was later that evening that Sophia took her first steps in the Reiner house. She let go of a low table and toddled towards her grandfather. She giggled and laughed as he swept her off her feet and held her high in the air.

The boys ran and played outside. While they explored their surroundings, Brownie stayed at their sides the entire time. In fact, keeping the boys inside long enough for their lessons became a real problem.

Angelina kept a tight rein on the children. She made them complete a certain amount of schoolwork each morning before they were allowed to play. And every night, Malene had to chase the boys into the tub prior to going to bed. With the dirt removed, their little bodies glowed with a healthy tan.

She was home and it felt wonderful, all the way to her toes, but she also wanted her own place. After eight months on her own, her independence had surfaced, and she wanted her own house. Besides, her parents were spoiling the children, and she didn't want her hard work undone.

Her papa laughed as she prepared to leave for Creed's Crossing. "The last time you departed, you took the wagon. I've yet to see it. This time you are taking the coach."

"Oh, Papa, if you want it, Adie would send it to you."

"Don't bother. I bought another." I will ride with you to the reservation. Your friend, Mark Hunter, promised he'd take care of you from there."

"Yes. I wrote him. He told me the same thing."

In one long day, they traveled all the way to the reservation. They had started their trek when light had begun to turn the sky purple and the stars were fading. They had barely crossed the border when two young scouts greeted them. No longer afraid, Malene said goodbye to her papa.

"You are in good hands with these young men." Her papa gave her a hug and a kiss, then turned to Marcus. "Keep those letters coming."

Malene looked into her papa's tear-filled eyes. "I promise, he will write."

To keep from crying, she slapped the reins and moved forward. She called to the young men. "I will follow you."

In less than a half hour, she pulled to a stop by a lone tipi. She had talked to the children about the Indians prior to their trip. Marcus and Dill were very excited, but Angelina was apprehensive, yet she smiled politely. Everyone spent the night in the tipi and they were served a meal of chicken stew. Malene decided it wasn't as tasty as she would have made, but it filled everyone's tummy.

She rested on a furry pallet made from coyote pelts and tucked Sophia next to her. Clara immediately went to sleep, as did Sophia, but getting the boys to settle down was next to impossible. They were curious about everything. Finally the boys closed their eyes and she dared to close hers.

She had probably only had a few hours of sleep when dawn began to break. The morning meal of cornbread was surprisingly good and sufficient. It didn't matter that she'd not had much sleep - she knew she'd see Mark before the sun vanished for the night.

Little Goat, who probably wasn't much older than fifteen, took the reins of the carriage. She let Marcus and Dill sit with the young teen. Just as Mark had assured her in his letters, they knew who she was and where she was going.

She sat in the carriage with her little family and rested her head against the back wall. It was not a smooth ride, but she slept most of the morning. She could hear the boys chatting with Little Goat and Little Goat telling tall tales. If she hadn't been so tired, she would have laughed. She closed her eyes and drifted off again, only to wake to the sound of thundering hooves. Her door jerked open.

***

Mark jumped inside the moving carriage. Angelina screamed, which set off Clara and Sophia. "This is the welcome I get?" Before Malene could open her mouth, Mark covered hers with his. Her fingers clawed at his shoulders as she took his breath. He whispered in her ear, "I have missed you, my beautiful woman of the sun."

Brownie snarled, and Mark held his hand for the dog to sniff. "It is good, my furry friend. No one else gets to do this to Malene. You understand that?"

The dog settled down as if he were used to

Mark being there, but little Clara was curled into a tearful ball in Angelina's lap, and Sophia wailed.

He picked the toddler up and cuddled her in his arm. "Have you forgotten me?" He ran his finger over the child's cheek and over her bright reddish curls. "I brought you into this world, my darling. Your memory is too short."

Sophia looked up at him. Her tear-filled expression turned to a grin. His heart swelled. He had his child and his woman. His gaze turned to the pretty woman traveling with Malene. "You must be Angel-enna."

Malene giggled. "An-gel-le-na."

He rolled his hands palms up and repeated the name.

"Yes." The woman nodded as she spoke.

"Pleased to meet you." He reached over and tickled Clara, but the child screamed at his touch.

Malene pulled Clara into her lap. "This is Mark. He is different, but that is no reason to fear him."

Mark took the little girl's hand in his. "Yes, I am different because I am Apsáalooke, or of the Crow tribe. I am a man. My skin is darker than yours, but it is only skin."

Malene put her hand on his shoulder. "Mr. Titus has skin darker than yours. Clara is shy and somewhat timid."

He grinned and looked at the child in his arms. "Sophia remembers, my darling daughter of the fiery sun."

Sophia wrapped her fingers into his hair and tugged. "You, little girl, have been taking lessons from Alisa Coleman."

Malene giggled. "You know Alisa loves you. You are her best student."

Sophia had grasped his hair in such a way that he thought he'd never get her fingers untangled from it. Then he swept his hair behind his shoulders and kissed her chubby cheek. "You are so beautiful, my sweet daughter."

Sophia's little fingers pulled at his lips and grabbed his nose.

"Is this the way you are going to treat me?" He chuckled. "Women! They can't keep their hands off of me."

Malene raised her eyebrows, as she tucked Clara beside her. "So who are these women who have been touching you?"

"Since you and Sophia have been gone, I haven't had any women. I need to be touched." He leaned across and kissed her.

"I've missed you so much, Mark, so very much."

He sat Sophia on his lap so she could look out the window. "Many things have happened while you were gone. And I have a prize for you."

"A prize? You mean a surprise?"

He nodded, but his heart thumped and fell. "I am not stupid, but your words confuse me."

She smiled, but the real warmth of her smile came from her eyes. "You do so well. You must teach me your language. I know I will not do as well as you."

"Yes. You will learn our language."

"What is my surprise?"

"I not tell. You will see."

He traded places with Clara and put his arm behind Malene. She snuggled to his chest and he rested his head against the back of the carriage. His world was perfect. He had Malene and Sophia. It would take time to win Clara's affection, but he was certain it would happen. The wish for a son of his own passed through him as he held his woman.

When Sophia's eyes began to close, he passed her to Angelina. Maybe he, too, could enjoy the luxury of rest. He closed his eyes as contentment washed over him.

He opened his eyes and slipped Malene's head to his lap. Sophia lay in Angelina's arms. The child's eyes were closed and he stared at her tiny, pink rosebud mouth that seemed to be busy sucking on nothing. He lifted his gaze to Angelina who was looking out the window. Her skin was a color someplace between his and Malene's. Her dark hair fell in deep curls. She was a beauty, but nothing like his Malene.

Clara had light brown hair with a hint of gold running through her long curls and pale brown eyes. She eyed him suspiciously.

He smiled back. "Do you like to ride horses?"

She shrugged.

"Ever ride one?"

She shook her head.

"Then I will teach you to ride. You and your brothers will each have your own horse. I will help you to pick one out. Everyone here rides horses."

Clara scrunched her nose. "Why is your hair long?"

"Because I do not cut it. Why is your hair long?"

She smiled. "Because girls have long hair."

"All my people have long hair. Some of the

old men have hair that will touch the ground and they wear it with a puff on top."

Clara raised her eyebrows.

He nodded. "And sometimes we paint stripes on our faces."

"The men last night had stripes on their faces, and we slept in a real tipi."

"Did Malene tell you that she was scared of me when she first saw me?"

Clara shook her head.

"She was. I had stripes on my face and a long strip of hair that was covered in feathers. My Indian name is Many Feathers, but I traded my feathers for my land."

Malene stirred and cupped her hands around his leg.

"See. She can't keep her hands off of me."

"I heard that," Malene mumbled.

He chuckled then briefly turned his attention to Angelina before looking out the window of the carriage. Anxiety began to build within him. His normal confidence seemed to have left him. He had pinned all his hopes on today, and that today was here. He had to convince Malene to stay, and the house was not finished.

***

Malene opened her eyes and sat up. Heat flowed over her cheeks because she had her head on his thigh. It wasn't the least bit proper, and Mark somehow made her do things that weren't. "How long has Sophia been sleeping?"

"A long time." Angelina looked at her timepiece. "Almost three hours."

"I'll never get her to sleep tonight." She took the child from Angelina and the young toddler began to cry. Malene put the child to her breast. When Mark touched Sophia's cheek, the look on the baby's face was enough to make Malene laugh aloud. "That's her food source, and she's not into sharing."

"She'll get over it." Mark chuckled.

Malene looked at Angelina who appeared to be shocked. "It is all right. If it were not for Mark, Sophia would not be alive...I might not be alive. Mark brought her into this world. She was stuck."

Angelina nodded.

Mark grinned. "Pass Sophia to Angelina. I want you to see something."

Malene did and Mark opened the door to the carriage and stood on its step. Then he pulled her out with him. Scared they both would fall to the ground, her stomach twisted into a large knot.

"There!" He pointed to a spot in front of them.

Before her were buildings. "Your ranch?"

"Our ranch and the house I built for you."

She gripped the edge of the doorframe. "House? You really did build a house? Please let me back inside before I scream."

He eased her in and followed. "Yes. Yes.

And why would you scream?"

Her heart pounded. She crossed her hands over her chest as if holding it would somehow slow the thumping within her. "I don't want to fall!"

"I will never let anything happen to you."

A few minutes later, the carriage pulled to a stop. Mark jumped out and lifted Clara to the ground, then Angelina and Sophia. "Come on, Brownie, your turn." Then he turned to Malene. He slipped his arms under her legs and lifted her from her seat as his lips crashed over hers.

The unexpected kiss made her feel more alive than she had in months. Her heart sang, and her body warmed with his touch.

"For you, my darling. It is all for you." He lowered her to the ground, and she was standing in front of a very large house.

"Is it a house or a shell like Frank built for Adie?"

"It is not completely finished. I try to finish

before you come. I built it for you. I know you do not want to live in a tipi."

He had told her of his house in his letters, but standing in front of a house…tears rushed to her eyes as total confusion swept over her. All of her dreams were shattering and falling through her stomach.

He wasn't joking. He was serious. He wanted her as his wife. She had four children. Three weren't even hers. One man had abused her and another used her. Mark wanted her enough to build her a house and go into ranching.

She swiped her tears. Bear and his wife Abigail Coleman could not raise their children to call them Mama and Papa, for such a marriage was illegal. A white person could not marry someone of color, and Mark was a red man. The world began to spin and a fog enclosed her. She reached out for him.

***

Mark caught Malene and gathered her into his arms as if she were a child.

Her eyes fluttered open. "What happened? Put me down."

He chuckled and lowered her feet to the ground. "You are so demanding."

"We must talk."

"Yes. There is much to talk about, but first we eat." He pointed to the swing. "I built one for you. I said I would."

She nodded and chewed her bottom lip. This was not the reaction he expected.

He introduced everyone to Rose. "There is still much to do. But it is also spring, and I had crops to put in the ground." He held Malene's hand as he showed her the main rooms, then he showed her another. "For teaching the children."

After touring the downstairs, he took her upstairs. "Half the house is for Rose and Robert, and half is for us. I made us a big room with a room for Sophia so she is close. When she is bigger, she can have her own room." He took her up another flight of stairs. "More room so Adie and Frank can come, or your parents, and no one must give up a bedroom. And I have running water. See."

She looked and nodded, but she was very pale.

He swallowed and with it went his pride. He had expected joy, but it never happened. "We eat, and tonight we talk. You are upset, and I do not understand."

Rose fixed a simple supper of chicken soup made with potatoes, onions, and carrots, then a salad of plain lettuce, and served it all with fried cornmeal cakes. Malene barely ate it. He wondered what was so wrong.

He'd tried so hard to build her a beautiful house. He would make the moldings and install them. And he would make fireplace fronts with store-bought mirrors like the pictures in the magazines. She never said a word about the stained glass in the window panels. They had cost a fortune, but he didn't mind the expense. He wanted everything to be perfect for his wife.

***

After supper, Malene let the children play outside. They had been cooped up for two days and they needed to have fun. Rose took them with her while she milked the two goats. Malene stood next to the fence and watched as each child tried milking. The chicken coop was huge. The children gathered eggs and brought them to Rose. Clara smiled through the whole thing, as did Dill. Marcus was more sedate, but he seemed to accept the ranching lifestyle.

Malene was crumbling on the inside. Had she not wanted this? It was all here. A noisy, happy household where the children could wander and play, a place for their lessons, and a big kitchen where everyone could eat? She didn't mind sharing the house with Rose and

Robert. The part of the downstairs was communal. Rose and Robert had their own parlor that was separate from the rest of the house. They had their own staircase to the bedrooms upstairs and a wall that separated the sets of bedrooms. It was like two houses put together. The kitchen was the separator and the laundry area was also shared.

Mark had even made a special set of rooms for Angelina. She had her own bedroom, sitting room, and even her own bathroom, like an apartment. The house was nearly as large as the one in San Francisco. Except this house was made like two houses back to back.

The sun had set when Malene chased the children inside. She bathed them and prepared them for bed. Each chose a room. The beds were primitive boxes and cushioned with pelts, but the children didn't seem to mind.

She walked to the front of the house and looked at the bedroom that he wanted her to share with him. That room had a feather mattress that he had made. Her heart fell into her stomach. She didn't want to be married, not really. Nor did she did want to ever feel pain again. A single tear ran down her cheek and she wiped it away.

Mark's hand rested on her back. She handed him the candle that she carried and moved away from him. Placing her sleeping daughter in the tiny bed that was inches from the floor, she tiptoed out of the room.

"Yes. We must talk," he whispered, as he escorted her down the steps and onto the porch.

She sat on the swing and burst into tears. "I cannot marry you. I cannot marry anyone. I have my own money, enough to build my own house, and take care of the children for the rest of their lives. The grandparents who do not love them, throw enormous amounts of money at them."

"I do not care that much about money, except it buys things. I must earn white man's money for this house and to make a ranch. I lived without money most of my life. I earn money now because you want to live like the white man. I understand that. I must live with the white man's standards, but I am still Apsáalooke."

"It is more than that...how do I tell you? I never want the pain of a man again."

He pushed her sleeve up. "A man who would brand his wife is not a man. He is a vicious animal."

"It is more than that. When a man is married, he wants a marital bed." Heat rose over her cheeks.

He put a single finger to her lips. "I told you, when there is love, there is no pain, only pleasure. I do not have the words for what he did to you. It was cruel and...forced."

His lips took hers. Soft and sweet, he touched her. Her milk let down and the front of her blouse became soaked. He pushed the material that covered them away. His fingers were on her skin, his lips traveled down her neck to her chest. She heard the moan that came from her throat. His arms were around her, and she was no longer on the swing, but on the floor of the porch.

She arched her back. His hands roamed her body. Hard and callused, they left trails of heat. The air was cold, and she was hot. His mouth devoured her. It was impossible to get enough of him. Her tongue toyed with his. A rough hand touched her most feminine part in such a way that she thought she would die. She gasped for breath and gripped his muscled back. She wanted to scream stop. She wanted to scream with pleasure. *Don't stop. Don't ever stop. Let me die like this.*

Her heart pounded, as her body betrayed her. The heat of his touch became too much. His mouth covered hers as she squealed with pleasure. Everything stopped. The whole world was on hold for those brief seconds. He brought her back with sweet kisses and rolled her on top of him.

"There will be no pain when you are with me, only pleasure. I love you, Malene, and you love me."

She could not look at him. Instead, she buried her face into his neck and tried to remember how to breathe.

"When you say yes, I will take you as a man takes a woman, and you will find even greater pleasure."

The heaving of his chest lulled her.

He gathered her into his arms and sat up. "You have nothing to fear."

She tried to button her blouse, but as usual, her fingers wouldn't work. His kisses always left her trembling. He buttoned her blouse for her.

"Go to bed, my darling. I will be up later. I slept with you after Sophia was born, and I will sleep with you again. You did not fear me then. Do not fear me now."

He helped her to her feet, said goodnight,

and wandered towards the barn.

Her whole body trembled. The glorious feeling he had created lingered. She crossed her arms over her and grabbed for her upper arms. Watching him walk into the night sent a pang of longing through her. Never had she felt so alive.

She peered through the darkness and saw him leave on a horse. Closing her eyes for a moment, she deeply inhaled, trying to clear her desire before going inside. As she climbed the staircase, each stair hammered in the loneliness that she felt when separated from him, the same loneliness that flooded her when she was in San Francisco.

She readied for bed and climbed on the feather filled mattress. He had tried so hard to make a house for her. Guilt besieged her, only to be replaced by another wave of desire, then confusion. Sleep evaded her. He was out there someplace watching over her and his ranch.

She wanted him beside her. Wanted to feel

his body tucked to hers. It was wrong and she knew it. But she loved him. Silent tears flowed.

Morning light bathed the bedroom. When she looked beside her, Mark lay there naked. Her heart caught in her throat. In her attempt to slip from the bed, his hand caught her and pulled her over his body.

"You are my wife. We belong together. You need to get used to the idea. We are one with the spirits." He kissed her and then rolled away from her.

Her insides turned to jelly. Quickly she pulled on her clothes, gathered her dirty ones, and the ones she had taken from the children. She hadn't washed clothes since she left the Coleman house, but it was one chore she did not mind.

She tiptoed into the laundry room and stared at the tub. It was a newfangled thing. She'd seen them in a catalog. Somehow, she'd figure it out.

Rose came in and pushed her out of the way. She watched as Rose stepped on a treadle. A few minutes later, Rose handed her a skirt that was washed, rinsed, and ready to be hung on a line. Never had she seen so many pieces of laundry washed so quickly. She smiled at Rose and the woman smiled back.

They hung the clothes outside in the fresh air and then came inside. Mark was dressed and holding Sophia in one arm. He held a small cup in his other hand and had lifted it to the child's mouth.

Appalled, Malene barely found words. "What are you giving her?"

"Goat's milk. She is old enough." Mark grinned as the child slurped another mouthful.

Malene put her palms to her forehead. "Are you trying to tell me how to raise my daughter?"

"No. I need to make her a better bed so she does not wake me up."

She took the child and put her to a breast.

"Our schedule is off from all the traveling."

Mark kissed her. "You will be fine."

When she finished nursing Sophia, Malene poked around the kitchen cabinets and found flour, salt, potatoes, and butter. It was a start. She found a knife and peeled two small potatoes. Rose looked at her and Malene smiled. They would have tasty, soft rolls tonight.

Rose put a cast iron pan on the stove, and this time, Malene give her friend a little push.

Mark chuckled. "She knows English, but she doesn't speak much. You will learn from each other."

Malene fried eggs for the adults who were present and when Angelina appeared with the children, she gave them the choice of fried or scrambled.

Rose toasted leftover cornbread and coated each piece with a strong tasting butter. It wasn't until Malene drank some milk that she realized why the butter tasted the way it did.

It wasn't made from cow milk; it had been made from goat milk. Alisa Coleman had goat milk, but she used it for cheese. Apparently, Mark didn't have any dairy cows, just goats. But when the butter was mixed with a few drops of honey and spread on the cornbread, it was delicious.

The children devoured everything, then ran outside to play. Angelina watched over them, as did Brownie. Clara found a playmate. Jumping Buck's daughter, Pretty Flower, was almost the same age. The two little girls had no problem with the difference in languages and seemed to be thrilled with their new friendship.

Malene sat on the porch swing. Memories of last night flooded her mind and left her totally confused. Mark made her feel things she had never felt before, and it scared her. Yet she wanted to tumble back into his arms.

The vision of him lying naked beside her, made her inhale. He was a beautiful man. She knew that. The renewal of the memory of that day at the Coleman pond sent her heart fluttering. She wanted to touch him, to feel every curve. But reality hit her.

She rubbed her forehead. The two little girls ran onto the porch. Pretty Flower stopped and climbed up next to Malene. The child grabbed Malene's blonde braid, then looked into her eyes. Yes, she must have seemed very different to this child who had only known other Indians.

Malene took the girls by the hand and wandered a short distance away. She showed them how to make chains with the flowers. The three of them sat in the grass decorating each other in blooms.

Angelina called the children. Clara took Pretty Flower's hand and went to her teacher. It was time for lessons, and Pretty Flower was about to get her first bit of formal education. Malene waved to Angelina and the young woman waved back.

There was work to be done and Malene did not need to waste time in the grass. If Clara could become fast friends with Pretty Flower, there was no reason why she and Rose couldn't be best friends, too.

But under everything, was the feeling that she had to somehow tell Adie she wasn't going to arrive as scheduled. Mail was too slow. She needed to leave and see her sister as promised. She'd beg Mark to take her.

Sophia followed Rose's son all over the place as Rose handled many chores. Rose also had another child strapped to her back.

Malene wandered through the rooms and imagined them with furniture in them. *Rose needs furniture, too.* Malene decided she should have brought more furniture with her. That thought struck her like a bolt of lightning. Was she subconsciously considering staying here and being Mark's wife?

Mark did not appear for dinner, but showed up before supper with a pheasant.

"Hunting?" Malene asked.

***

Mark could feel the grin that lifted his cheeks as he answered Malene. "I won't turn down what I am given."

"We shall eat this tomorrow. Rose and I have a tasty meal this evening."

"Where were you today?" Malene asked, as he led her to the porch swing after they had eaten.

"I have much to tell you and I did not want to worry you." He told her of his encounters with Albert Goddard. "Robert and I spend time watching from the rise above the house. We both worry that he will return."

The color drained from Malene's face. "I am sorry."

"It is not your problem, yet I thought you wanted to know."

"Do you think he knows about us?"

Mark shook his head. "No. He hates Indians. And I think he hates that I am doing well. We have not seen him in many moons, not since the fire. But we watch for him. No one has seen him, no bank robbery, no stagecoach, nothing. It is as if he's vanished. But I cannot trust him." He inhaled and held it before blowing the air out of his lungs. "A wolf will return for his prey. He wants me."

Malene broke into sobs.

"Do not cry. When he is dead or captured, then I will rest. Until then, I've worked very hard for what I have and I will not let him take it from me."

She curled against his chest, and he rubbed her arm.

"Do not be afraid." His voice was soft as his words enveloped her.

"I need to go to Adie. She is expecting me, but I do not want to leave you. She is going to worry because I am not there."

He laughed. "I told her I was keeping you. I

was going to surprise you with the house and give you time to think about marrying me."

"You did? She did not tell me that."

"She knows and promised me that she would keep our…secret. But I did not tell her about Albert Goddard."

"That makes me feel better. I was concerned that she would worry." She looked up at him. "Why do you feel so good to me? Why do you make my heart flutter?"

"Because you love me as I love you. There are problems being with me. Alisa and I have talked about it. Life is full of dangers. I have lost one wife and I do not want to ever lose you." He nestled her tighter.

"When I was in San Francisco, I missed you. I missed talking to you. I missed these quiet moments together. When I am with you, everything is right, even if it is wrong."

"It is never wrong when we are together. I am trying to help my people. By doing for you, I am helping them, but they do not see that. They think I...I turned my back on who I am. I think forward to the future. My people do not understand that our ways are dying. We must live in a white man's world. If by doing this I can keep my brothers and sisters from starving, then I have done much good."

Malene nodded.

"I do not want my people to ever lose their traditions or skills. There has to be a balance between our past and our future. Our children must know who they are and from where they come." He gave Malene a little squeeze. "I have great dreams."

"I have dreams of my own house near my sister with my own land. I can add to Frank and Adie's land and give them more land to use. I want the children to grow up where they will be safe to run and play. I don't need a man to support me. I can live alone and be happy. I proved that in San Francisco. But I also realized while I was there, how important my family was to me." She put her hand upon his chest and sat up. "You have ruined my dreams."

"That is because you forgot how much you loved me. You make new and better dreams of us." He put his hands on her shoulders and kissed her. "Now, go to bed, for it is my turn to watch over the ranch and keep everyone safe."

He watched as she went inside. He grabbed his rifle, and took off on his horse for the ridge. At least tonight, he did not feel the need to release his seed. She was everything to him, and she still had not figured out that she was his woman. *Her mind needs to find her heart.*

A light breeze whipped around him. It was as though it tried to whisper in his ear, but he could not hear the words. He knew he could never let his guard down as long as Albert was alive. The wind whispered again.

11

Malene tried to settle into the ranching life. She began to learn Rose's words as Rose learned hers. Pretty Flower soon became Priscilla; she and Clara were inseparable.

Waking up to Mark's body next to hers sent a rush through her system that was undeniable. There were mornings that her fingertips grazed his skin and mornings that she didn't dare touch him for fear of setting her own body aflame. She loved the way he looked, the curves of his muscles and his obvious masculine parts.

His back contained several jagged lines, the childhood scars of a nasty tumble into a rocky gully. Silky black hair fell to his waist. She wondered how a man that big and powerful could be so gentle with her?

Sophia stirred. Without being confined to a crib, the child could get up and roam. Malene went to her and took her into the bathroom to prepare for the day. The child's diaper was dry.

Malene undid the diaper and sat the child on the toilet. "Sit here, while I wash your face."

Sophia babbled as Malene ran a cloth over the child's face and in her mouth. Sophia bit down and Malene discovered another tooth.

"You are getting a mouthful of teeth." Then Malene heard the sound of Sophia relieving herself. "Oh! What a big girl you are!"

Sophia laughed and tried to clap her hands together, but when she let go of the seat, the child's little derrière discovered there was water below her.

Malene giggled. "Now I must wash you, silly girl."

She put a little warm water in the tub and bathed the child, then let Sophia play with the washing cloth. Malene lathered her hand with soap and formed a ring with her thumb and forefinger. Lightly blowing against the thin layer of soap film, she created a bubble. Sophia squealed with delight and popped it. Malene blew several more.

"Ah, that is what all the noise is about," Mark said as he opened the door.

"You don't open the door and walk in. What if I were in the tub?"

He shrugged. "Then I would enjoy seeing my beautiful woman."

Malene didn't dare turn around, for she could hear what he was doing. "Do you not understand that some things are private?"

"You sound like Alisa. We all do it. Besides, I will not hide from my wife and child."

"You will hide from this child, and I am not your wife."

He kissed the top of her head. "You *are* my wife. You need to admit what is in your heart. Your heart is important."

She lifted Sophia from the tub and dressed her. Mark was gone from the room and she was certain he had not had enough sleep.

Her thoughts turned to Albert. She had tried

to escape him, yet he was near. *Swindler becomes bank robber. What will he do when he finds me?*

She gathered the children's laundry and took it downstairs. After she washed and hung everything on the line, she planned to make cheese curds from the goat milk that was stored in the cold cellar. She lifted the pail from its dark room, sniffed it, and knew it would make great cheese. How could she explain to Rose that the next young calf they butchered, she needed the stomach to make rennet? Until then, she would be forced to use the apple vinegar, except there wasn't much vinegar. She groaned.

If I am going to stay here, I will need to buy basic pantry items.

It hadn't taken Malene long to realize that the food that Rose was used to making was plain and limited. Teaching Rose to cook new things was fun, and Malene truly enjoyed her time in the kitchen with Rose. The woman was about the same age as Adie. Also Rose's personality was much like Adie's, friendly and outgoing.

The house was empty, devoid of all the basic items, even the kitchen lacked beyond a few pans and bowls. In her mind, she began to imagine the place filled with the things she had brought from San Francisco. *Maybe I should have brought more with me?*

While making cheese, a white man appeared on horseback. Malene wiped her hands on her apron and greeted him. "Hello, I'm Malene Reiner."

"Adelwulf's daughter?" the agent asked.

"*Ja.*"

"I have some mail for you. Mark's been too busy to collect it lately." The man stared at her intently. "Mark has hinted that you'll be staying here with him."

She sucked in a breath. "We're discussing it."

"May I speak openly with you?"

Her heart thumped. "What's on your mind?"

"You do realize that your living here is acceptable by the tribe, but will never be accepted off the reservation."

She tried to calm her quaking insides. "*Ja*. I know. Mark is of color."

"It's worse than that. He's an Indian."

She nodded. "People are bigoted. If they knew him, they would see he is a good man. But they only see what they want to see - his color."

The agent nodded. "What do you see?"

She could feel the tug at her cheeks as she beamed the man a smile. "I see an intelligent man who is trying very hard to help his people. He's still learning our ways. I see a man who has strong convictions to do what is right, no matter how difficult."

"And how do you feel about living here?"

That was one question she wasn't ready to answer. She wanted to read the letters from her sister.

***

Mark tried to be everywhere and do everything. Instead, he found himself falling behind. He had hoped to have more land plowed. Plus, he had calves to brand and no time to do it. The constant watching for Albert Goddard was something he didn't need, but it had to be done. The man would be back, and with Malene there, he felt certain the ranch was in greater danger.

Malene wanted to visit her sister and that required taking a few days off. He needed more help. There was no way out - he'd have to ask the tribe for additional men, and that meant swallowing his pride.

After talking it over with Robert, he made the trip to the main encampment. A few men were hunting, but the rest sat around waiting for something to happen. His people had lost their way. He wanted to yell at them. Nothing was going to happen unless they made it happen. He went to Angry Bear's tipi.

"I seek your wisdom," Mark said as he

entered the tipi. He paid his respects to Angry Bear's wife, and gave her a freshly killed quail. He explained his situation to the tribal elder.

Angry Bear lit a partially smoked cigar. "You have grown too big, too quickly. There was a time when each man took care of his own and shared his excess. You are trying to share everything."

"I don't want my people to starve. Our old ways are gone, we must learn new."

"You have proudly accepted a new name and wear the white man's clothes. You no longer live as an Apsáalooke. Now you have white man's problems."

Mark pressed his lips together. He nodded. The man was right.

Angry Bear put his fist to his heart. "You are still Apsáalooke in here."

Mark watched the man's wrinkled face as he spoke.

"You have provided many chickens to the tribe and other food. Your connections to the white man have brought many sales of horses. You see the future. Not everyone likes what you see."

Mark nodded. He was being reprimanded and praised in the same breath. In the end, Angry Bear promised him six young scouts. The Hunter ranch would provide food for the men. It would be a heavy burden, but it was necessary. If he wasn't watching, he could do other things, as could Robert.

"Before you leave...have you married her without telling us?"

Mark swallowed. "No. I am waiting for her to see into her own heart."

"You are a young man with plenty of energy." Angry Bear put his cigar out. "She cannot marry you by her people."

"We are very aware of that."

The old man smiled. "But we will celebrate your union."

"I only have my sister. I will not burden her."

"My wife is making a dress. Your Woman of

the Sun will be welcomed as if she were our own."

"*Ahó.*" Mark bowed his head. "That means much to me. I am honored." He left the tipi and headed back to his own place. He'd have help and another financial drain, but he needed the manpower.

Tired and hungry, he arrived late in the evening at his house. Malene had the children in bed, but she immediately fixed him a plate of food.

She touched his arm and smiled at him as he sat at the primitive table. "You've been gone a long time."

"I am getting scouts for this area of land. I will not have to watch for Albert alone."

"That is good."

"Very. When they have learned the area, I will take you to Adie, but I cannot stay. I must come back here."

She looked at him with great concern on her face. "Will you watch tonight?"

He nodded.

"But you have not slept."

He lifted a shoulder and let it drop. "I am a great hunter."

"You think you can do anything," she said flatly

"Yes. I must."

***

Malene climbed into bed and realized how much she worried about Mark. She worried because she cared. She wanted him in the bed with her, to feel his body next to hers, and to listen to him breathing. Instead, there were only night noises. Then worry took over. What if he fell asleep and Albert came? What if Albert set fire to the house?

An eerie feeling cloaked her. The air was still and she was hot. She listened to the patter of Brownie's toenails on the wood floor as he came down the hall to her room.

"What's the matter, Brownie? You can't sleep either?"

The dog whined and walked towards her door.

"Do you need to go out?"

The dog yipped.

"Shh!" Slipping out of bed, she grabbed her shawl.

Brownie scurried down the stairs and waited by the front door with his nose pressed to the door jam. The fur on his back stood up in a stripe from the top of his shoulders to his tail. Without thought, she opened the door, and Brownie shot into the night. Instead of returning immediately, he began to sniff.

Her skin crawled as she watched the dog. Someone was out there and Brownie had picked up the scent. She stepped back into the doorway and found herself against a hard body. She inhaled as her heart stopped. A hand covered her mouth.

"What are you doing?"

It was Robert's voice. Her whole body relaxed and Robert removed his hand.

"Brownie wanted to go out," she whispered.

Robert moved her out of the way and stepped onto the porch. He walked soundlessly to the far end, slipped over the railing, and out of sight.

She wiped sweat from her forehead and tugged at the nightgown that clung to her wet skin. Brownie took off in the direction of the sawmill. The sky lit up with a flash of lightning. Slowly she counted the seconds until she heard the distant rumble. She wanted to call Brownie back, but that little inner voice told her to remain quiet. Another flash of lightning filled the sky. Her heart pounded as she counted the seconds to the rumble.

Brownie started barking, and Malene froze in place. Another bolt lit up the sky and she saw what Brownie had found, a doe and two fawns. They bounded away from the house.

Brownie returned with his tail wagging,

stopping every few feet to lift his leg against something. Malene wiped the sweat off her brow. A moment later, Robert returned as thunder rumbled through the still night. Drops of water began to fall. First it was a light splattering and then it turned into a deluge. She was certain it was too much rain and too hard on the young crops in the fields. Concern over Mark's safety made her shudder.

Robert leaned against a porch support post. Crossing his arms over his chest, he asked, "What are you doing up?"

"Brownie wanted to go out."

"You said that, but there is more."

She shrugged. "I didn't mean to awaken you. I wasn't asleep when Brownie asked to go out."

"There's not a man on this ranch who is sleeping with his ears closed."

"I'm sorry." She tugged on her shawl, hoping she had covered everything. "I was worrying about Mark. He's not had enough sleep."

Robert shook his head. "Mark is fine. He does not want you to leave, but you need to go to your sister. Nothing is ready for you. He has too much and you make more."

She eyed Robert and wondered if he was being truthful or hateful. She turned towards the doorway. Robert's hand caught her shoulder. "He loves you. Let him make things good for you."

She pulled from his touch and ran up the stairs. Tears clouded her vision. Robert was right. It was as if she had been stabbed.

Adie wanted her and she was here with three extra children and Angelina. There was no reason for her to even come back to this house. Mark would find another woman who would love to be married to him and provide him with many children.

She knew how to handle the carriage. Certainly, making her way to the Coleman ranch wouldn't be that difficult. It was not winter. It would only take a few days. She only had to find the Coleman path.

***

A few days later, Mark awakened to a strange silence in the house. He poured a cup of coffee, and when he saw Rose, he asked, "Where is everyone?"

"Malene took everyone for a long ride. She made a big basket of food and left."

Mark's stomach turned over, and he ran back upstairs. Everything was gone, even in Angelina's rooms. She had picked the one day he could not chase after her. He knew exactly where she was headed. He was going to take her next week. They had talked about it and made plans. *She's worse than a headstrong bull!*

He jumped on his horse and rode to the top of the rise. There he found Robert on watch. "You knew?"

Robert nodded. "She wanted to be with her sister before the baby is born."

Mark raised his hand.

"No. Let her go. Little Goat is with her."

"You knew all along?"

"Rose did. Rose made her take someone with her."

"He is but a boy."

Robert shrugged. "She'll be back."

"Why did you not tell me?"

"Rose told me last night."

Rage tore through him as he jumped on his horse. He didn't have time for anger, nor did he have time to chase after Malene. It felt as if something had reached inside of him and ripped part of his heart away.

He didn't dare leave the ranch. Too many months and too much hard work had gone into the transaction with the McLaughlins. He was trapped between white man's money and his love for Malene.

***

Malene arrived and was greeted by Alisa Coleman. Adie waddled out from the house. Her bulging belly looked three times too big.

Adie smiled. "*Ja*. I know."

"Now I know why you said this baby must come early." Malene wished Mark had come with her. She feared for Adie.

"Alisa is making me stay here. She doesn't want me alone."

Malene shook her head and introduced the children and Angelina. It didn't take her long to settle in. Malene shared a room with Angelina. Alisa tucked the Hamilton children in with the other Coleman children.

It was noisy and fun. For the first time in more than a year, Malene totally relaxed. She had so much news, and news of Mark's ranch.

Adie giggled. "I know what Mark has done. Frank helped him with the house. Twice we rode up to help with the house."

"Did he tell you about Albert?" Malene asked.

"*Nein!* What does he know about Albert?"

Malene told as much of the story as she knew.

Alisa nodded. "There have been many robberies this past year. Joseph had to go to Laramie, and he came home telling of a Wells Fargo heist and two train robberies. You think your Albert is behind all of it?"

"According to the Wanted posters, yes. And he tried to kill Mark and Robert. I did not tell Mark I was leaving. He has been so busy trying to do all the spring planting and keeping watch over the ranch. I did not want to add to his burden."

Adie sipped her tea, then asked about their parents.

"Mama was thrilled with Clara and Sophia. Papa spent much time with Marcus and Dill. I think Papa wished he had sons instead of daughters." Malene grinned at her sister. "Marcus had written him several times and Papa always answered the child's letters.

These boys are starved for male attention, yet they miss their mama."

Alisa began to fix the evening meal. "It will take them time. Now they have you and they are surrounded with love. They will be fine."

Marcus and Dill followed Joseph to the barn after dinner. The whole atmosphere at the Coleman ranch was more relaxed. Malene pitched in and helped with the evening chores.

Two days later, Adie broke her water and delivered two babies. Adie was thrilled and exhausted. Two baby girls snuggled into the cradle by their mother's bed. Alisa tied a small length of ribbon to the first baby's arm so everyone could tell the twins apart. Emma and Anna were declared healthy by Alisa when she weighed the babies on the scale from the kitchen. Adie glowed, for each baby was over six pounds with strong lungs.

Frank strutted around downstairs. This was a first for the Colemans. Never before in the family had there been twins. Virginia sat next to the cradle and slowly rocked it. Issy and Clarissa popped into the room long enough to peek at the babies before returning to their chores.

Malene was glad she came when she did. If she had waited, she wouldn't have made it in time for the birthing. That night, she wrote to Mark.

***

Mark almost didn't want to look at the letter from Malene. He was angry that she had left. He worked long hours trying to make the ranch successful, and she walked away from it...and from him. Alone on the hilltop in the fading light, he pulled her letter from his pocket and read it. He was pleased to hear Adie had healthy twin girls, but he had suspected she carried more than one child. Two babies were a rare occurrence. Unfortunately, the letter gave no hint of

Malene missing him or wanting to return. Had he done everything for nothing?

The scouts took a huge burden off of Robert and Mark. Together the men managed to accomplish more than they dreamed. Then one day, the agent rode to their house. He had a letter for Mark and Robert from the United States government. They had been awarded a total of three thousand dollars for the body of Harris and the arrest of Wilson, wanted bank robbers.

The men sat up several evenings discussing how to best use the money. They each decided to take five hundred, give a small amount to Broken Spear and Jumping Buck, and put the rest into the ranch. Reserving a small portion, they bought cattle. By next fall, they'd be making real money.

Later that summer, Rose gave birth to another child. Two sons and a daughter, Rose was filling her part of the house, but Mark's stood empty.

Mark worked on the molding and the fireplaces. He put wainscoting in the dining room, bathing rooms, and down the long halls. The house was beautiful, but it was empty like his soul.

As summer was drawing to a close, Mark knew he had to do something. His heart ached. Malene belonged to him and he wanted her back.

He picked up the blue and gold pen that Malene had given him. The memory of receiving her package struck him as he held the pen between his fingers. The pen was very special and she deemed him worthy of such a fine gift. Taking a few deep breaths, he began to write.

The house is ready, & I have purchased coal to keep it warm. The summer has been dry, but the fields have survived. I want you, Malene. It is time to come home & bring our children back to me. I miss holding Sophia in my arms & watching her grow. I need to teach Marcus & Dill to ride &

hunt. They are both old enough. Priscilla misses her friend Clara. Bring our children back.

I have money for furniture. Pick what you want from those fancy magazines & I will buy it & have it shipped here.

I must go to Buffalo the end of September to buy a used saw. I will come get you, if you tell me that you are ready for me.

Come home. We can marry by my people on the reservation. The wife of Angry Bear has prepared a traditional dress for your wedding. I do not want to spend another winter without you. You love me, Malene, & I love you. You belong here. Come home.

***

Malene, Adie, and Frank rode into Creed's Crossing. Frank stopped for the mail and brought out a Wanted poster for Albert Goddard. This time his hair looked darker and his face was clean-shaven, except he had a scar on his cheek.

"Seems he robbed one too many trains, the railroad has put up a huge sum of money," Frank said, as he showed the women the flyer and handed the mail to Adie.

Malene wiped her forehead with the back of her hand, while her sister sorted the mail into piles.

"Two for you." Adie handed over a letter from Mama and one from Mark.

Malene pocketed both of them and headed for the general store. She had ordered clothes and shoes for the boys, along with a few things for Clara. She was glad everything had arrived. She found a pretty pattern for Clara and then Adie started looking at fabrics.

Most of their late evenings were spent sewing or knitting, so when Malene spotted some silver-gray wool that was very soft, she wanted it. She knew how cold winters could be, but Angelina had no idea. Having money meant she could buy things when she wanted something, and she wanted warm clothes for the winter.

Life was different on a ranch. With her parents, she never ventured outside on a cold day. But living on a ranch meant running out to the chickens, slopping the pigs, or handling some other chore. And every time the door opened, there would be a blast of cold air coming into the house.

She spotted flannel cloth and chose several pretty colors. She would make a few things for her and Angelina, then use the leftover material for Sophia, and the twins. As she pulled the bolt of lilac flannel from the shelf, she discovered another bolt of creamy pink. It would be lovely on Clara. Laden with enough material for a full wardrobe, she paid the store clerk and piled everything into the wagon.

When she heard footsteps behind her, she thought it was Frank. She turned and found herself face to face with Albert. Air went into her lungs as a lump formed in her throat.

"You say one word, and I will kill you," he hissed. His face was covered in a pale reddish beard and his hair looked almost blond, except it was filthy.

Goose bumps covered her arms as ice water circulated through her body. "Stay away from me. I don't care where you are or what you do. I'm not saying a word."

"Give me your money," he snarled.

"I just spent it."

"Give me what you have left."

She reached in her pocket and found her coins. "Here. Go away."

She stomped into the store. Her insides had turned to mush and her head swam. "Adie, please buy a few sticks of candy."

Adie looked at her and frowned. "They don't have anymore peppermint."

"Please. I don't care what flavor."

Adie picked out three sticks and paid for them. "What is wrong with you?" She handed a lemon stick to her sister, then whispered,

"You are shaking."

"It's Albert. He's outside," she mumbled back.

"Oh, no. Frank is picking up supplies."

"We've got to get out of here and get Frank. Albert demanded money. He took my coins. I told him I spent the rest. He threatened to kill me."

Adie took her hand and pulled her to the store window. "I don't see him. Do you? How much money did you give him?"

"I did not count it… Maybe two dollars. I'm scared."

Adie nodded. "You are right. We need to leave here."

Malene picked up the package of Adie's purchases and Adie carried the basket that contained her twins. They loaded the wagon and pulled it next to the farm supply store. Frank walked out and began loading his supplies.

"Hurry up!" Adie pleaded.

Frank shook his head and went back into the store. Malene thought she'd melt. Her insides shook with every beat of her heart. Seconds felt like hours. She was certain that Albert would return. Frank kept bringing things out of the store and putting them in the wagon. After he added a wooden barrel into the back of the wagon, he jumped into the driver's seat.

Once out of town, they told him what happened.

"Maybe it is best if you two do not come to town for awhile. There's no point in taking chances with your lives."

Malene answered Frank, "I already thought that."

"He probably took the money and went to the saloon."

"I thought that, too. But I didn't want to find he was still lingering between buildings." Malene felt her body shudder.

"We need to turn him in." Frank slapped the reins and the horse picked up speed.

"No, Frank, don't," Adie said. "It is too dangerous."

After supper, Adie and Frank took the twins back to their house. Malene settled Sophia in for the night and then read the letters from Mama and Mark. Her mother's letter was chatty and full of motherly warmth. She had enclosed several pages from a magazine on the latest fashion and another on gardening. Then Malene opened Mark's.

Tears streamed down her face. She had to make up her mind and tell him yes or no. As much as she wanted to say no, her heart kept saying yes.

She tiptoed down the front stairwell, hoping for a quiet cup of tea, but discovered Alisa working on a piece of needlepoint.

"What is wrong, my dear friend?" Alisa looked up from her needlework.

"I thought a cup of tea might help me think."

"Make enough for two and I will sit with you, for sometimes thinking aloud helps."

When Alisa entered the kitchen, Malene passed Mark's letter to her friend. "I have one thing in my heart and another in my head."

Alisa sat and read the letter. "What is your head saying?"

Malene poured the hot water over the tealeaves. "That I do not need to be married. The Hamilton family is paying me to raise these children and provide a home for them. They do not want them. I thought I would buy a partial square or maybe a whole square and allow Frank to use it. Then I would build my own house."

"But Mark has built one for you."

She nodded and took a seat. "I arrived at the wrong time. Mark was busy. The house wasn't finished, and food was limited. Even the garden had not yet begun to produce."

Alisa rolled her hands over facing her palms up. "Now the house is done and he's ready for you."

Malene nodded. "I love my sister, too, and I

love being with you."

"The reservation isn't that far away." Alisa pressed her lips tightly together for just a moment. "A house is a house. It contains walls and roof. The house in San Francisco sounded lovely, yet you were not happy there because you were away from the people you love."

"*Ja.*"

"You left here a young woman with a newborn who had lost all hope for her future, so you were willing to settle. But you came back as an independent, mature woman with four children. You were strong enough to leave the comfort of your parents with the ideology of having your own place here." She took a sip of her tea and then looked at Malene.

Alisa took another sip and then continued. "Then you discover that Mark has created his own ranch and built a lovely house for you, except he wasn't ready for you. You knew that your sister wanted you. You took the initiative to leave him and come to your sister." She picked her cup up once again, stared into it for a moment, and then put it down.

Alisa smiled. "You are a very strong woman. You walked away when others would have preferred to be kept in warm, loving arms. You gave Mark the freedom to finish without worrying about you, four children, and their teacher." This time she lifted the cup to her lips and sipped. "What is your problem?"

Malene put her elbows on the table and put her hands over her face. "Do I love Mark enough to spend my entire life with him?"

Alisa laughed. "You were going to spend your life with Marshall, because your father deemed him a good man. I know Mark is a good man, and he'll be an excellent father to the children. You don't need money. You have your own." She drained her teacup and poured another cup. "Love isn't something that is planned. It happens. Frank was a lovesick puppy from the day he met Adie."

"What about you and Joseph?"

"His grandmother and my grandmother knew each other. He would write me and tell me about the ranch. But he also told me his deepest thoughts. I fell in love with him. He was different from other suitors. They were concerned about their neckties or dust on their shoes. Joseph cared about his family and his livestock. He cared about me and wanted me to be happy."

"That sounds like Adie and Frank."

Alisa nodded. "You have a man who cares about you. And you care very much about him. Do you think it gets better than that? Do you really think if you built a house here you'd be happier?"

"You're saying to follow my heart."

Alisa pushed her chair back and stood. "No. Follow your head. Your heart will not change. It's your mind that needs companionship. Your heart is already with him."

Malene washed their cups and put them

away. Alisa was right. Many Feathers stole her heart from the very beginning. She recalled their first encounter. She was so afraid of him, yet he showed her nothing but kindness. She remembered the feel of his calloused hand on her face and the way he had held her hand. He was fearsome with his face painted and his long, jet-black hair. That bizarre hair adornment, that was nothing but feathers, gave him a strange appearance. Through all of it, he treated her as if she were a queen. Had it not been for him, she probably would have died in childbirth. And when he kissed her, he sent fire through her body.

Her thoughts drifted back to Albert. She was but a schoolgirl when she met Albert. His touch did nothing and eventually sickened her. Marshall was kind, but again, there was nothing. He needed a caretaker for his children and probably a woman to warm his marital bed. But Many Feathers was different.

He'd slept in the bed next to her. Sometimes

his hand would find hers, but he never took from her. Only when they kissed, did his kisses become more. She had been a willing participant, and she knew she could stop him, but she enjoyed his maleness.

He was brazen and he made her blush. He was soft and tender, yet strong and hard. With time, she had learned not to fear him as a man. She had fallen in love with him.

She lifted her skirt and silently climbed the steps to the room she shared with Angelina. Malene had to make a decision as to where she would find her own happiness that would last a lifetime.

The following morning, Malene took Sophia, put her in a buggy, and went to Adie's house with the material she had bought. "*Gutten morgan*, my sweet sister. We have a lot of work to do."

Adie's home was plain. She had only a small amount of furniture, and Malene suspected that it probably had come from the Coleman attic. Two chairs were covered in blue fabric that had been one of Adie's fancy dresses. Malene admired the new fender in front of the parlor fireplace. It was as if they splurged and bought several nice things while making do with lesser things. Malene was kicking herself for not bringing more from the house. *Had not the agent said it would be easier to sell without furniture?*

Together they sat on the floor, laid out the patterns, and then cut the material. They joked about being a factory. Adie cut, Malene pinned, Adie sewed, Malene hand sewed, and they continued for days at the crazy pace. When they were done, Malene, Adie, and Angelina had several new outfits, Clara had new dresses, and so did Sophia and the twins.

Alisa had given them her cache of leftover lace, ribbons, and braiding. Malene attached bits to collars and skirts for the children. None of it was exactly high fashion, but everything was lovely. Malene preferred riding skirts and blouses, whereas Adie preferred a simple skirt or dress.

Malene had purchased yards of toweling. Adie machine hemmed them and Malene added touches of embroidery to them. They each made aprons with it and Malene made two aprons for Alisa. The scraps they made into long, narrow pockets for those womanly times. Each pocket could be stuffed with other rags. Nothing went to waste. Malene leaned back and was thrilled with her hard work.

Adie had returned to her normal shape very quickly. Malene had not. It wasn't until she came to the Coleman ranch that she went back to her normal self. Malene admired her younger sister, for it had taken Malene a year to get back into her old clothes. Adie had done it in weeks. But the thought of squeezing into a corset had no appeal. Malene realized she no longer really cared what the latest fashion was. It was the children that mattered to her.

Yes, she had changed. Alisa was right. She

wasn't that young idealistic woman. Her dreams had been shattered.

"Malene!" Adie whined. "You are far away in thoughts. Do you want to ride with us to Sheridan in September?"

"When in September?"

"We'll leave here on the twentieth."

"Why are you going to Sheridan?"

Adie giggled. "Frank wants a big bull."

Malene chomped on her lower lip. "What if I brought Angelina and the children with me and only went as far as Buffalo?"

"Why would you do something like that?"

"Because Mark is picking up a saw in Buffalo."

Adie rolled her eyes. "Tell Mark we'll pick up the saw and bring it to Sheridan. That will save him a day." Adie looked at her sister wide-eyed as it dawned on her that her sister wasn't just turning the trip into a little outing. Then she stammered, "You're planning to go back and stay with Mark?"

Malene nodded. "The house is finished and as hard as it is to admit, I do love him."

Adie threw her arms around her sister. "I'm so excited for you. I want to see you happy."

"It's not that simple."

"*Ja,* it is."

"No it's not, but it's where I want to be. I miss him."

That night, Malene cried as she wrote to Mark. No matter how hard she tried to envision another life with a different man, she couldn't. Mark's smile invaded her very soul. For a little personal happiness, she'd forever have to pretend that he was hired help in public. What would she do if Angelina didn't want to go? What if he wanted more children?

12

Mark opened the letter. He wanted to yell with joy. He would meet them in Buffalo anyway. The old sawmill there contained more than just a saw, besides he wanted to see it before he bought it. Running a sawmill was profitable and they had plenty of work. More saws meant they could do even more. More work meant more money, and Broken Spear and Jumping Buck liked the idea of living in a house. They wanted their own houses and their own pieces of land.

It was a ripple spreading through Mark's people. Some still resisted, but he'd had several ask if he could give them jobs. Alisa had said to teach by example. He was doing that.

He wrote back to Malene and hoped that his letter arrived before she left.

***

Malene talked to Angelina about moving back to the reservation.

Angelina smiled. "I am here for you and the children. I will go wherever you do. Mark and Robert are good men, and Priscilla needs an education, too."

"Thanks, Angelina. I feel as if you are part of my family. It's as if I've gained another sister."

"I hope this time we have real beds. I know Mark tried. I am spoilt."

"I have all my furniture. It is only a matter of getting it there." *And that's not going to be easy.*

Malene wrote to her parents. She knew her parents wanted her to marry someone who could take care of her. That almost made her laugh aloud. Mark was the one man who did care about her, and he was very capable of caring for her. Besides, she didn't need his money.

She asked her papa if he would hire someone who would deliver all her furniture to Mark on the reservation on the twentieth of

October. She would pay any expenses. She went on to say that Mark had finished the house for her and was slowly creating a ranch that would be bigger than the Colemans'. She knew she'd hear from her mama, because her mama wasn't thrilled that Malene had stayed with Mark for so long on her way to Adie's. Sharing the house with him meant she'd be living with him, and it wouldn't take much for her mama to figure out that they were going to live as man and wife. She chewed on her bottom lip, wrote a few more lines, and added her closing.

On September twentieth, she said goodbye to Alisa and the rest of the Colemans. Their trunks were on the wagon that had once belonged to the Reiner parents, which gave everyone more room in the carriage. But that didn't calm Malene's beating heart or the butterflies in her stomach. She prayed that she had made the right decision.

***

Mark left a day early for Buffalo. He wanted to be certain that he was there when Malene arrived. Robert had offered to come, but Little Goat came instead. The young man looked forward to another trip off the reservation. Being he liked Malene and the children, made it even more exciting for him. Mark knew it would be young men like Little Goat who would hold the future of the tribe in their hands. For now, the most Mark could do was encourage his young friend.

A storm rolled in that first night, drenching both of them. The white man's clothes were not waterproof like the traditional tribal clothing. Behind the storm was cold air. Mark peeled off his wet clothes and put on dry ones. He knew they were not welcome to stay in a hotel, so they drove through Sheridan and stopped outside of town for the night.

The days were shorter and there was no

point in driving a wagon through the darkness. They pulled the wagon off the road and then found a spot away from the wagon to sleep. The only noise they heard was of elk in the area, but Mark knew never to let his guard down. Albert Goddard was out there and if he wasn't, there were plenty more like him.

He wanted a good saw. The agent had told him about this one and had made all the arrangements for Mark. It was government surplus, since they had closed the fort. Many members of the tribe didn't like the agent and didn't like his ways. Mark had learned to work with the man. So far, it had been beneficial. Saws were expensive, and if this one was in good shape, it was worth the trip.

But the thrill of seeing Malene constantly churned through him. Yet with it came a sadness, as he could only offer her a tribal wedding, not a white man's. He hoped she had gotten his letter that said he would meet her in Buffalo.

He slapped the reins and hurried the horses. He stopped in Buffalo long enough to pick up some food, then drove past the old fort town and pulled away from the road near a little rise. From the top of the rise he could see a fair distance.

He and Little Goat ate and waited. They waited through the next day and into the night. Maybe she had changed her mind. He'd wait another day. If she still didn't appear, he'd get his saw and head home. She was the most headstrong, obstinate woman he knew.

Another day passed and he knew he'd have to leave. He stopped in town and inquired as to the whereabouts of the man he needed to meet. A few hours later, he had several saws, tools, and two beautiful lathes. "What I need is another windmill to run everything."

The man laughed. "Not a problem. Here, take it."

The massive windmill was lying on its side.

Mark had no idea how he'd get it home, but he wasn't about to pass up a free windmill. "Have an extra set of wheels?"

The man walked to a building and picked through the debris. "Ain't nothing in here."

"What about that?" Mark pointed to an old wooden platform with what looked like train wheels on it.

"That old thing? If you can get it out of here, you can have it."

Little Goat and Mark pulled the thing from the building, but the wheels were rusted and refused to turn. Mark handed Little Goat some coins and sent him in town for vinegar and lard.

***

Traveling with two infants, a toddler, three children, and a dog was not easy. Malene was certain that Mark had given up and had gone home. Then again, maybe he hadn't gotten her letter. Sadness draped her.

Frank promised to take her to the reservation, if she had missed Mark in Buffalo. That eased her mind, but it wouldn't erase her disappointment.

Frank pulled to a stop at the hotel. "We'll spend the night, grab a few extra provisions, and with luck, the children will wear themselves out while there is still plenty of daylight."

Malene knew it was her fault that the trip was delayed. Frank came to help her down, and as he put his hands on her waist, she heard her name being called.

She looked in the direction of the voice and spotted Little Goat. She waved. Excitement built inside her.

The teen ran to her. "Malene, Mark will be so happy to see you." He turned to Frank. "Maybe you help him?"

Thrill was replaced with ice water that ran through her veins. "Is something wrong?"

Little Goat nodded. "His wheels won't turn."

Frank looked at Malene and chuckled. "If his wheels won't turn, then he's got a very big problem. That man's wheels turn faster than anyone's." He smiled at his wife. "Can you and Angelina handle the children until we get back?"

Malene looked at her sister.

Adie nodded. "Go with them, Malene."

Frank took the carriage to the livery and then helped Malene into the wagon. They traveled a little ways outside of town and found Mark by a section of the old fort.

He ran to greet them and Malene almost fell into his arms with her enthusiasm. His lips found hers, as he swung her around. Her heart pounded, and her body warmed from his embrace. She knew she had made the right decision. No matter what problems they might encounter, they would have each other.

"What's wrong with your wagon?" Frank asked.

"It's not the wagon." He took the supplies from Little Goat. "Follow me."

Frank looked at the contraption. "Was it used for hauling heavy equipment?"

Mark nodded. "The wheels are rusted." Mark poured vinegar on a piece of old cloth he had found. "I'm going to see if this works."

Frank found another bit of cloth and began working on another wheel. When the last wheel was finished, Mark said, "Going to try to break them free."

The three men got behind the cart and began to push it in spurts. Malene poured a few drops of vinegar on each wheel. With double axles in the front and the back, there were eight metal wheels.

"This one is turning, and this one." She ran to the other side. "All of these are." She went to the other side and dribbled more vinegar on the two that had refused to budge. "Success!"

The cart rolled about four feet, squealing the whole time. Mark took the lard and rubbed it between the axle and the wheel. "Try again, nice and slow. I like my fingers."

Mark coated each wheel hub in lard. The grating sound lessened until it was gone, and the wheels turned freely and almost silently.

Frank looked at Mark's wagon. "Looks as though you bought the place out."

Mark chuckled. "I needed this to take that."

"Are you crazy?" Frank asked.

Mark nodded. He backed his wagon up to the windmill and then rolled the cart behind the wagon. I'm putting it between the two."

Malene watched as the men tugged, pushed, tugged, and pushed some more. Finally they angled the windmill between the wagon and the cart. Mark and Frank lashed the thing into place.

Mark laughed. "Guess I don't have to tie the cart to the wagon."

Frank shook his head. "That's not going to be a problem. You think six horses are going to pull this?"

Mark nodded. "I brought six because I wasn't certain how much the saws would weigh. As long as I don't try to run the horses, they'll be fine."

"What did this cost?" He pointed to the windmill.

"Nothing. And the cart was free. But if you notice, there are no pipes to the windmill."

"Free is worth it."

Malene tugged her shawl around her shoulders. "I don't want to complain, but it's getting cold and dark."

"Maybe Little Goat ride with you? I want to keep the weight off my horses."

They made their way back into town, but Mark veered off to the north. "I'll see you in the morning."

Malene's heart fell as she watched Mark ride off. She prayed he'd be safe while they slept in the comfort of the little hotel.

At breakfast, she ordered extra to take with her, knowing how much he enjoyed bacon.

Alisa had given instructions on how to cure pork and Malene had carefully written them in a book. She still had much to learn, but she knew she could do it.

When they exited the hotel, Mark was waiting for them. He took Sophia from her and held the child in his arms. He ran his hand over the child's hair. "She's so beautiful. I have a daughter of fire."

Sophia giggled. She knew no stranger, but Malene didn't want to disappoint Mark. He kissed her tiny cheek and she batted at him. Mark caught the little hand and kissed it over and over until the child dissolved into giggles.

Malene could feel the smile on her face. Seeing Sophia and Mark together warmed her very soul. He truly loved Sophia and lavished the Hamilton children with attention.

"I'll go get the carriage," Frank said, getting off the wagon. "You going to be all right with the children until I get back?"

Malene nodded and watched Frank walk

back to the livery.

"There's a bakery," Adie said. "I'll find something wonderful for us."

Malene nodded and then looked in the direction of Mark and Sophia. Her gaze caught more than just Mark holding the toddler. Albert stood across the street. Air went into her lungs and refused to leave. "Adie," she whispered. "Don't go. Stay here."

"What's an injun doing with a white man's child?" Albert called.

***

Mark looked up and recognized the man. "This child is very special, for she belongs to Malene."

"Give her back to her mother."

Mark looked the man in the eyes and saw a hatred that he'd never seen in a human. It reminded him of a crazed animal. He shifted Sophia to his left side, freeing his right hand.

He was no longer the prey. Human stench and spirit water wafted in the air. The lone wolf before him was trapped by his own stupidity.

Albert tossed more insults. Each time he opened his mouth, he created more problems for himself. It remind Mark of a mouse squealing as a hawk approached. The more the man squealed the more attention he drew to himself.

Mark always carried a rifle in his wagon, but he'd taken on the habit of the white man by wearing a pistol slung low on his hip whenever he traveled. Now he was thankful he did.

***

Adie recognized Albert instantly even though he had lightened his hair. She walked to the wagon and reached under the seat. Less than thirty feet from Albert, she kept her gaze on him and he kept his on Mark. Her heart pounded. Mark was probably no more than twenty feet from Albert, and Angelina, Little Goat, and the Hamilton children were on the hotel porch behind Mark.

Silently, Adie slipped the old rifle from under the seat. Another wagon rumbled between the two men. She wished that Frank were still at her side, for he, too, carried a pistol.

She wasn't but ten years old when her father and Dan showed her how to use a gun. Her father whispered in her ear as if he were standing beside her. She knew exactly what she had to do. But this wasn't the backyard, and there were other people around.

Several people had stopped and were watching the banter between the men. Albert was tossing accusations at Mark, as if he were the criminal. Adie hoisted the gun to her shoulder and cocked the lever, hoping no one heard the click over the rumble of another wagon passing through the town. She rested the barrel on the wagon and watched. Albert wore a gun, but so did Mark. She prayed Frank would show up.

"Scraping the bottom of the pigsty, Mal? Not a white man out there that will have you when you've carried another man's child. I should have known you were pregnant. You're a lousy whore."

***

Malene swallowed. "Why would I tell you? So you could push me down the stairs again or beat me until I died?"

Albert laughed. "You were a useless excuse for a woman. It's a shame you didn't break your neck."

Malene could see Mark's hand at his side, unfortunately he still held Sophia on his other hip. Her heart thundered in her chest at such a rapid rate that she was certain it would explode. She looked behind Mark and realized that Angelina had gathered the children and was moving them towards the general store in an attempt to put some space between her and Mark.

Albert was goading Mark, but Mark wasn't responding. Malene's eyes remained focused on Albert's hand and the gun on his hip. She knew he was fast. She'd seen him practicing too many times. He prided himself on his quick draw.

Albert put his hand on his gun and a shot rang out. Albert stumbled. A second shot was fired and the man fell. He raised his gun and another shot sent it out of his hand.

Blood ran from Albert's mouth and Malene vomited.

***

Adie ran to where Albert had fallen. His eyes were half closed and he lay there with blood spurting from his chest. Her insides quaked. "Please tell me he's dead. Please!"

An older man walked up to Adie. "Young lady, you're in a heap of trouble."

Gray fog enveloped her.

***

Mark sat in the sheriff's office, along with Adie and Malene. As much as he wanted to hold Malene in his arms, he knew he couldn't. Malene and Adie clung to each other.

When asked, Mark produced his pass. The sheriff shoved some paperwork in Mark's direction. "Put your mark here."

Mark stared at the man sitting across the desk from him. Dark brown hair fell across his forehead and curled over the collar of his sweat-soaked shirt, and the man's badge looked too heavy to be hanging from the thin white cotton. Mark picked up the paper and read it twice. "I'm not signing that. I didn't do anything."

Adie read it behind Mark. "That's not what happened. Everyone knows I shot Albert."

The sheriff shook his head. "Missy, I'm trying to keep you out of a heap of trouble."

"Trouble?" Adie stood and placed her palms with a thud onto the man's desk. "There's a reward on that man."

Malene took the paper and read it. "Albert is a wanted man. I know that. I was married to him. My father obtained a legal divorce."

"Do you have those papers?"

"Yes. It will take me a few moments to produce them."

The sheriff nodded and excused her.

Two hours later, the Wanted posters were located, Malene had her proof of divorce, and they all agreed on what had happened. They all signed the paperwork, but Mark insisted on a copy that he could take with him. The sheriff balked, but created a copy, and everyone had signed that one, too. Adie was entitled to the full amount of the reward. It made the three thousand dollars that Robert and Mark had split seem like egg money.

Mark knew that there were other Alberts out there, people who hated the Indians based only on the color of their skin. He didn't understand it, and he never would. But Albert was dead, and a huge burden fell from his shoulders. He would spend the rest of his life protecting his ranch, but the immediate danger had been lifted.

With luck, he'd never again have to stand guard over his land every day and every night. It was over. The nightmare had come to an end.

They sent a letter to Alisa Coleman telling her what had happened, and that they would be delayed. When they were done, it was decided everyone would spend one more night in town, then Frank and Adie would follow Mark to his ranch. No one wanted anything else to occur and Mark had a heavy load.

***

Malene entered the house and almost swooned when she saw it. "It's beautiful. You've done so much."

Mark smiled at her. "I told you I would build you a house."

"This must have cost a fortune."

"I used some of the reward money. Much is from our sawmill. I only copied what I saw in magazines."

Malene wandered through the rooms amazed at how lovely it was. Deep molding ran around the base of the walls. It framed doorways, windows, chased the stairs, and edged the ceilings. The fireplace mantles were beautiful and each one was inset with a large mirror. Several rooms contained stoves instead of a fireplace. No matter where she looked or which room she was in, Mark had done everything possible to make the house perfect.

And he had definitely succeeded.

When she went into the kitchen, she saw Robert leaning against a doorframe. His hair had been pulled into two braids and he wore a pair of waist overalls without a shirt. His muscled body had turned a dark red-brown. Two years ago she would have blushed at seeing a man without his shirt, but Robert looked totally natural standing there. She smiled and said, "*Kaheé.*"

He grinned. "*Kaheé* and welcome home. I told you."

"Is your side done, too?" She pointed past him to the room on the other side of the doorframe.

"We will finish my side this winter. Rose understands why we finished your side first." He came to Malene and hugged her. "This time you will stay?"

"Yes. This is my home. It's where I belong." She looked around the kitchen that contained several four-door cabinets and a big butcher-block table. "This time Mark is ready for me."

"We are all ready for you. Even Rose is excited you have returned."

That evening she wrote a note to Hamilton Wholesalers & Importers Trading Company in San Francisco requesting the rest of the furniture from the house. She wanted it freighted directly to her on the reservation. She hoped the agent had a telegraph in his office.

When Mark walked into the bedroom, her breath hitched.

He closed the bedroom door and the door to Sophia's room. "Will you be my wife?"

She nodded. "Yes. That is why I came. I don't understand why, but I love you. I fell in love with you when we first met."

"You were afraid of me, afraid of your own shadow, and afraid to follow your heart." He pulled her to her feet and covered her mouth with his.

Her body trembled as his tongue parted her

lips. She pushed him away.

"What is wrong?"

"I am scared…I'm still scared of you and of the pain."

He took her hands in his and kissed them. "When there is love, there is no pain."

Fear paralyzed her, yet she wanted to help him undo the buttons on his shirt. She wanted to see his beautiful body. The image of him had invaded her dreams and her daily thoughts for months. But her body trembled too much to do anything except watch. His skin had darkened in the summer sun, and his chest and upper arms seemed twice as large.

She took a deep breath. Her gazed was riveted on him as her fingers fumbled with the buttons on her shirt. Curling her lower lip inward, she sunk her teeth on it to stop the trembling. He dropped his pants and she stifled a moan. Heat flowed over her cheeks.

He stepped to her. Her fingers found her button again as she gazed into his dark eyes.

Fear mixed with excitement ran through her. Quivering insides rolled themselves into a tight ball and made it difficult to breathe.

She attempted to take a deep breath, but the air left too quickly, and she had to try again. His fingers replaced hers, as his lips found her ear. Words she did not understand flowed to her heart. One by one, her clothes fell to the floor.

His arms wrapped her and held her tight to his muscle-hardened body. His hands caressed her back, while his lips plied her with a million tiny kisses that tingled. She clung to him.

He kissed her until she melted. He touched her until she was certain that her body would burst into flame. And when it was over, she understood what he'd been trying to tell her.

She had never been kissed in so many places, nor had she ever touched a man the way she touched Mark. She didn't want it to end. He had pulled her on top of him and she rested her head on his chest. Exhausted and exhilarated, she listened to his heartbeat His fingers caressed her back. The undulating movement that came with each breath he took and the beat of his heart lulled her to a peaceful place where she relaxed.

"Tomorrow, we will go to the chief and celebrate our marriage." His voice reverberated in his chest.

She knew what she had done. Tears flowed onto his chest. There was no turning back, for she had become an Indian's wife. She had Mark, but she also had invited problems, for her people would never accept her marriage.

***

As morning light filtered into the bedroom, Mark made love to his wife one more time. He had awakened a hunger deep inside of Malene that she had hidden away. And he loved it.

It was noises coming from Sophia's room

that forced them to separate. He opened the door between the two rooms and Sophia toddled out. Malene scurried into the bathing room with Sophia, and Mark followed.

Malene attempted to chase him away. He laughed and filled the tub with water. "My wife does not need to hide from me."

That morning, the children, Angelina, Rose, Robert, Adie, Frank, Malene, and Mark made their way to the main encampment. The sun was setting as they arrived. Mark found Angry Bear and informed him of the marriage. Angry Bear's wife took Malene and dressed her in a ceremonial dress that had been made for this wedding.

When Mark saw Malene, he sucked in a breath. She was dressed as if she were the bride of an important man. The dress was made of buckskin and was lavishly beaded and trimmed in fur. Her hair hung in two long braids that were tied with beaded bits of leather. Her moccasins were also covered in beads.

He wore buckskin breeches and moccasins. Angry Bear draped his chest in beads, and feathers taken from chickens. His hair had been pushed into a pompadour, and several crow feathers were placed into it.

Formally attired, Malene and he were presented to the tribe and to the chief.

Adie squealed when she saw them and Frank grinned. The children watched with wide eyes as the ceremony began. Drums played and the men danced and chanted. It was not the same as when he first married, for this time Malene was being welcomed, and he was being recognized for his accomplishments. He danced with his fellow tribesmen and noted Robert's wide grin. Malene, Adie, Clara, Angelina, and Rose were encouraged to dance with the women. Mark danced with Marcus and Dill, then held Sophia in his arms as he watched Malene and his sister dance. He and Robert taught Frank to drum.

Prepared for this day, Mark brought gifts with him, and gave them to his people. The party seemed to last forever, and when it ended, they all went to Angry Bear's tipi.

Malene and the children fell asleep, but Angry Bear wanted to talk to Mark and Robert.

The old man pulled out a pipe and lit it. "My days on this earth are nearing their end. I will not always be around to protect you. There are many who oppose what you are doing."

Mark nodded.

"You have had sorrow and you have had happiness, but are you strong enough to battle your own people over your principles?"

Mark straightened his tired body. "I have come this far. I cannot give up."

***

In the morning, they started their journey to

Mark's ranch. By the time they arrived, they were all exhausted. Malene fed everyone a simple meal, bathed the children, and tucked them in for the night. Every time she looked at Mark, she blushed, for she could barely wait to be in his arms. But it did not take her long to discover how exhausted Mark was, for all she had were his arms around her and the gentle breathing of his deep sleep.

She snuggled tight to him. Content to know how much he loved her, she basked in the glow of their love. She never dreamed she could be so happy. All she had ever desired was a handsome husband, a beautiful house, and a family. But she had something more important than those things - she had love. No amount of money could ever buy that.

Three weeks later, Adie and Frank returned to the Hunter ranch. It was after breakfast that Adie asked, "Robert and Mark, Frank and I would like to discuss some business with you."

Malene was slightly shocked at her sister's boldness, but in a way it was not a surprise. Adie could be very forthright, especially when it came to money and business. Malene made more coffee for everyone and listened to her sister.

Adie placed Albert's Wanted poster on the table. "Frank and I have discussed this. We are all starting ranches. Mark and Robert have suffered losses as a result of Malene's former husband. If Malene had been the one standing by the wagon, she would have done exactly what I did."

Frank took his wife's hand. "No one needs this much money. We wish to divide it."

Malene shook her head. "Adie is much better with a gun. It is her reward."

"No." Frank picked up his cup of coffee. "We want to share it. You and Adie are sisters. Mark and Robert deserve a piece of this."

Robert put his hands up. "I was not there."

Adie lifted her coffee cup. "Yes, but you

were trapped in the sawmill when he tried to kill you and Mark."

Robert frowned. "And we were paid for those men."

Frank pressed his lips together for a second. "Yes, but you have both lost many hours of sleep trying to protect this land and this house for Malene. This money will buy cattle, seed, and plows. There will be bad years and things will go wrong." He looked directly at Mark. "Malene has money, but you are a proud man, and I doubt you will accept her help."

"I will never take from Malene."

Frank smiled. "We know. Therefore we want to share the reward with the two of you. For the ranch, for our futures as ranchers, we want you to have it."

Malene touched her husband's shoulder. "My sister is right. You have a heavy burden on you."

Robert looked at Mark and then at Adie. "Give us a few minutes alone."

The two Indians left the kitchen table and walked outside. Malene looked at her sister. "It's very generous of you."

Adie giggled. "I'm only sharing with my sister, for I want to see her prosper, too."

Malene nodded. "That is a huge sum of money."

A few minutes later, Mark and Robert returned, and Mark smiled. "We will accept your offer."

There was a thundering sound that sent them all out of the house. In the distance, they could see what appeared to be a wagon train headed their way. Malene looked at Adie and squealed, "My furniture!"

Twenty-three freight wagons pulled up to the house. Adie and Rose went to work preparing food for all the men. As each crate was opened, Malene gave orders as to where each piece was to go. The empty house that once echoed every footstep, now had rugs and real furniture. Rose's side was also filled.

There were plenty of pieces for Adie and Frank, and several pieces for Alisa and Joseph.

That evening everyone dined on a hearty soup, soft white rolls, and apple pie.

Malene paid the fees to have the excess furniture delivered to the Coleman ranch. Adie could sort it all out when she got home.

With the furniture, came a packet from Hamilton Wholesalers & Importers Trading Company. Malene opened the packet after supper when the shippers had left. The house had been sold and the money from the house had been transferred to her bank account. The sum was staggering. Marshall had left her a very wealthy woman.

Before Frank and Adie left, Frank helped Mark set up the new windmill. It would be awhile before it was operational, but at least it was in place. The sawmill would have its own power and plenty of it.

***

Mark smiled as he took his wife into his arms. He had plenty of bedrooms and plenty of time to fill them. With luck, he'd have many sons of his own, but until then, he had four wonderful children, their mother, and his very own ranch. He had learned the ways of the white man, but he was still Apsáalooke.

His lips touched Malene's, as he unbuttoned her nightgown and slipped it off her milky white shoulders. The flimsy cotton fell into a puddle around her feet. He held her tight to his naked body. Kissing leads to much more, and Malene loved to be kissed.

The End

Did you enjoy reading *A Rancher's Woman*
by E. Ayers?

Please let your local bookstore know! Independent authors count on your reviews and input to help them succeed. You can write to the author directly at the following website: http://www.ayersbooks.com

About the Author

Born and raised with wealth, E. Ayers turned away from all of it and married a few days after turning eighteen, to the shock and dismay of family and friends.

A firm believer in love conquering everything, there was never cause to look back. The newlyweds' life-long love became the springboard for many future novels.

Fascinated with the way people deal with everyday problems, E. Ayers has always been an observer and a listener. A simple problem for one person is a mountain for another. Utilizing those common predicaments, the subsequent novels have touched many lives.

Today finds E. Ayers writing while living in a pre-Civil War home with a dog and a cat. Rattling around in an old money pit provides one's muse with plenty of freedom. A perfect day is spent at the keyboard, coffee in hand, and everything in the house actually working as it should.

As the official matchmaker for all the characters who wander through a mind full of imagination and the need to share, E. Ayers enjoys finding just the right ones to create a story.

YOU CAN VISIT CREED'S CROSSING AGAIN... AND AGAIN!

Please enjoy this peek into
A Snowy Christmas in Wyoming,
a novella from E. Ayers.

Caroline Coleman hadn't seen the place look this good since she was a teen. The flowerbeds were mulched and tidy. There was a new coat of green paint on the shutters and front door. Garlands of fresh pine wrapped the porch rails that encircled the log house, and a pretty, matching, pine wreath hung on the front door.

She knocked once and opened the door. "Grandmamma. It's me! I'm home."

"Thank goodness, you're here," a voice from a distant room called back. "I was worried about you coming in with this snowstorm on its way."

The stress of her journey slipped from her shoulders as she breathed in the familiar scent of home. Caroline let go of her rolling suitcase and looked around. Inside, everything looked the same, even though it was decorated for the holiday. A beautiful Douglas fir tree, covered with ornaments, stood in front of the window. Its tiny lights twinkled as if they were welcoming her.

The house was neater, cleaner, and there was a basket of toys next to the sofa. But everything else was exactly the way it had been all of her life. That familiarity wrapped her in a warm blanket.

"Darling, I'm so glad you're here. You're needed. This storm is going to be bad," Barbara Coleman said.

Caroline turned to her grandmother. The woman was holding a toddler whose eyes were filled with tears.

"What are you doing? Babysitting?" She hugged her grandmother and offered to take the child, but the child clung to the older woman.

"I guess you could call it babysitting. I'm trading, and I got the best end of this bargain. This is Sarah Anne Coyote. Isn't she a cutie?" Barbara took the child to a highchair in the kitchen. "Coffee?"

"Thanks. I'll get it. How did you wind up with a child?"

"Long story. You remember Margaret Simpson?" The older woman started fixing a snack.

"Double T ranch, of course."

"Her kids are selling everything since she died. Remember when I told you I was buying some of her land?" She put a handful of baby carrots on a plate, and stuck them in the microwave.

"Yes." Caroline poured a cup of coffee, then watched her grandmother fix a cup of milk with a sipping lid, and hand it to the toddler.

The child's enormous chocolate brown eyes were still washed in unshed tears and her long eyelashes were clumped with moisture.

Chubby hands grabbed at the handles on the sippy-cup and tipped the cup of milk to her mouth. She watched Caroline with a reserved curiosity.

"Are you thirsty? Did you just wake up from a nap?" Caroline asked the child.

Little Sarah pursed her lips and banged on the tray in front of her. "Milk."

"How old is she? She's adorable. She's got the prettiest eyes."

"Thirteen months. She's a little handful. She's really coming out of her shell since she's been here." Barbara put several crackers spread with cheese on the child's tray. "Eat, sweet baby. You like creamed cheese." The microwave beeped and Barbara lifted the plate of baby carrots off the unit's carousel and put them on the child's tray after checking each one. "She's such a good thing. Just never thought I'd be playing with a baby at my age."

"Why did you nuke her carrots?"

"It slightly softens them. Makes them easier

to eat. She doesn't have all her teeth."

"Grandmamma, you still haven't told me how you've wound up with a child."

"Well, I'm buying the eastern portion of Margaret's land, which includes her house and barn because it backs up to mine."

"Nice house."

"Yes, it is. I'm hoping to rent it. The one barn is in perfect shape, but the other barn has some problems and that's going to take more money."

Caroline rolled her eyes. Sarah giggled.

"Anyway, when Margaret died, her foreman lost his job."

"Oh, no. Sarah is one of those Coyotes?"

The back door opened and Andy Coyote walked into the kitchen. "Miz Barbara…"

Caroline stared at Andy. He wasn't the scrawny kid she'd known most of her life, and if it hadn't been for the scar across his cheek, she wouldn't have recognized him. His shoulders were broad and he'd grown very tall. The long straight nose, strong cheekbones, and his coloring conveyed his Crow Indian heritage, except he was taller than most.

"Excuse me, I didn't know you had company." He took his jacket off and hung it on the peg by the back door.

"Company? I doubt that anyone would call me company," Caroline shot back at him. She couldn't remember the last time she'd seen him, maybe high school.

He looked at her for a brief second, then grabbed a mug, and poured a cup of coffee.

"Caroline, you remember Andy?" Barbara asked.

"How could I not remember Andy?" Memories of the young man and his family flowed through her brain like a bad news story.

Sarah squealed with delight as Andy took her in his arms. "How's my baby girl?"

The child pointed to Caroline.

"Yes, that's Caroline," Andy said with a big

grin. "Have you been playing with her? I thought you just got up from your nap."

"She did just get up from her nap as Caroline came through the door. I brought her in here for her snack. She hasn't had a chance to play."

He pulled his mobile phone from his pocket and looked at it. "We're in trouble."

"What kind of trouble?" Barbara asked as she cleaned up the crumbs off the child's tray and handed the toddler the last tiny carrot. "Are you talking about the storm?"

Andy turned on the TV and watched the weather channel. "I've been watching the storm track on my phone. I'm gonna need help getting that herd down here. I can't do it alone. If I can find help, I'll leave tonight. That is if you don't mind keeping Sarah for me."

Barbara turned to her granddaughter. "Caroline'll go with you."

Andy turned around and stared hard. "You? You think you can ride herd?"

"Darn right, I can ride. Won't be the first

herd I've ever brought in, but I..." She bit her tongue.

"But what?"

She forced a smile. "Let's just say I always ride with a gun, and I know how to use it."

"Good. So do I. We'll leave at six. Make sure you're saddled and ready to go."

Hot anger boiled through Caroline. "I'll be ready."

She stormed out of the kitchen, grabbed her suitcase, and headed for her room.

***

"She'd better be able to ride. This isn't going to be an easy cattle drive," Andy said.

"That little thing knows every square inch of this ranch and this business. My husband used to say, 'Let her go, and when she's done, she'll come back.' I hope he was right."

"Ma'am, I don't need a prissy female. I need a man for this job or I'll never get that herd back here."

"Oh, she can do it. She and her grandfather moved herds all the time. She's knows what she's doing and she knows this land. Listen to her."

Andy kissed his daughter's nose and put her to the floor. "Are you sure you can handle her overnight?"

"I can handle your daughter overnight." Barbara laughed. "Just don't try to handle my granddaughter, or she'll be bringing you back in a sack."

"Miz Barbara, one female in my life is plenty. I don't need anymore."

***

Caroline cinched the saddle and adjusted the stirrups before tying on her pack. Her mind drifted over the stories of Jessie and Clare Coleman and the things that they endured to start this ranch in the 1840's. She had vowed to write their story one day. Clare was barely fifteen when she married Jessie and went west with him. The handwriting in that diary was difficult to decipher, but Caroline managed to read it when she was a teen. Snowstorms were nothing new, and if Jessie and Clare could survive them, there was no reason why she couldn't do it today. Except instead of doing it with her grandfather at her side, she had Andy Coyote. She grimaced as bile rose from her stomach.

"You ready to ride, Caroline?" Andy asked.

"Yes, I'm ready." She pulled her scarf over her head and shoved her old felted Stetson over the hot pink angora.

"Don't wimp out on me. I need another man for this job, not a fancy Washington, D.C. TV news anchor."

"Well, I have a job to do, and the idea of having you along for the ride has no appeal. As far as I'm concerned, you're strictly brawn, and you'd better do as I say."

"This is gonna be hell," he mumbled as he

yanked on his horse's reins.

"That's right, and don't forget it." Caroline put her foot into the stirrup.

Caroline pulled her scarf tighter around her face. An occasional snowflake floated down as they rode. She wasn't going to let on that she was dead tired, but she was certain that if she'd blink her eyes, they wouldn't open again. She had worked yesterday doing the six and eleven o'clock nightly news broadcasts, and then caught an early morning flight out of D.C. Three hours of sleep was not enough.

"Caroline!"

She gasped and righted herself.

"You're falling asleep."

She looked over at Andy and frowned.

"If you talked to me, you might stay awake," he suggested.

"What would you like to discuss?" she snarled.

He chuckled. "You want my opinion on the Senate's newest budget?"

"Oh, save your breath."

"I didn't think so. Why don't you tell me what it's like living in the big city and having a hotshot job?"

"Nothing to tell. I have a condo overlooking the Potomac River. I have a driver who takes me to and from work. The clothes I wear are chosen by someone else, even my hair is styled according to the network's consultant, and I don't have a say so in any of it."

"I think you look mighty pretty. Miz Barbara and I always watch you while we eat our dinner."

"Why are you living in the house with my grandmother?"

"And not living in the foreman's apartment in the barn?"

"Yes." The idea of a Coyote living under her grandmother's roof bothered her. As far as she was concerned they were all filthy criminals.

The only sounds were theirs, the horses' breaths, the soft slap of leather reins, and the thumping of hooves on the frozen earth. Finally he answered, "She didn't want me out there in that small apartment with the baby. She thought it was easier on Sarah if I stayed in the house."

"Where's Sarah's mom?"

"Don't know and don't care." He nudged his horse to pick up the pace.

"Nice attitude."

"Yours sucks, too."

"I don't have a child," she retaliated.

"I have two. I'm not allowed near my son."

She shook her head. "What did you do to prevent visitation?"

"Fathered the boy."

"How old is he?"

"He'll be fifteen in February."

Her mind spun back in time to Andy and Katelyn as teens. They were inseparable. The fun loving, petite female with wide set eyes had always been a fierce competitor in 4H and was an amazing trick rider. Then Katelyn vanished. "So the rumors were true?"

"Half true. I never raped her. We were kids and thought we were in love. When she found out she was pregnant…her dad came looking for me with a rifle in his hand. Three years later, the judge threw it all out. I was forced to sign an order to stay away from Katelyn and my son."

Somehow she understood the wealthy family's rage. She could also imagine Katelyn's tears at being torn from the boy she loved. But Andy was a Coyote, and those boys were hellions. "She still here?"

"If you mean still in the county, no. According to a few friends, she's living outside of Boulder, raising horses, and happily married to some hotshot lawyer."

"And your son?"

"He's with her. She'll tell him the truth someday."

"What about Sarah?"

"Another big mistake. Sarah's not, but her

mom was. I'll be honest. My life was a mess. I was living in Casper when I meet Jessica. We went out a few times and then we started living together. She was hot. Then one day she tells me that she's pregnant. Two weeks later, the warehouse where I'd been working closed. I started searching for any job I could find."

Andy's momentary silence hung in the cold air.

Caroline straightened her back and rolled her shoulders. Fatigue was robbing her body, but she wanted him to keep talking. He was right. Conversation kept her awake.

"It was a bad situation. I needed money and there were no jobs. Eventually, I found a job working back here for Double T. They needed a hand. But Jessica didn't want to come. She wanted to live in the city. Had a big fight. I tried a half dozen times to patch things up. Then the phone quit working and my envelopes were returned with no forwarding address. When Margaret Simpson died, her kids kicked everyone out and started selling everything off. I got lucky and got a part-time job working at Kalab's Store."

"Doing what?"

"Anything. Didn't matter to me. It was a job. Had to cover the payment on my truck and put food in my belly. That's where I found your grandmother. She was complaining to BillieJo Kalab about not being able to do everything. That evening I came out to her house. I begged for a job and a place to sleep."

"My grandmother does not complain about anything."

"Well, call it whatever you want, but those two women were commiserating about how hard life was."

"Oh, big word."

"Knock it off, Caroline. Just 'cause I didn't run off to some big university in Virginia doesn't make me an idiot."

She nudged her horse. "You never were an A student."

"No, I wasn't. But you don't have to get uppity with me."

She looked over at him. "You calling me a snob?"

"I really don't care what you are, as long as you can get this herd back to where I can take care of them. Your grandmother doesn't need to lose her livestock because they've frozen to death."

She hid her snarl. "So how did you wind up with Sarah?"

"I'd been here about three weeks when Miz Barbara got a phone call. Seems Social Services tracked me down. Sarah had been abandoned. She was in bad shape. If it weren't for your grandmother…I don't know what I'd do."

"She's adorable."

"She is. I'll do anything to make sure nothing ever happens to her again."

"A Rancher's Dream is unique, poignant, and wonderful."
Jeanie, 5 Star Reader Review

E. AYERS

*The elusive dream of his own ranch rested before him,
a reality still shrouded in a morning mist that reflected the
green of nature, of money, of success, and of a future.*

Historical Fiction

A Rancher's Dream

Victorian American Western

A Creed's Crossing Historical Novel

Now Available
A Rancher's Dream by E. Ayers
Also available in LARGE PRINT!